George Parsons Lathrop

True, and other Stories

George Parsons Lathrop

True, and other Stories

ISBN/EAN: 9783744750141

Printed in Europe, USA, Canada, Australia, Japan

Cover: Foto ©Andreas Hilbeck / pixelio.de

More available books at **www.hansebooks.com**

TRUE

AND

OTHER STORIES

BY

GEORGE PARSONS LATHROP

AUTHOR OF "AN ECHO OF PASSION," "NEWPORT," ETC.

FUNK & WAGNALLS

NEW YORK 1884 LONDON
10 AND 12 DEY STREET   44 FLEET STREET

CONTENTS.

TRUE.

CHAPTER I.
HER EYES WERE GRAY.................................... 5

CHAPTER II.
THE DE VINES........................... 13

CHAPTER III.
TWILIGHT.. 23

CHAPTER IV.
A VISION.. 38

CHAPTER V.
BIRTHDAY TOKENS................... 46

CHAPTER VI.
A NEW LESSON IN BOTANY..................... 55

CHAPTER VII.
THE RACES, AND THE MOTTO............ 67

CHAPTER VIII.
ADELA'S LEGEND... 80

CHAPTER IX.
LANCE AND SYLVESTER.................................... 92

CHAPTER X.
THE LIKENESS... 106

CHAPTER XI.
LANCE RETURNS............................ 116

CHAPTER XII.

SYLV'S TROUBLE... 123

CHAPTER XIII.

LANCE AND ADELA.. 130

CHAPTER XIV.

DENNIE'S TROUBLE... 138

CHAPTER XV.

ELBOW-CROOK SWAMP...................................... 148

CHAPTER XVI.

"I LIVE, HOW LONG I TROW NOT"........................ 159

———

MAJOR BARRINGTON'S MARRIAGE..................... 166

———

"BAD PEPPERS".. 198

———

THREE BRIDGES.

I.

THE IMPORTANCE OF A HAT............................... 222

II.

FATHER, DAUGHTER, AND—WHO ELSE?................ 227

III.

LISTENING... 236

IV.

THE THIRD BRIDGE... 242

———

IN EACH OTHER'S SHOES.................................. 250

TRUE.

CHAPTER I.

HER EYES WERE GRAY.

It might have been yesterday, but in simple fact it was three hundred years ago, that something happened which has an important bearing on this story of the present.

Antiquity is a great discourager of the sympathies : the centuries are apt to weigh like lead on an individual human sentiment. Yet we find it pleasant sometimes to throw off their weight, and thereby to discover that it is a mere feather in the scale as against the beating of a heart.

I know that when I speak of Guy Wharton as having been alive and in love in the year 1587, you will feel a certain patronizing pity for him—because he is not alive now. So do I. But then it is possible that you will be interested, notwithstanding—because he was a lover. Would you like to hear what experience he had ? I promise not to go through the history of those three hundred years. The story of Guy is merely the starting-point of my narrative.

He was in love with a sweet English girl, Gertrude Wylde, who lived in Surrey ; and she, for her part, was the daughter of a small tenant-farmer there, well connected as to family, but not well furnished with worldly goods. Guy's father was a country gentleman ; but that circumstance failed to affect the young man's eyesight and emotions injuriously ; he beheld Gertrude, and he loved her. I can see it all, now, as if it were something that had happened to myself—how they strolled together in those wondrous lanes hedged with hawthorn and brier and hazel, which stray so sweetly over the rolling lands about Dorking ; how they met beneath the old yew tree where, half way up Box Hill, it hung out its foliage black as night, spotted with strange waxen blossoms of scarlet, like drops of blood upon a funeral-pall ; how they wandered in the untamed forest of great box trees at the top ; what joys they had, what anxieties beset them.

"And will thy father indeed take his leave of old England so soon ?" he asked her, when they had reached the brow of the hill.

"Yes, in truth," she answered, sadly enough, looking out over the white chalk highlands, and the arborous glades and open downs, to where the waters of the English Channel showed soft against the hazy sky at the horizon, like a blue vein on a circling arm. "And that means that I must take leave of *thee*, Guy."

"Never, my darling !" cried Guy, drawing her to him. "If thou goest, I go as well."

"What ! Forsake all here—estate and fortune and family ? Nay, dearest, that can never be." But, as she spoke these words, Gertrude pressed her face upon his shoulder and gave way to tears. Then presently, raising her head and gazing up into his face : "How should it be possible ?" she asked.

"Easily enough, if thou wilt," he replied. "I would go as thy affianced husband."

Thus it was settled that he also should join the colonizing expedition with which Gertrude's father had resolved to embark, under the patronage of Sir Walter Raleigh. Its goal was Roanoke Island, Virginia.

As the lovers walked homeward in company, and parted to go their separate ways, they felt as if their feet already trod the shores of the New World. "But when we are there," said Wharton before he left her at the turnstile that ushered the way to her father's farm— "there we shall have no more partings."

Alas, he was but a poor prophet!

Difficulties came up. Wharton's father violently opposed the plan that Guy had made. That, however, might not have prevented its execution, had not a fatal thing happened just at the critical time. On the eve of the sailing of the expedition, Guy's father died. That which his bitterest activity while alive failed to effect was accomplished by his white and silent presence as he lay dead in the old manor-house. At such a moment Guy could not go away; the unspoken edict of death restrained him absolutely. Besides, the elder Wharton's affairs were left in a confusion which it would take long to clear up.

So the ship sailed without Guy; but you may be sure he was at the wharf when she weighed anchor, and that he bade a tender farewell to Gertrude, promising that he would follow with the first convoy that should be sent to re-enforce and victual the new colony. At the instant when he had to leave her, she said, as if answering his words, uttered many weeks before at the turnstile: "Yes, dearest, we shall meet soon in that other world, and there shall be no more parting."

Guy did not think of the exact expression, just then; but as he travelled back to the manor-house, now his own, he kept saying to himself involuntarily : "That other world ? God grant it may not mean the world beyond !" When he stepped within the door, his eye rested on the inscription over the great fireplace of the hall :

> " I live, how long I trow not ;
> I die, but where I know not ;
> I journey, but whither I cannot see :
> 'Tis strange that I can merry be."

Many a festival had been held beneath the unnoticed shadow of those solemn lines ; the laughter and the cheer, the sobs and murmurs of many a voice forever hushed, had echoed from the wall where the verses were graven ; but it seemed to him that the motto had never gained its full meaning until now.

> " I journey, but whither I cannot see."

Gertrude had gone out into the great void of the unknown spaces ; and he was to follow her—whither ?

It would indeed have been strange if he could have been merry ; and, to say truth, he was not greatly so ; but he kept up his hope indomitably.

At last everything was arranged : he was ready to go. But he had to wait for the relief expedition to sail. In those days it was a great undertaking to prepare for a journey across the Atlantic. Raleigh was busy, perplexed, anxious : three years went by before Admiral John White started from Plymouth with three little ships (one for each year) and two shallops. But when he did start, Guy was on board.

It had been agreed with the colonists that, if anything went wrong and they should find it best to look for a new site, they should remove to a spot fifty miles inland among the friendly Indians, and should carve upon a tree the name of the place to which they were going. In case misfortune befell them, a cross was also to be carved above the name of their destination.

When, after a five weeks' voyage, Admiral White's vessels approached the shore of Hatteras, they anchored some miles out, for safety, and sent a boat in to the shallow Sound. Guy was in the bow of the boat which ' steered for Roanoke Island. The crew, when they had come near enough, blew trumpet-blasts as a signal of their approach, and sang songs of home—old English glees and madrigals—that had often echoed in the fields, the groves, the farmhouses of Surrey and Kent. Attracted by the sound the colonists, they hoped, would make their appearance the sooner. But how strangely these familiar strains fell upon the ear in the primeval solitude of those lonely waters, on that lovely April day! So strangely, indeed, that one might almost fancy the colonists did not recognize them any more, and hence failed to respond. Yet the trumpets continued to ring out on the air, and the gay songs were trolled cheerily, as the boat drew near the landing-place.

It may be imagined what an eager lookout Guy kept up at the bow. He believed every moment that, at the next, he should see Gertrude emerging from the woods and waving her hand to him. Still, not a sign of life had been given when he stepped ashore.

The little party began to be oppressed by forebodings. They set out through the forest, eagerly searching for some token of their countrymen's presence; but no voice answered their calls, except those of unaccustomed birds and astonished squirrels; and no trail was found upon the light brown soil, other than the marks of an Indian moccasin or the curious dottings made by the feet of furtive animals.

At last, however, the seekers came to a tree which confronted them with three rudely carved letters cut upon its side.

C. R. O.

That was all. There was no indication of the cross, the symbol of distress. The men burst into exclamations of delight ; yet Guy, though his heart bounded high with reviving hope, suffered a terrible suspense. The sturdy tree had, as it were, found a voice and spoken ; but it had uttered only one vague, baffling syllable. Of what use was that feeble clew ? Still he pressed on, having no idea which way to turn, but guided by some inspiration ; and presently, shouting to his companions, he pointed to another conspicuous tree which bore upon its blazed trunk the full name of the colony's new abiding-place. The letters missing from the first inscription had doubtless been worn away by storms. The word engraved upon the fibre of the second tree was " Croatan."

The friends of the colonists did not know precisely where Croatan lay ; and though Guy urged an immediate exploration, the rest thought it impracticable. The distance from the ships threatened danger of being separated from the expedition by some accident, and left alone without supplies. So, having read the brief message of the departed colonists, the boat party returned to the little squadron and reported.

A storm arose ; anchors were lost ; the supply of fresh water had run low ; and a council called by the Admiral decided that prudence required taking a southerly course to find some safer harbor ; advising also that an attempt should be made to capture some Spanish vessels and return with the booty and provisions to find the lost colony. In vain Guy pleaded, with anguish in every

word, that at least one of the ships should cruise near
the coast off which they now lay and await the first
favorable moment for prosecuting the search. The
Admiral and his captains were inexorable; and the
southern course was taken.

None of the vessels ever went back to the aid of the
English at Croatan.

The captain of that one on which Guy Wharton was a
passenger turned her prow toward England after a
little time. Once more at home, Guy made every
endeavor to have a new fleet equipped; but all his
attempts failed. He was on the point of selling everything he owned, in order to fit out at least one ship and
carry substantial aid to the exiles, when certain com-
mercial ventures, in which a great deal of the property
left to him was involved, went amiss and left him helpless. Restless, unhappy, almost broken-hearted, he
entered on the struggle to re-establish himself; no opportunity occurred for him to sail to Virginia again; and
so much time passed by, that such an undertaking came
to look hopeless. Even could he have gone, what would
he have found? Perhaps Gertrude by this time had
died. Or, perhaps, thinking herself forsaken or forgotten, as the whole community of emigrants seemingly had
been, she might have married one of the colonists.

The old hope went out of Guy Wharton's life; but
though, after some years, he took a wife, he never lost
the pain which this tragedy of his youth had planted in
his breast.

And they, meanwhile, the vanished exiles—what was
their life; what were their thoughts? How long their
hope survived, no one can even guess. Without resources beyond those which the friendly Croatans themselves had; living a rude and simple life among the

natives in that wild and lonely land ; did they watch day
after day for some sign of sail or fluttering pennon coming
up the river, or listen for some sudden bugle-note or
gun-shot, announcing the approach of relief ?   Did
Gertrude keep up her faith through the weary years,
hourly awaiting her lover ?—fancying she heard his voice
close by ?—then waking again to the reality of the lonely
stream, the fluttering forest-leaves, the uncouth habita-
tions, the garments of deerskin and the swarthy savage
children at play ?

God only knows ; for of all those hundred and fifteen
wanderers, men and women, not one was ever seen
among the civilized again.   They passed from the region
of the known and the recorded into the vagueness of
unlettered tradition.   From the midst of history they
were transplanted into myth.   They faded out amid
those dusky tribes in the forest, as the last streak of light
in the west fades into darkness at nightfall.

A hundred years afterward the Indians of the Hatteras shore were described as declaring with pride that
some of their ancestors were white and could "talk
in a book," like the later Englishmen who were then
established in Virginia.   It was taken as confirmation of
this story, that some of the Indians who told it had gray
eyes.

Her eyes were gray.

CHAPTER II.

On a little headland at the southern end of Pamlico Sound where it narrows in to the waters of Core Sound, a small dwelling-house, half hut and half cottage, looked forth over the liquid expanses with an air of long habitude and battered self-reliance. It had but two meagre windows, and its chimney was short and black, suggesting an old tobacco-pipe; but the little house leaned comfortably against the low sandy ridge at its back, and did not seem to mind any of the imperfections in its own facial aspect. Along the ridge live oaks and red cedars flourished gracefully, and the ancient structure was closely enfolded at either side by thickets of that kind of holly known in the region as *yaupon*, the polished leaves and warm red berries of which glistened cheerily in the sunlight. Indeed, the whole place, dilapidated though it was, had the reassuring appearance of a home; and when from its narrow doorway a beautiful young woman stepped forth into the breezy afternoon, nothing more was needed to complete the effect.

If it was a home before, it now looked the ideal of a home.

The young woman turned to the holly bushes at the left and began clipping from them some of their lighter branches, which she let fall into a large basket, held gracefully against her hip with one rounded arm, while the other plied the shears. She was tall, but not fair. No daughter of the gods, but firmly and robustly human; yet, at the same time, there was in her humanity something noble and inspiriting. Am I not going too fast? Why talk in this way about a young girl in a calico gown, cutting holly-sprigs beside a tumble-down old cabin on the Nawth Ca'liny shore? No, she was not fair as to complexion; her skin was richly browned by out-door life, though a clear rose-tint shone faintly through the brown. She was beautiful, nevertheless; and yet—and yet what was it? It seemed as if that outer hue could never under any circumstances wear off. But a mere glance at her features would convince any one that she was not of octoroon or metif parentage. Only it was as if the sun, watching over her loveliness from birth, and searching into the depths of her nature, had warmed her blood until it had darkened a little and her pulses had spread a shadow in their flowing.

Suddenly she desisted from her work and, bending her head forward, gazed off across the light green waves that stretched for miles between her and the low-lying strip of sand that barred out the sea. Had she heard a distant hail from the boat that was scudding fast toward the headland? At any rate, there was the burly little craft, careening to the lively breeze amid a shower of spray, with a recklessness characteristic of the young helmsman, whom the girl's bright eyes would have recognized even farther away. And now, as the craft abruptly veered to windward, to approach the landing, her master's careless handling received a startling illustration, for she almost broached to; the sails were laid aback, and for an instant the boat threatened to capsize.

There was one passenger, an old woman, who sat near the helmsman; and at this juncture she snatched from her lips a short clay pipe, emitting a shrill cry of fright, together with an alarmed whiff of smoke—as if she herself had unexpectedly exploded.

"Lord save our soulds, Dennis! What be you thinkin' on?"

"All right, auntie!" cried the young man, heartily. "The critter 'll come straight in half a turn." And, exerting all his force, he caused the dug-out to round into her course again, with the breeze on her quarter. Two or three minutes later she touched the shore.

The young woman, having thrown down her basket, stood ready to greet the new-comers.

"Well, Deely dear!"

"Why, Aunty Losh, it don't seem possible that it's you come back again. And so you're really here."

"Yes; a'most really—though, as you see just now, I come nearer drowndin' in front o' my own door, Deely."

Dennis submitted his stout frame to a convulsive laugh, which for an instant gave him some resemblance to a dog shaking himself on emerging from the water. "Drownded in half a fathom," he exclaimed, hilariously. "I'll be dog-goned if that ain't the cutest, aunty! Why, I'm almost sorry we didn't overset the old boat, just to show you. It would have livened you up fit to kill."

"Dennis!" exclaimed Deely, her eyes flashing indignantly, "you ought to be ashamed."

"Oh, never mind the boy," Aunty Losh soothingly interposed. "It's his natur' to be wild, ye know. He ain't never happy unless he's in some dare-devil scrape. But where's Sylvester?"

Deely, with eyes cast down, appeared needlessly embarrassed. "He went up to Beaufort to market," she explained.

Something in her tone caused Dennis to glance at her rather fiercely, as if he were jealous. " Yes, that suits *him*," he muttered, with a trace of contempt. " Market business is just about what Sylv is good for ; that's what it is."

" It aren't right to speak so of your only brother, Dennis," said Aunty Losh, mildly.

" Oh, dog gone it !" (Dennis reverted to his favorite expletive.) " What does it matter whose brother he is ? I speak my mind. Deely, don't look so down on me. What's the trouble ?"

" Only you're so rough," said the girl, laying her hand on his arm. " You know I love you, don't you, Dennie ? But it goes against me to hear you talk so."

He placed his own rough hand on her smooth one and patted it softly for an instant ; then he moved it somewhat brusquely from its resting-place on his shoulder, and Deely drew away a step or two.

" I *catch* all the fish," he said, " and Sylv *takes* 'em for himself." There seemed to be an undertone of double meaning in his remark. But the next instant he changed from gloom to sunny cheer. " Come, aunty, you mustn't stand here on the mud. I reckon you've been away so long you'll be kind o' glad to see the inside of the old cabin again ; hey ?"

He was tall and sturdy, this Dennis De Vine ; and though he could not have been described as handsome, his reddish hair and ruddy coloring, united with the glance of his blue eye and a certain good-humored Irish daring of expression, made his presence gay and attractive. Aunty Losh was quick to act on his suggestion, and they all went into the cabin, which despite its limited frontage spread out sufficiently, within, to afford rooms for the old woman and her two nephews.

"Now, aunty," said the girl, "the tarrapin is most ready, and I'll brew you a good cup of yaupon. I was just cutting some to dry when you came." And thereupon Adela, taking a handful of the seasoned leaves from their place of storage in a cupboard, swung the kettle from the fire and proceeded to infuse this local substitute for tea.

"My patience, but it's dear to my buddy and heart," Aunty Losh murmured, as she sipped from the smoking cup. "An' now tell me what's happened while I been away."

"Why, Sylv wrote you everything that happened hyar," Adela reminded her, in some surprise.

"Oh, I know, I know!" was the rejoinder. "But it didn't seem nachul-like when I had to have folks read it to me. I didn't mo'n half get it in."

"There ain't nothin' very novel," said Dennis, "except old Sukey strayed off on to the main yistiddy." Sukey was the cow.

"Sho! It'll allays be so, long as I live. Nothin' but stray and find, stray and find. Ye *mout* hev dug that ditch across the neck, Dennie, when ye knowed I wanted it so bad. If you'll do it one o' these near-comin' days, I'll knit ye a new pair o' socks."

The headland on which Aunty Losh's house had been built was connected with the main only by a narrow neck, and it was one of the grievances of her life that her cow and her two or three sheep, when turned loose to graze, could so easily make their way to the adjoining territory.

"I'm fearsome o' the tides," Dennis explained. "They run so strong that mebbe they'd cut a wider channel than you want, aunty. But I'll try it; I'll dig that ditch by-and-by—or arterward."

The talk then turned to other matters, and Miss Jessie Floyd was mentioned, the daughter of an ex-Confederate colonel who lived a few miles inland on an "estate" of some dozen acres, magnificently entitled "Fairleigh Park."

"Miss Jessie's been down hyar two or three times," Adela said, "to buy bluefish and tarrapin for the manor; and she was very kind to the boys. Wasn't she, Dennie?"

"That she was. She brought us jelly, one time." Dennis gently smacked his lips, in a reminiscent way.

"I reckon she hain't brought any money, though," his aunt skeptically meditated, aloud. "Any company up at the manor?"

"Why, yes," said the girl. "There's a young gen'l'man from the Nawth—a sort of English chap, I reckon; anyhow, he comes from New York. Mr. Lance; that's what they call him. I hain't seen him, but Dennis can tell you."

"Certain shore," said Dennis. "That's his name. He's got ideas about buildin' up. He wants to eddicate folks all round—sort of free snack of knowledge for everybody."

"I reckon he'll be eddicating Miss Jessie to fall in love with him," Adela observed. "That's what."

"Well, I sha'n't find no fault with him if he do," Dennis returned. "Only he needn't come down hyar away with his ideas and all. 'Pears like him and Sylv 'ud be chancey to take up with one another, though."

"What makes you think that?" Aunty Losh asked, with a trace of apprehension.

"'Cause Sylv don't think of nothin' now but book-larnin', and he's been hevin' talks with that ar fellow."

"Sylv 'll be goin' off and leavin' us one o' these days," the old woman mused, as she put a match to the short pipe she had been filling for herself.

"Oh no, aunty! You ortenter think he'd be so mean!" Deely protested, with energy.

Dennis turned upon her, angered. "You keep still, d'you har!" he exclaimed. "What matters if he do go? I reckon I can take car o' you and aunty, all by myself, when it comes to that."

Deely was evidently impressed by his dictatorial manner, but she assumed a haughty air. "*I* reckon it's about time for me to go," she retorted, "if you can't be more civil. Just when aunty hain't no more'n set her foot inside o' home, too." And, despite her tone, there was a slight appearance about the girl's lips and eyelids as if she would like to cry.

"Oh, well; I didn't mean nothin', you know I didn't," Dennis answered, becoming penitent. "And when you go," he added, "I'm a-goin' with you as far as your dad's."

The rising trouble was thus allayed, and all three were soon engaged again in talking over the news, or the local affairs of the last few weeks. For Aunty Losh had achieved one of the most remarkable events of her life, in going to see some of her relatives at Norfolk, Virginia. She had much to tell about the journey and the ways of the people in that great city, and dwelt especially upon the hardship she had been compelled to suffer in drinking "China tea," instead of that far superior docoction, yaupon. The young people, in their turn, gradually discovered many little items which they must impart to her.

Aunty Losh, strange as it may seem, was the sole female representative of a stock which once gave promise of making itself distinguished. Her lineage was traceable from a certain Major De Vine, a young Irishman who, stirred by the sympathy that led the natives of two widely separate but oppressed countries to join the cause of the American colonies, had enlisted in the cavalry corps raised by Count Pulaski to join the Continental army, during our Revolution. Pulaski was a Pole, and De Vine an Irishman, but they had the same inspiration : they fought for freedom in America with the hope that their own people might also become free. De Vine performed many a gallant deed, in the course of the war, and rose to be a major ; but the consciousness of his good service was his only recompense.

At the peace he retired from the struggle poor, and ill fitted to make his way by other means than the sword. He settled in the South, where the soil was not favorable for such a man as he. What little property he possessed was soon lost. Moreover, he and his children having surrendered to the reigning prejudice against work, there was no way open to a retrieval of even the meagre comfort they had at first commanded. The family, failing to make any advantageous alliance by marriage—which, indeed, would scarcely have been possible in their circumstances—soon declined into still deeper poverty. The Major died, followed by all his children excepting one son, who drifted across the border into North Carolina ; and his posterity became a part of that strange population known as " poor whites."

Listless and inefficient as those people are, germs of energy are known to have been fostered among them, which have sometimes developed ; and the De Vines always retained enough of their ancestral vigor to counteract their ancestral pride, as well as their sense of unmerited misfortune, and to keep them somewhat above the general hopeless prostration of the class into which they had fallen.

Aunty Losh, widowed by the Rebellion, and left childless, had settled in the little hut on the headland, with her two nephews, mere boys at the time, but now grown to efficient manhood. The elder one, Dennis, was stalwart and courageous, and became a successful fisherman on a small scale. Sylvester had also assisted in the common support, and together they had made a little headway. But in Sylvester the ambition for something higher had awaked : he had not only learned to read, but had actually become a student, and was now taking steps toward what seemed to his aunt and brother the attainment of a distant and dangerous witchcraft—namely, making himself a lawyer. Neither of them believed that he would ever accomplish this chimerical design, but Sylvester's scheme was always present to them in the guise of an impending danger, which was just as dreadful as if it had been realized. In fact, it was worse, because it seemed to them a spell in which he had been caught, and to which his life would ultimately be sacrificed. They regarded him with the mingled envy and commiseration that we are apt to bestow upon those who have the strength to devote themselves to an idea which we think is going to prove a failure.

Dennis, on the contrary, had never troubled himself to learn anything beyond that which his own instinct and contact with the forces around him could teach. There was a vague tradition stored up in the dust-heaps of Aunty Losh's mind, to the effect that his ancestor, the Major, had once at the siege of Savannah cut his way through the British with a detachment of Pulaski's Legion, and that in so doing he had slain with his own

hand eleven of the enemy. Well, it was with the same
sort of desperate rush that Dennis cut his way through
the problems of existence. He was good for a short,
sharp struggle, but he was not steady, and had no ability
to plan long manœuvres or patient campaigns.

A streak of fierceness remained in him, also, derived
from the man who had been so deadly to his enemies
when placed in a perilous dilemma. As there were no
British opposed to him, it did not manifest itself in just
the same way; and, thus far, being temperate in his
habits and having no foes so far as any one knew, he had
not slain anybody. But his passionate impulses asserted
themselves plainly enough at times, to the discomfort
not only of others, but also of himself.

Here they were, then, these three people, the remote
offspring of that old Revolutionary officer, living
humbly on the North Carolina shore, unlike as possible
to what Major De Vine might at one time have supposed
his descendants would be, yet bearing his blood in their
veins, and acting out every day his traits or those of
some still earlier progenitor, with as much exactness as if
what they did and said had been a part written for them
in a play.

They knew nothing about the romance of Guy
Wharton and Gertrude Wylde, so far back, so musty
with age as it seems, yet so alive and fragrant, I think,
when we pluck it out from the crumbled ruins of the
past where it grew. They knew nothing of the deposit
of stones in the waters up by Shallowbag Point, near
Roanoke, which—being of foreign character—are probably the ballast of one of Raleigh's vessels thrown over-
board there, in the stress of weather; nothing, except
that Dennis had learned to steer clear of it at low tide.
But when you consider the destiny that had befallen

the family of the gallant young Revolutionary fighter, how much did it differ from that of the English colonists whose race had been extinguished in savagery? The change which had taken place was, essentially, of the same kind.

CHAPTER III.

TWILIGHT.

WHEN the group at Aunty Losh's cabin had finished what they had to say, Adela Reefe rose to go ; and Dennis, taking his gun from a corner of the room, prepared as a matter of course to accompany her.

"Sun'll be goin' down," he remarked, languidly, "by the time I'm a-comin' back, and I'll have a right smart call to get a few birds."

"I wish ye was goin' t'other way," Aunty Losh said, fretfully. "Ye mout see suthin' o' Sylv. It's quare he don't come 'long when he knows his old aunty's a-waitin' for him."

"Oh, he's young, aunty. You got to give him some play," said Dennis, with fine sarcasm, though he knew well enough that his younger brother was more mature and better balanced than he.

But his demeanor underwent a change as soon as he had passed out of the doorway with Adela. The air of lazy jesting disappeared ; his face became earnest, and he walked with a kind of meekness beside the girl, looking at her guardedly with a devotion that did not lose the grace of a single motion of her lithe figure. Leaving the headland, they took the direction of Hunting Quarters, a fishing village several miles distant, where Adela lived alone with her father, a nondescript personage depending for his livelihood upon equally nondescript and fragmentary lore of a supposed medical character. Old Reefe, to say truth, was held in awe by some of the simple neighborhood folk, as a man possessed of mysterious and magical powers.

The two had gone some distance without speaking, when Dennis began abruptly : " I got somethin' to say to ye, Deely, what I was waitin' to say till aunty come back. It didn't seem everyways fair to say it afore."

" What in time is it wouldn't be fair for you to say to me, Dennie ?" she asked, turning her face quickly toward him, her lips parted in a smile, or perhaps only in eagerness.

" Why, when you was comin' over, tendin' me and Sylv and the cabin, it didn't look like it was right," Dennis said. " But now there's a free course, and I want to lay for home."

" That's a good word," Adela threw in, seeing him pause.

" Yes, and you know what I'm after. I want ye to say when you'll marry me."

Deely, at this, was quick to avert her glance. She remained silent.

" Well, what's in the wind now ?" he persisted. " Ain't ye goin' to pass me an answer ?"

" What *can* I say to you ?" she returned, earnestly. " I love you, Dennie, as I told you long ago ; and I want to be your wife. But where are we to go ? What have we got to live on ?"

Adela's speech varied from the customary manner of the locality to a more precise and refined utterance, according to her mood ; for she had shared in Sylv's progress to the extent of taking lessons from him in reading. This had caused her to observe Miss Jessie Floyd's pronunciation, and that of the few other cultivated persons whom she occasionally saw, so that she had learned to copy it. The instant she found herself in opposition to Dennis, she unconsciously assumed that superior accent, the effect of which upon him was by no means mollifying.

"Oh, don't go for to go on that tack now !" he exclaimed. "I've hearn enough on it a'ready. I mean squar' talk now, and I ain't goin' to be fooled, neither."

"Answer *my* question, then," said the girl, peremptorily. "That's no more than fair."

"Why, there ain't no trouble," Dennis assured her, becoming amiable again. "I reckon we can make out to live together as well as we can separate one from t'other."

"How ?"

"Just like we do now. 'Pears to me the fish 'll bite as easy when they know they've got to make a dinner for we uns, stead o' for Aunty and Sylv, and the tarrapin 'll walk up to be cotched, and ground-nuts and rice 'll allays be plenty."

"Yes, yes, Dennie ; but who's goin' to take keer of Aunty Losh ?" said Adela, dropping back into the easier way of talking.

The young man's face fell, and he wrinkled his forehead. "That's a fact ; that's a fact," he murmured, sadly. "Poor ole aunty ! She's been a true mammy to we uns, and it ain't nachul to leave her be by herself. But Sylv mout take keer on her, Deely."

"Sylv's younger than you," she objected. "'Tain't his portion to do that."

"Mebbe he ar young," said Dennis ; "but he's got a darn'd sight cuter head, some ways, than I have. And you mind now what I say, Deely, this hyar thing has got to stop one o' these hyar days. If it hadn't been for Sylv's mopin' over them books, and a-glowerin' and tryin' to make his self too wise, I'd a-been a heap better fixed."

"But Sylv wouldn't a-been," was the answer ; "and he's worth thinkin' on a little."

Dennis laughed scornfully. "A little ! He's a heap too much wuth thinkin' on."

Adela ceased walking, and faced round upon him, at the same time brushing away with one hand a tress of her crispy black hair, which the wind had blown across her eyes. She wanted to meet his gaze directly. "What do you mean by that ?" she demanded.

Dennis was her match for belligerency. "I mean," he said, "that that ar youngster takes up too much 'tention. Thar ar'n't no time for considerin' on no one else. It's allays Sylv's ways and Sylv's idees, and he can't do nothin' for himself, but some one else hev got to do it for him. An' here am I, one month arter another, findin' the ways for him and aunty to live, lettin' alone myself, whiles he goes smellin' arter them old books what's made o' yaller hide that ain't no better than the skin off'n our Sukey's back. An' that's whar the bits and the dollars go, that you and I might be enjoyin' if 'twarn't for his dog-goned concayt of lawyer's jawin' and politics and parla*ments*. That's what ! An' I'm tired on it, I tell ye. What I mean ?" Here the young fellow's handsome, free-colored face became clouded with passion that darkened it as with the shadows of a thunder-cloud. "I mean, Deely, that if you are a-goin' to put Sylv up agin me, every chance comes along, thinkin' o' his good and not o' mine, ye're not nigh so lovin' o' me as ye are o' him. D'ye un'stan' me, now?"

Adela shrank back slightly, as if he had levelled a sudden blow at her. Then she replied: "If that's all ye got to say to me, Dennie De Vine, ye can just go back on your tracks to the cabin, and I'll go to the Quarters alone."

Dennis forgot his anger in anxiety. "But there's the tide-way ye can't cross," he said.

"I've done it afore now, by myself," replied the girl. "'Twant for nothin' you learned me to row and sail. Ah, Dennie"—her under-lip trembled as she spoke—"it ar'n't right in you to treat me so. If you'd only remember those times when we were children! You was always good to me, then. Why ar'n't you good to me now? I feel just the same about you as I did in those way-off days. I never loved any but you—and old dad."

The poor child's head was drooping, as she finished; and, but for pride, she would have wept.

"All right, then, Deely," began Dennis. "If that's so, I'm sorry—I started for to say, I'm glad. Only, give me your squar' promise that you won't let him stand in the way no more. I've kept my hand to the helm, and I've waited. I've been waitin' a long time. Sylv won't never be no 'count, if he go on as he ar', and we won't be no 'count, nuther. Only say the word that you'll marry me soon, and that you ain't goin' to let Sylv stand in the way."

"But you said I cared more for him than I do for you," Adela objected, less inclined to make peace than before.

"Well then, you can say you don't," he suggested.

"No, I'll never tell you so!" she cried, her eyes

flashing. She laid a hand upon her bosom, which was heaving. "There's somethin' here, Dennie, makes it hard to say it. I can't! I can't!"

What she intended by this was no more than that, if he could not trust her without such assurance, it was impossible for her to speak. But Dennis took it quite otherwise.

"By God, it's true, all an' all!" he stormed. He paused an instant, seemingly dazed, and then went on: "I didn't fairly believe it afore, but a little black devil come allays whisperin' it into my ear, when I was alone, and I couldn't get him out'n my mind. It was Sylv, Sylv, Sylv—my own brother! Oh yes, you can bet I began to see it, then! I done my best, and I've waited; but it's *him* you love, and now I'm to be throwed over, *I* am. *I'm* the one that don't count nary fip. An' now I believe it, you needn't be afeared. I believe it, and I *know* it."

Adela was stung by his doubt, and, recoiling from it, made her next move in precisely the opposite direction to that which her heart prompted her to take.

"You've done your best?" she echoed, tauntingly. "And what's that? Mighty little. You can't read, like—like Sylv."

"Sylv be d—d!" shouted her lover. "If ye say another word, I'll kill him!"

Adela Reefe stood before him, quite calm and unshaken. However she might fear his violence toward others, she felt no alarm for herself. She knew her power.

"No, you won't kill him, Dennie," she said. "You're not wicked: you can't do that wrong. But I'm goin' to tell you what you'll do. You're to leave me here, and go back by yourself, as I said."

Dennis tossed out a little defiant laugh. "No, I ain't a-goin', nuther. You'll see me walkin' right alongside o' you till we get to old man Roefe's, and then I'm a-goin' to tell him the whole yarn, and we'll fix the weddin'."

"You will go straight back to aunty's," she re-affirmed, quietly.

Dennis's features softened into a pleading expression. "You'll let me go as far as the tide-way?" he petitioned.

"No."

He hesitated, but presently turned and walked a few steps over the ground they had just traversed. His gun was slung in the bend of his right arm. Once more he reverted to her, appealingly, but without a word.

"You must go," said Adela, gently, standing on one of the little hummocks into which the land was broken, with the glow of the sinking sun irradiating her brown and rosy cheeks, her dark gray eyes, and wild black hair.

Dennis obeyed. She remained stationary, watching him as he withdrew.

But before he had gone out of earshot, he called out to her, defiantly, like a truant schoolboy: "I'm not goin' back to aunty's. Some o' those birds yonder got to smell powder, fust."

Accordingly, he sauntered along over the uneven ground, scanning the narrow territory, the stretches of adjacent marsh, and the clear, pink-illumined air around him, for snipe or plover. He was the picture, outwardly, of careless ease and confident health; but, inwardly, he was far from being placid. There was a turmoil of clashing sentiments and impulses within him, which he did not understand. He was not sure as to what he thought, nor could he have told what he felt: he knew only that he was thwarted, miserable, and angry. He was hurt and helpless, and drifting on toward some fresh injury, the nature of which he could not foresee and did not so much as try to guess ; for he had no more control over the passions that tossed his soul than if they had been a raging sea. Yet, all the while, his gunner's instinct was alert, and the winged creatures doomed for his prey could not, even had they been gifted with understanding, have guessed that he was about to avenge his own wounds by those he would inflict on them.

Adela waited a few moments where she stood ; for she, too, was distressed, and hardly knew which way to turn. The thought of the dreary home of the herb-doctor, to which she must return, was not alluring ; but she could not go after Dennis, either, to make up with him. Suddenly she heard a short, hollow report, that was lost immediately in the echoless spaces over land and water. She started ; an indescribable dread seized her. Why, at that instant, did she think of the foolish threat —empty as his gun-barrel—which Dennis had made against his brother ?

It was nothing but a flying plover that he had knocked out of existence ; she could guess that well enough. But she did not stay to reflect. Like a frightened thing seeking shelter, she sprang from her place, along the open stretch, taking the opposite edge of the open ground to that which Dennis had chosen, and ran lightly on under shelter of the low hillocks, so as to reach some spot abreast of him.

A strange sight—this maiden running so featly under the sunset-light on one side, while her unconscious lover strolled along the other ! She glided over the sod with a swiftness and an intuitive caution worthy of an Indian. Then all at once she halted, so promptly that it might have been with a premonition of the shock of sound that came almost simultaneously from a second discharge of the gun—nearer, this time ; much nearer ; so near that Adela, standing still, quivering but not breathless, heard the faint rush of several shot that fell with a sharp "pat" on the ground, close by her. Glancing up, she saw a small bird driving through the sky, with dropped feet and frantic little wings, which seemed to melt away out of sight in a moment, as if by magic. Dennis had tried too high a shot and missed his aim.

Adela did not flinch, but she continued on her way more slowly.

Dennis also proceeded, popping at the feathered game now and then. He did not fire again toward the quarter where Adela was lurking ; she half wished that he would. The dangerous greeting of those leaden pellets would be better than no message at all. She longed to cross over and speak to Dennis, but could not persuade herself to. He, meanwhile, gathered only two small birds ; the rest that came in his way either escaped or fell out of reach among the sedges. Slinging the little creatures into his pocket, indifferently, he went on ; and when he reached the point where he should have diverged toward the cabin, he resolved to strike into the pine-woods and meet the Beaufort road.

Moody and dissatisfied, he was not inclined to shut himself up in solitude at this hour with Aunty Losh ; for he knew that Sylv, though he had set out for Beaufort before sunrise, was not likely to have accomplished the return journey before now. It was a distance of more than fifteen miles ; Sylv had taken his load of fish on a borrowed wagon which must be left at the town, and therefore would be obliged to foot the whole way back. Dennis preferred to wait on the road and meet him there.

Possibly Adela had suspected that he would do this.
At all events, on arriving where she could see him if he
had been going toward the hut, she discovered that he
must have taken the other course, and she, too, protected
by the trees which now were frequent enough to afford
a cover, slipped cautiously into the piny woods.

Dennis had not gone far along the rough thoroughfare
when a second figure appeared, moving toward him in
the gradual twilight, between the ranks of long-leaved
pines. It was the figure of a man, young and of
vigorous frame, but slightly bent; though that may have
been due only to fatigue or revery. His face was darkened, rendered still more serious in its thoughtful expression by a straggling beard, which, however, grew in
a picturesque entanglement that added character, instead
of obscuring it. He was dressed with a modest style
and care that made an outward difference between him
and the ordinary dwellers on that shore, but his clothes
were of simple "sheep's gray." Under his arms he
carried two books, heavy tomes, the smoky yellow of
which, discernible even in that fading light, showed that
they were the ripe husks in which the fruits of the law
are stored.

This was Sylvester.

Dennis waited in the shadow of the trees until Sylv
came nearly abreast of him.

"Hullo, Sylv," he said.

The younger brother gave a start, and stopped abruptly
in the rutty roadway, looking toward the speaker.
Then, with a smile of singular frankness and sweetness,
he said in a low, unperturbed voice: "Why, Dennie, I
wasn't looking to find you here. Seems queer, but I
was thinking so hard, all alone, that you almost
frightened me."

He spoke with great precision, as was natural in a person of his studious turn, but without the least primness or affectation. Carefully transferring a ponderous volume from its place under his right arm-pit to his left hand, he held the other hand out for a greeting. "Seems as if I'd been away a week," he said, wearily. "Has aunty come?"

Dennis made no motion to take the proffered hand. "Yes," he said, "she's thar, and she's waitin' for ye."

His manner was so unusual, so withdrawn, that Sylv was surprised, and let his right arm fall to his side.

"Why, what's the trouble?" he asked. "You're not like yourself, Dennie. You are dispirited."

"Anybody could see that," answered the senior in a surly tone, "without those thar long words. Yes, I am sort o' down; I'm out o' gear. That's the fact."

"Well, let's go along to the cabin," Sylv proposed, throwing into his words a soothing tenderness as unconscious as that of a woman's voice. "Whatever's ailing, we'll consult over it there."

"No," said his brother, refusing to stir. "I want to talk to you hyar."

"I'm downright tired," Sylv objected, mildly. "I've been walking so long. I made a good trade, though, Dennie. See here."

He laid his books down in the road, and put his hand into his pocket. Then he withdrew it suddenly, looking alarmed, and began to search another pocket. Dennis waxed visibly impatient. Finally, plunging into a third receptacle, Sylv brought to light five silver dollars. "That's what I got!" he exclaimed, triumphantly.

"That all!" cried Dennis. "Oh, I knowed it, I knowed it! And those thar books—you worked shares on 'em."

"Yes, I found I could get those, too," said Sylv, with honest exultation.

Dennis emitted a groan. "Ye've done it agin," he muttered, gloomily. "Now look hyar, Sylv, ye wisht a second; I'm goin' to give ye my mind. You're a-takin' the life right out'n me and ruinin' my hopes, and I ain't stood out about it afore; but dog-gone me if I don't stand out now. I wouldn't 'a' keered if it hadn't been none but me and aunty, but—" Here the unhappy man's voice broke. His right arm was occupied with holding his gun, but he raised his left and wiped away upon the sleeve the moisture which had gathered in his eyes. "But when it comes to Deely," he continued, "I ain't a-goin' to let things run as they hev."

With the instinct of the collector, Sylv stooped and picked up his books; but, as he rose, he offered to Dennis the money which he held. "I don't understand," he said, looking puzzled. "What are you talking about?"

Dennis remained immobile in the shadow of the pines, ignoring the younger man's gesture. "Keep your money," he said. "D'ye think I'm a highway robber, to stop ye for what ye've got? It's bad enough that ye barter away our livin'; but 'tain't that I'm a-thinkin' on. Ye've took Deely away from me. That's worse; a heap sight worse!"

His brother gazed blankly at him, apparently not understanding. "Deely?" he said. "*I* didn't take her. What d' you mean. Where is she?"

"Coward!" cried Dennis, growing violent.

At that word Sylv quivered visibly, and drew himself up, with a pride he had not shown before.

Dennis, after pausing, went on: "D'ye dar' to tell

me ye don't know what I mean? Deely's home, but I've been a-talkin' with her, and I know it's so and ain't no other way. She sees how you been a-playin' it on me, but 'tain't no 'count to her. She wants you to go right on, the same way. 'Tain't nothin' to her that you hold us off from bein' married, by that foolishness and studyin' o' yourn. It's cl'ar as day she thinks a heap more on you than she does on me. An' I tell ye ye're the one that's to blame. Ye done it, and ye knowed it. Ye took her heart away from me."

A new perception broke upon Sylv. He contemplated Dennis with a sort of curiosity, and a smile stirred the loose dark beard about his lips. Any one but his angry brother might have seen that he regarded the idea of his being enamored of a woman with a disdain curbed only by a sense of the comic.

"So you stand up here and tell me that, do you?" he retorted. "Well, all I've got to say, Dennie, is that you're acting like a fool."

Dennis's hand clutched the stock of the gun, nervously, under the strain of the effort he made to control himself. "No, I ain't," he declared. "I been a fool afore, but I ain't one now. I see the whole thing, I tell ye. She's set her heart on you, and you've set yourn on her."

Sylv braced himself a little, and looked resolute. "Now I give you fair warning," he said. "I tell you square that I don't care about Adela Reefe more than as a sister—my sister and your wife that is to be. Are you going to deny my word?"

"Yes, I am," the other asserted, doggedly.

"And you're going on, after that, to assert that I took her love away from you?"

"Yes, I am."

"Then I say, *you lie!*" Sylv returned, hotly. The same passionateness that ruled Dennis was present in him, also, though well concealed under his habitual calm ; but it had broken loose now.

In an instant Dennis lifted his gun to an aim. "No man can say that to me," he thundered.

His finger slid down to the trigger, and he drew the hammer back.

Sylv stood in the road, unmoved, the books under his arms. "It's too easy a shot," he said, quickly, but in a low voice. "Besides, I can't fire back."

"You won't have any call for that," Dennis assured him, grimly. He spoke coolly, but his rage completely mastered him.

"Stop !" cried Sylv, when the gun-mouth seemed about to burst into flame.

"Stop !"

The syllable was repeated from the woods close by them. Was it an echo? No ; that was impossible ; there was no echo in that place, and both men knew it. Besides, there was a different tone in the voice which seemed to ring out from the shadow of the pines—an accent of alarm and agony, unlike the peremptory cry which Sylv had uttered.

Dennis brought down his gun, instantly. "What's that?" he exclaimed, thoroughly unnerved. He felt as if some supernatural warning had been given him.

"It sounded," said Sylv, "like—" Here he checked himself, and stared across the road, trying to make out something among the trees.

Dennis turned in the same direction, and in a moment they had both moved thither, and were straining their eyes to discover the source of the sound. But their scrutiny was in vain : nothing appeared. It is true, they fancied a noise as of some one stirring, some one making a hasty retreat ; but that might have been only the wind that came with stealthy swiftness from the ocean side and set all the murmurous branches in movement. Was there a figure flying through the piny arcade ? Of that, also, they could not be sure ; for the twilight had increased more and more, and darkness seemed to ooze through the air like a palpable exudation from the gummy trees.

The brothers faced half around and exchanged a peculiar glance that was tinged with awe. But Dennis fell to trembling.

"Hyar ! Take it !" he said, in a voice of horror. "Take the gun, Sylv. I was crazy. What was I a-doin' just now ? Oh, take it away from me ; don't let me touch it !"

Sylv, on the point of complying, paused and said slowly : "No, Dennie, I won't take it. You didn't think what you were doing. I trust you."

Still shaking, Dennis looked at him with a dumb, bewildered gratitude.

"Come," said his brother, stepping again into the path.

Dennis followed him, but as they left the spot he said : "It war like Deely's voice, Sylv. She saved me, this time."

CHAPTER IV.

A VISION.

THAT which Adela had seen and overheard so startled and horrified her, it raised such a war of emotions, that she was unable to reflect upon what she ought to do. In coming through the woods, obedient to the vague need she felt of following Dennis, she had heard the rising voices of the disputants, and when she reached a spot where she could command a view, she beheld her lover with his gun raised, on the very verge of committing murder.

For a moment her every faculty was paralyzed. Had the weapon been levelled at herself, her dread would have been less freezing : she could have been brave and active on her own behalf. To see another person threatened with mortal danger, and he the brother of Dennis, was different. In the presence of impending crimes, human beings seem to yield to a painless lethargy like that which is said to overcome the victim of a tiger, even before the claws have made a single wound. The extreme of terror suspends the faculty of feeling, as of action ; and this is what renders possible the enactment of the most dreadful deeds in broad day, before a crowd of witnesses.

To shriek would have been the easy resource of some women. Adela Reefe did not know how to shriek. She might have bounded forward, to stay Dennis's hand or divert his aim ; but her muscles failed her as if they had been caught and webbed with invisible cords. Besides, any sudden movement might have resulted only in precipitating a tragic end,

Just then it was that Sylv called out ; and Adela echoed him, half-unconsciously, but with a wilder earnestness. The two exclamations dissolved the spell that had held her. The crisis was over, and the catastrophe had been warded off. What was she to do next ? If she appeared, the effect of her sharp outcry might be lost ; Dennis might be maddened to some fresh outbreak worse than the first, by the knowledge that she had seen him in that awful situation. The difficulties, the quarrel that might ensue, were she to confront the brothers then, would be full of peril. There was nothing for it but to hide ; and, gliding from tree to tree, she made her escape.

It was a long time before she finally reached her father's house at Hunting Quarters that night ; for, driven by the agitation which followed the episode in the woods, and troubled by a cloud of doubts, wonders, and anxieties that rose upon her mind, she wandered restlessly along the shore, as homeless and unfettered as the marsh-ponies that were tossing their manes above the dim, low line of that outer strip of land which, across the Sound, ran out thirty or forty miles under the evening sky toward Ocracoke and Hatteras.

Now it happened that Mr. Edward Lance, the guest at Colonel Floyd's, had been out on a solitary excursion of scientific inquiry, diversified by fishing, along that same sandy barrier. He stayed later than he expected ; and, boating over to the main in the nightfall, he came walking along the uneven and indented shore, on his way to Fairleigh Park, while Adela was still abroad.

Lance was sorry to be so late, but he had abundant material for agreeable revery with which to occupy himself until he should get back to the society of Miss Jessie and her father. Some three weeks had passed since he had come to the hospitable shelter of the colonel's roof, and he had had time to become much interested in other things than the errand which had originally brought him hither.

The young man, it should be explained, was a New Yorker, whose tastes were cultivated and progressive ; fortunately for him, he likewise had money enough to admit of following his bent.

"He is the son of my agent's former partner in business," Colonel Floyd had told his daughter, when he received the letter which led to his sending Lance an invitation to visit them. "You don't know his name, my dear, and indeed it is unfamiliar to me. Mr. Lance senior died some years since, before my relations with Mr. Hedson, who was in business with him, began. But I understand that he is an accomplished young gentleman, who wishes to inquire into the resources of our State—more especially the coast-belt."

"That's where *we* live, isn't it, pa?" Miss Jessie inquired.

"Yes, my child," said the colonel, impressively. "He desires to study our fisheries and other industries— with a view, perhaps, to establishing some manufacturing or agricultural enterprise. It would not be at all strange, Jessie, if he were to put capital into something in our neighborhood. I think he may invest. Yes ; he is probably seeking a field for his capital."

Colonel Floyd said all this as if he were reading a letter or quoting from a cyclopædia. That was his habitual way of saying things. I should hardly call it an affectation, but he seldom spoke at any length without producing the effect of his being a standard work of reference, which would always tell you exactly what you wanted to know, and would state it in the best language.

He was a slender man, with a small but well-shaped head encased in closely cut hair that had begun to silver ; the gray and the black intermingled, and shone with a glimmering changefulness, like the sheen of mica. He wore spectacles, and had that precise, tactical expression noticeable in Confederate veterans of the war and so wholly at variance with our conventional idea of the romantic Southern type. As the colonel held the lease of a turpentine plantation which he was working, near his own modest estate, he was naturally interested in the development of the " coast-belt," and was disposed to welcome the young Northern capitalist of whom his agent, Hedson, spoke so highly.

" What do you say, my daughter ?" he asked Jessie, after a pause. " Would it be agreeable to you to have a visitor ? Shall we invite Mr. Lance to stay with us ?"

He inspected her kindly through his glasses, as if she had been some harmless little prisoner of war.

" It shall be just as you like, pa dear," said Jessie, artlessly. " And if Mr. Lance is coming—why, there's no other place for him to stay. Is there ?"

The unsuspicious would have been forced to suppose, from the forlorn manner in which Miss Jessie cast her eyes around, that she regretted the absence of any convenient hostelry for the stranger's harborage.

The veteran, however, saw through her, or fancied that he did. At all events, he knew that the solitude of the Park, with only a few liberated slaves and the old housekeeper for company, could not be much more desirable for his daughter than the presence of a promising young man like Lance.

Accordingly, it was settled that Lance should come. Here he was, then, fully established, and—thanks to the perfect hospitality of the old officer—rejoicing in an unexpected sense of being thoroughly at home in those warm latitudes. It was now the end of July—a hot time to be so far South—but Lance's satisfaction with his new surroundings was so great, that he had decided to remain through the summer, and already began to think that that period would seem all too short.

While his scientific eye had been riveted upon the processes of turpentine manufacture, on the number and kinds of food-fish inhabiting the shallows or the sea, and on the feasibility of turning Elbow Crook Swamp into a luxuriant market-garden, a finer vision—which he possessed in common with some others of us who belong to the masculine side of our species—had been occupied with the dainty yet commanding outline of Jessie Floyd's face; the saucy charm of her dark hair parted on one side; her novel, half-childish, yet imperious ways.

He was thinking of her, now, as he traversed the bit of open, marsh-bordered land alongside the pines, where Dennis and Adela had taken their unpropitious walk, that day.

The sun had set long before; the twilight had deepened and deepened until all at once it seemed to meet, in its meditativeness, a thought, an inspiration, a celestial surprise—and the moon rose, silent and beautiful, like the embodiment of that thought.

A panorama of memory passed before Lance's mind, embracing pictures of all the things he had observed during the day, and all that he had seen since he came to North Carolina. He stood there alone, with the ocean moaning subduedly beyond the sandy dunes, four miles away, yet audible through the plash of the nearer waters of the Sound, across which the warm breeze brought its voice to him. He saw in fancy the green waves, the ardent sunshine, the low shore with huts or hamlets clustering occasionally in some favoring nook, surrounded by evergreen oaks and other verdant growths ; the chalky lighthouses, the random sails of shore-fishers ; the green, inaccessible marshes that fringed so much of the mainland. The poor folk he had met in his rambles, hearty, simple, ignorant and super-stitious, came back to his eye in groups, with the sur-roundings amid which he had happened to encounter them. The gloomy recesses of Elbow Crook Swamp filled in the background of his memory-pictures ; wild birds rose and flew across the sky, as it seemed ; and all the while Lance was oppressed with a sense of the great natural resources of the region, against which its loneli-ness, the prevailing ague, and the shiftless languor of the population opposed themselves as a dead-weight on all improvement. Yet, stranger and alone though he was, his soul expanded with the idea of somehow better-ing the condition of affairs and making life there brighter and more prosperous.

Then he, too, emerged from revery as the twilight had from its sombreness, and faced clearly the new thought that glowed upon him like the large, sweet moon so dreamily brooding in the sky.

Suddenly he was aware of a shape looming up in the faint moonlight not far from him ; the form of a woman, half of whose body was concealed by a curve of the ground, in such a way that it might have been thought she was just rising out of the earth.

The woman was looking seaward. She did not observe his presence.

Such an apparition would, in any case, have given pause to a preoccupied man upon whom it came without warning ; but there was a special reason why it should affect Lance in an extraordinary manner. Her face offered itself to him in profile, and was so irradiated by the nocturnal light that it came out clearly against the sky. Seeing it thus, Lance was instantly—I might say, appallingly—struck by its resemblance to a face he had many times seen, one that, in fact, he had been thinking about only a little while before.

The face was like a darker profile of Jessie Floyd, touched with moonlight.

At first, of course, Lance thought that he must be suffering from hallucination ; that the day's exposure to the sun had affected his brain and brought out in a visible form the thought of Jessie, which had been so constantly with him. But the unknown woman stirred, and he saw that she was real. Hereupon he scanned her more carefully, guessing that at least the resemblance which he traced was an illusion. No ; it remained intact. He could not get rid of it. Clearly, the resemblance was real, no less than the woman.

I have hinted that Lance was of a modestly scientific turn ; but he also had in his constitution many susceptibilities whereof science as yet knows little, and the phenomenon so abruptly thrust upon his notice stirred these susceptibilities to their depths. He did not at all know what to make of it. A fear crossed him that he was becoming as superstitious as the ignorant folk on whom he had lately shed the balm of his pity. What did this strange presence and resemblance mean or portend ? Was there not some omen hidden in them ?

Another thing disturbed him, affecting his mind very much as a sudden contact with the supernatural might have done. In Lance's family, which had sprung from England, fragments of an old story were still extant, about an ancestor who had been involved with one of the colonizing expeditions to Virginia. He did not recall every particular of the story, but sundry items of it were quite distinct. It was said that this early predecessor had fallen in love with an Indian girl, from whom he had been cruelly separated ; or that he had come to these virgin shores in search of some one whom he had lost : accounts differed as to that. But Lance's belief was, that this long-dead member of his long-dead English family had been in quest of his plighted wife, and that he had somehow missed her, returning to England alone. Virginia, in those days, included the territory of North Carolina—the very place to which Lance had drifted, propelled by a rather vague purpose and a desire for knowledge as well as recreation. There was nothing very remarkable in this, perhaps. The young man himself had not thought much about it ; for one does not have time, in the present age, to linger over little coincidences and bits of ancient family gossip. The old tale had once or twice flitted through his mind since his installation at the colonel's manor, but it was not a thing he would have considered worth mentioning.

Nevertheless, because of those occult susceptibilities which I have mentioned, at the moment of encountering this mysterious woman with her face turned seaward, the remembrance flashed up over his mental horizon like a kindling beacon-fire. A marvelling awe took hold of him, and for his life he could not have shaken off the fantasy that made him conceive of her as a projection from the shadowy past, an image that typified the lost mistress, or the forgotten Indian maiden, with whom his ancestor's life-history had been linked. The circumstance that she was gazing eastward also had an effect upon him ; he could easily have persuaded himself that she was waiting for her vanished lover to come to her over the waves.

But the fancied resemblance to Jessie—that was the most bewildering element of all. Why should it occur to him ? And why should he feel such an unwonted shiver running through his veins ?

The simplest way to banish all this nonsense was, doubtless, to go forward and speak to the girl. The good nature of the inhabitants, Lance knew, made such an informality excusable ; but, as he was about to try that solution of his perplexity, and find out who this woman really was, the figure began to descend the slope on the farther side from him, and disappeared so noiselessly that she seemed to have crumbled and dropped back into the earth from which she came.

Lance stood still ; that curious warm shiver thrilled his veins anew. Then he turned away and resumed his tardy progress toward the distant manor-house, muttering aloud : " How can I be such a fool ?"

But the vision, notwithstanding, remained imprinted on his consciousness, and troubled him.

CHAPTER V.

BIRTHDAY TOKENS.

THE next morning ushered in Miss Jessie Floyd's birthday anniversary. The emancipated housemaid, ancient Sally, had given Lance timely warning of this occasion, and he had taken the precaution to send to New York for a present which he thought might be acceptable.

The question as to what sort of a gift he should select had been a hard one to decide. If the truth must be told, he had allowed himself the inappropriate but impassioned notion that he would like to give her a ring ; inappropriate because he had not yet succeeded in effecting those preliminaries which justify a young man in giving a ring to a young woman ; though, except for that, it was exactly what would best have conveyed his sentiments. Just why an ornament for a lady's hand should have this potent significance, when it is her ear that receives the lover's confession, was not perfectly clear to him ; yet it was plain that there was no insurmountable objection to his offering Miss Jessie a pair of ear-drops. He therefore ordered some pearl ones, hoping to please her. To please himself, he ordered a ring. But the little packet which lay beside her plate at the breakfast-table, that morning, contained only the ear-drops. The ring was securely locked in Lance's private consciousness and his trunk.

Perhaps in order to appease his own self-reproaches for cherishing this jewelled secret, but also to prevent any embarrassment in Jessie's receiving a costly trifle from him, Lance thought it best to let Colonel Floyd know of his intention beforehand. He did so, late in the evening, after returning from his solitary expedition.

"I hope this will be quite agreeable to you, sir," he ventured, with becoming deference, when he had explained.

The colonel remembered that he himself had once been young, and probably found it easy to gauge the effort it cost his youthful friend to maintain this deference in a case where he was positive that he had an inalienable right to do as he pleased.

"My dear Lance," he replied, "neither my daughter nor myself can need any outward token to assure us of the kindly feeling you entertain toward us. That is the only reason why I might regret that you have decided to offer one. A simple congratulation or good wishes would have been enough, I assure you ; but I appreciate your thoughtfulness, and Jessie, I am sure, will be delighted."

"Thank you, colonel. Then it is all right," said Lance, decisively, feeling as if he had just snapped the cover tight over the pearls and rescued them from loss.

They were sitting in the room which the colonel, with innocent grandeur, called his library, surrounded with a few editions of English and Latin classics, flanked by rows of obsolete works largely relating to politics ; and they were engaged in the unscholarly pastime of sipping whiskey and water. It may be that the beverage had softened the colonel into a pensive mood.

"Speaking of congratulations," he said, "these anniversaries begin to make me think that my Jessie perhaps hasn't got so much to be congratulated for."

"I think she has a great deal," said his guest, with some fervor. "More than I have, at any rate. She still has her father—" his listener smiled sedately—"she has her old home, and—and herself !"

Lance had not known in advance that he was going to wind up with those words, and was himself rather astonished at them.

The colonel braced his neck and looked at the young man somewhat narrowly for an instant ; after which he subsided, and observed, good-humoredly : "That is saying a good deal, too. What I had in mind, however, was the changed condition of everything here—the melancholy changes that have come since the war.

When Fairleigh Park, sir, embraced five hundred acres instead of twelve, and when I had a hundred good niggers, it was a very different matter. Why, sir, even in this poor house there was hardly a stick or a rag left on my return from the field. My books"—here the colonel waved his arm with proprietary pride at the faded volumes on his shelves—"my books fortunately had been removed to Wilmington, where my wife and daughter were in the care of friends ; but a foraging party of the Northern soldiery came here, sir, in my absence, and, though there wasn't a soul opposed them, they broke the mirrors, chopped my piano into kindling, stabbed and maimed the pictures on the walls, and tore the hangings into shreds. Yes, sir, that was the noble revenge they took upon me for daring to fight in defence of my native land. Ah, I must not recall those things," he added, recovering himself. "Thank God, we are a united country once more, and I don't regret my share of the loss. But I was also thinking, sir, of Jessie's mother."

The veteran leaned his head on his hand, unable to speak further. There was a quivering of the muscles in his good old, honest, disciplinarian face, that touched Lance's heart.

"I can understand what a loss that has been to you," he said, gently—"and to Miss Jessie."

The colonel raised his head again, and looked with determination at the opposite wall, mustering his self-control.

Lance resumed, with some hesitation, but impelled to speak at this precise moment, though he had not contemplated doing so. "I—I have reflected a great deal about Miss Jessie," he said.

Colonel Floyd's attention was prompt and watchful at

once. He regarded the speaker with mingled friendliness and jealousy. "You are very good, my friend," said he.

The younger man smiled involuntarily. "I see no great merit in my thinking of her. I can't help it."

His host hemmed, and gave evidence, by his restless manner, of being ill at ease. "I don't know that I fully understand you," he began, moved by a conviction that he did understand with the greatest distinctness.

"Well," said Lance, "I suppose it ought to be very easy to explain myself ; but I find it extremely difficult. I have thought about Miss Jessie—I wish it were possible to add in any way to her happiness."

The colonel rose. "Pray say nothing more," he begged, not unkindly, but with some reserve.

"I will say nothing, if you prefer, beyond this : that her welfare and her future cannot possibly be of greater moment to you than to me."

Lance looked at the colonel squarely until he had finished, and then he dropped his eyes. There was no mistaking the purport of his tone, which went farther than his words.

"My dear fellow," said the colonel, stretching out his hand, "from what I have seen of you I like you ; I may say, I esteem you. If you have anything to say which concerns Jessie more than it does me, tell it to her."

The other accepted his hand, and pressed it. They stood thus for a moment, before parting for the night, and Lance saw that the old soldier approved of him. A strange feeling also came over him, that his host and he met not so much on the basis of a possible father-and-son relationship as on that of brotherhood. There was a community in their love for Jessie ; each felt the depth of the other's devotion to her, different though it was from his own ; and to Lance this mutual trust was of good omen.

Before the breakfast-hour they met again in the pleasant dining-room. The colonel was mixing a mint-julep by an open window which gave upon the garden.

" I'm not feeling quite well," he said, " and so concluded to tone myself up a little. It's a great thing to have a Virginian's grave in your garden."

" Virginian's grave" was the facetious term, as Lance had learned, applied to a bed of mint ; in allusion to the theory that where a Virginia gentleman is buried the plant essential to his favorite beverage in life will spring up and multiply.

He laughingly declined to share in the refreshment, and the two said little to each other. Their talk of the night before lingered with them in the form of a slight constraint, mixed with suspense.

But Jessie put all this to flight, when she slipped into the room fresh as the morning sunbeams. She was quick to notice the white packet on the table.

" Oh, how lovely of you, pa," she exclaimed as she opened it, " to take so much trouble ! Why, they're exquisite !"

She held the case up admiringly.

The colonel glanced over at their guest, a slight smile wrinkling his bronzed cheeks with fine lines like those in old engravings ; and there was a trace of guiltiness in his look, as if he and Lance had been fellow conspirators.

" Don't thank me, my dear," he said. " It's Mr. Lance who was lovely."

" Oh !" cried Jessie. She fastened her eyes on Lance, with a sort of reproach ; and his heart sank. " They're beautiful, though," she continued. " Thank'

you *so* much, Mr. Lance. Then you didn't get anything
for me, pa ? Well, I shall have a kiss, anyway." And
she ran toward him.

The old man's gray mustache appeared to revive, as
he received the salute and gave one in return. "Look
under your plate, child," he said, " and you'll find something, will do to give you a treat when we go up to the
races at Newbern."

Jessie trotted back to her place, and the treasure
under the plate proved to be a gold eagle. Another
demonstration of filial fondness ensued, and they all sat
down in a good humor ; albeit Lance suffered a feeling
of unenviable exclusion.

But in a moment or two Jessie jumped up again,
and, with the earrings in her hand, went to the glass to
put them on. She faced around brightly from her reflected image there, to thank Lance again. " I never
dreamed of getting anything so nice," she said, frankly.

And Lance told himself that he, on the contrary, had
many times dreamed of some creature as captivating as
she was, but had never quite expected to find the reali-
zation. He wondered how, in this solitude and with no
one to set her the example, she could have grown up
into such charming womanliness.

The doors of Fairleigh Manor, excepting in the most
inclement weather, stood always open—a symbol of the
owner's frank and hospitable heart. And now when the
breakfast was over and Jessie had betaken herself with
the two gentlemen to the little morning-room across the
hall, a train of darkies—men and women—presented
itself at the entrance, bringing good wishes and simple
gifts to their young mistress. First of all came old
Sally, who folded the fair maiden in her faithful arms
and covered her forehead and neck with kisses. Lance,

with his abstract theories of equality and his concrete prejudices, which made equality impossible, was rather amazed at this proceeding. He did not relish the spectacle of the black face in such close proximity to the white one. Involuntarily he turned toward the colonel, expecting to find in him some support for his own displeasure ; but there was a kindly light in the colonel's eye, and he looked on with approval as the servants approached, one after another, to give greeting in their several ways—the women with less effusion than was permitted to Sally, and the men with awkward bows or friendly grins that attested their speechless affection. Those who shared in this demonstration were elderly servants who had once been slaves, though they were accompanied by a few younger ones—their children, born in freedom. They all brought flowers and leaves ; the fragrant yellow jessamine being a favorite form of tribute, alternating with festoons of the trailing vines found in Elbow Crook Swamp, baskets adorned with gray moss, and little ornaments of woven straw.

The colonel's face grew radiant and tender as he watched them. "Faithful creatures !" he said, in undertone to Lance. "Most of my people stayed by me when the fight was over. I told them they were free to go where they liked, that they didn't belong to me any more, and I couldn't tell whether I could give them work —much less support them. But they wouldn't go. They clung round me ; and little by little we all got on our feet again. They said : 'You's been a good massa to us, and we ain't gwine to leave you now yore in trouble, Massa Cunnel.' And so we built up, together, what small prosperity there is here now. I had fed and clothed them, Lance, and spent many thousand dollars in buying them, but they did not forget everything, as many white people do. I little thought it would be my old slaves who would help me out in the hour of need— I to whom *they* had always looked for help. But so it was. My God, it has been worth all the cost and the suffering ! We are more human than we were."

The veteran planter was deeply affected ; and, as he spoke, a mist seemed to clear away from the young man's mind, and he beheld the simple ceremony that was taking place, in a transfigured light.

Here, close to his-eyes, was an act in the endless changes and developments through which humanity is forever passing : the lifting up, the pulling down, the growth of new types and phases, the subsidence of old forms of life, accompanied by the survival of certain among their features.

One of the negroes, bolder than the rest, after wishing Jessie happiness all her days, said he knew it wasn't right to ask her for anything now, but if she " would only give him a little book to read in." . . . The book was instantly forthcoming. Jessie went to her secretary, and took one from the slender row of volumes on its upper shelf. But at this Sally came forward again.

" Why, missy," she said softly, in Jessie's ear, where Lance's pearl was trembling, " ole Scip ain't no 'count. He war on'y coachman, you know, befo'. He didn't nevah b'long to *you* and the missus. But I come from *yo'* side de house, yo' know I does ; and now yo' dun gone give him suffin', why I'd kin' o' like dat ar pink frock what you mos' got fru wearin'. 'Tain't good nuff for yo', nohow, missy, and ole Sally she'd be mighty glad on't, ef you don' want it no mo'."

So Jessie laughed, and sent Sally up-stairs to get the garment of her desire ; and from that moment on the reception was metamorphosed into an exchange of gifts.

The darkies brought in their vines and clusters, and laid them on the table or draped them with primitive art about the room, until it became a sort of bower, verdant and perfumed with their offerings ; and Jessie sat there like an unaffected little queen, distributing tokens to this and that adherent. She knew their humble demands were not prompted by greed, but that they simply loved the old custom of receiving something from their mistress, and could not give it up even though times were so greatly changed.

Lance had now fully entered into the spirit of the scene, and the fancy struck him that it was a repetition of the old story of savages on the New World shores worshipping the first white person who came among them.

What if these negroes had been the aborigines, and his Jessie—or Miss Jessie, rather—had been that Gertrude Wylde whom tradition told of, receiving their homage ? The idle query of imagination, thus propounded, brought up to him with renewed force the vision, still unexplained, which had crossed his path on the sea-shore.

CHAPTER VI.

A NEW LESSON IN BOTANY.

IN the cool of the afternoon the Floyds and their guest took a drive, rattling gayly on, in the old carry-all, which was the colonel's chariot of state, over many

miles of light-earthed road screened for the most part
by groves of pine.

The old gentleman discoursed to Lance a good deal
about the country and the people, and gave vent to his
natural regret that the class once dominant had yielded
more and more to a hard, pushing set, who were no
doubt doing much to increase the general welfare, but
lacked the graces and the repose of the whilom aristocracy. The young Northerner's own conviction was
that the old aristocracy had succumbed to a relentless law
of nature, for which he entertained the admiration that
he believed all natural laws were entitled to ; but he
could not help regretting somewhat the fate that had
overcome his friends and their kind ; and it was borne
in upon him strongly that so fine a flower of heredity
as Jessie appeared to be—however defective the structure
of the species to which she belonged—ought not to be
involved in this decadence.

You will observe that I am giving you his thoughts in
the formal and strictly rational phraseology which it
pleased him to adopt. Plainly speaking, he was very
much in love with Jessie, and did not care a rap about
natural laws or anything else, if they conflicted with her
happiness or his chances of winning her.

Meanwhile, as they passed Elbow Crook Swamp,
which the road skirted for a considerable distance, he
reverted, with every appearance of absorbed interest, to
his scheme for reclaiming that tract and converting it
into a source of wealth and the means of building up a
prosperous, highly intelligent community. The swamp
covered a territory of many hundreds of acres. It was
rank with cypress, evergreen, oak, and laurel, from which
parasitic gray mosses depended in endless garlands,
locked in the embrace of luxuriant vines, that hung or

crept down to the edge of that slow brown stream, the
angular turnings of which gave the place its name. The
rich, alluvial soil in which all this greenery rooted held
a promise of unlimited fertility ; but the only profit
which men derived from the splendid waste was found
in the cane-brakes, that yielded succulent fodder for
hogs or cattle. Lance imagined in this wild expanse a
possibility of great results, which might play in well
with his humanitarian schemes. He had brooded over
the matter ever since first seeing the spot ; but the com-
mercial and educational interest attaching thereto was
not the only one that kept him thinking about it. Its
mysteriousness, its lone solemnity ; the frowning masses
of dense and forbidding trees ; its impenetrability in
parts ; the danger and savageness of its hidden depths—
all these had wrought upon and excited him, until it became impossible for him to get the swamp out of his
mind, and he felt that it was somehow connected with
his destiny.

In answer to his exposition of his schemes, the colonel,
who was fond of a classical allusion, said : " That's all
very fine, Lance ; but you propose a labor beside which
Hercules slaying the Lernean Hydra would be insignifi-
cant. You know, that myth is supposed to refer to the
draining of a morass. Hercules was the first man who
discovered the still mythical disease of malaria, and tried
to kill it."

But Lance was not to be discouraged by banter.
When they got back to the mansion the colonel
judiciously disappeared, and the two young people
were left alone on the veranda. Lance began to talk
over his theories anew with Jessie, as they sat there
just outside the window of the morning-room whence
the scent of the pine-boughs, the jessamine, and flow-

ering vines drifted toward them in occasional puffs of fragrant air.

"The people here need so much help, so much enlightening," he said. "I can't give up the idea that something might be done in the way of elevating them."

"Oh, that's only because you're so restless," said Jessie. "You come from the North, and you find it so dull here that you have to think of something to keep you busy."

Her lips pretended that they were smiling with indolent mockery; but she looked so charming, and the contrast between her gray eyes and the Spanish jauntiness of her dark hair was so attractive, that the young man began to think opposition was the pleasantest form of encouragement.

"No," he said, quite earnestly; "I don't think it's mere restlessness. I mean what I say, and I can't help it. And certainly it isn't dull here for me."

He fixed his eyes for a moment on the boards of the veranda-floor, as if meditating. Jessie, in her turn, considered him. In his loose blue flannel suit, with a soft straw hat perched upon his thoughtful head, but throwing no shadow on his features, to which a small brown mustache gave additional emphasis, he certainly was handsome; she had never denied to herself that he was handsome, but she was just now especially impressed with the fact.

"I am going to tell you something curious," he said, lifting his eyes unexpectedly, so that she turned hers quickly toward the garden. He had evidently arrived at the result of his meditation. "It has several times occurred to me," he continued, "that my interest in this locality may have a queer, remote sort of origin that no one would ever suspect."

" Why, what's that ?" asked Jessie, in a dreamy tone, feeling sure now that he could not be going to speak of her, since she was neither " queer" nor " remote."

Thereupon Lance went on to relate to her the legend of Gertrude Wylde and Guy Wharton, as well as he could from the stories which he remembered to have heard half jestingly repeated in his father's household. "I am directly descended from Guy Wharton," he stated, in conclusion, " but my name is different, because the male line died out and my father belonged to the posterity of one of the daughters. It's true, all that romance happened a hundred miles or more from here, way up by Roanoke, and I didn't think of it in the least when I started to make this visit ; but, some way or other, the thing has come back into my mind, and I begin to fancy that by an occult law of thought it may account for my interest in this place—at least, partly."

Jessie was absorbed by his narration, as her attentiveness and her eager interruptions had shown ; but what she said was : " It must be a very occult law indeed." She also emitted a little impertinent laugh, which she did not mean to be impertinent.

Lance was somewhat taken aback. " I dare say it's all foolishness," he admitted ; " and there are other elements of interest which are much more obvious."

She was sorry to have brought such confusion upon him, and hastened to revive the conversation.

They got to talking about the negroes ; and Lance, alluding to the scene that morning, proceeded to speculate on the problem of the colored race. " There is something very fine in their relation to you," he said, " but it belongs to a phase that has passed away. They ought to be educated, too."

" I'm sure," Jessie answered, " we educate them as

much as we can.   Didn't you see me give Scip a book ?
And I've helped to cultivate Aunt Sally's æsthetic tastes
by letting her have my pink frock.   What more can you
ask ?"

"You insist upon making fun of me," said Lance,
forcing a smile, though a trifle mortified by her lack of
enthusiasm.   "But you know I'm right."

"Indeed I don't know it !" exclaimed Miss Jessie,
vigorously.   "You want to change everything, but you
can't tell what you would get by the change.   You
would like to cut down those splendid old trees in the
swamp, and turn it into fresh vegetables and berries for
New York.   But the trees are much nobler than the
berries, or even wild-flowers."

"Oh no, I beg your pardon ; they're not !" said
Lance.   "Most of the trees around here are simply
monsters.   They represent rude, primitive types of
vegetation ; they are the earliest specimens of Nature's
effort to produce flowering plants.   Why, the common
ox-eye daisy is a far more refined product than they."

"Oh, dear me," cried Jessie, "I never heard that.
How much you know !   But I like daisies, too ; I don't
want any of these things destroyed."

"They sha'n't be, then," Lance declared, with offhand
omnipotence.

After that, he branched out into an informal lecture
on the relationships of various plants and flowers, trying,
in the sketchy way that he had learned from cheerfully
popular books of science, to give her some conception of
the evolution of new types and the persistence of old
ones in the flora of the earth, together with the mani-
fold delicate ties of kinship between the different existing
forms.

"Then, they are all one big family !" said Jessie, her

face lighting with a sympathy that Lance reverently recorded as being maternal. She was as much pleased as if she had discovered a new set of thoroughly desirable relatives. "But oh, Mr. Lance," she added, quickly reflecting, "doesn't that prove that all these types have got to exist? You say that after one crude attempt has been followed by a better development, specimens of the old sort continue—like the pine trees. Now, it seems to me that it's just the same with the human family. We're all related, but we're very unlike; and while some of us have gone on improving, the others have stayed just as they were. The negroes and the poor whites around here are our monsters—for you say the pine trees are monsters—but if we have the pines, why shouldn't we have the others?"

She clapped her hands, in her glee at the argument she had discovered; and it must be admitted that Lance was nonplussed by her swift sagacity.

"But then you must remember," he said, after pausing, "that the human creation has a much greater capacity for growth than the vegetable; and we ought to help it forward in its growth. There's Sylvester De Vine as an example. See how he's rising above his condition! I take the greatest interest in that young fellow, and I believe I'm bound to assist him as far as I can."

"Yes, that's true," Jessie acknowledged. "But it's very nice to have all these contrasts. I don't want them abolished."

Lance could not but be aware that he didn't want them abolished, either. Would he have been willing to obliterate all the differences that existed between Jessie and the majority of the surrounding population? Did he want all other women to be just like her? On the contrary, the reason why he preferred her was that she represented a higher development, a "more specialized" form, an exception to the common mass of inferior beings.

"You're right," he said. "It *is* nice to have the contrasts. I admit myself vanquished."

In her triumph Jessie rose from the cane chair where she had sat reclining. "Oh, how splendid!" she cried. "I never expected such a victory. I must find pa, and tell him how I've vanquished you."

Lance also rose, but to detain her. "Don't go yet," he said; "I have something else to say. You have conquered me in another way, too, and I want to hear from you whether you will accept my surrender." In saying this he drew a little closer, and gazed with earnest expectancy into her face.

The sudden stillness and frightened silence with which Jessie at first met his advance were not exactly what one would expect in a conqueror. After an instant, however, she regained her self-possession. Her natural merriment and archness returned as she asked, with her head leaning sideward: "Is the surrender unconditional, Mr. Lance?"

"No. There is one condition, of supreme importance. Ah! Miss Jessie, you understand. Will you listen to me?"

"I can't promise, but I'll try," said Jessie, in a faltering tone. Imperceptibly, as it were, she resumed her place in the chair, and waited. The sun was declining; a faint rumor of odd clucking cries came from the turkey-field at the end of the grounds; but otherwise the air was still, and a spicy coolness stole in to them from the pine-plantations and the distant Sound. "Now tell me," she said, softly.

You may be sure Lance eagerly complied. With an eloquence that had never been his before, he told her what he thought of her ; how he loved her, and wished her to be his wife. In his confession he likewise mingled unpremeditated touches about the daisies and the pines, and all that marvel of nature of which they had been talking ; and he made her see how to him she was the culminating blossom of creation.

"If you could only guess," he ended, hopeless of conveying all that he wished to, "what a delight your presence is to me—how it is almost enough just to look at you and watch every movement that you make !"

So fine and frank was Jessie's maiden mind, that she no longer thought of concealment. "Why, then you know," she answered, with the surprise of a child, "exactly how I feel about *you* !"

I do not care to describe what happened after that ; for in the first place it belongs only to those two lovers, and in the second place I know it could not be described without tarnishing the pure beauty of it.

In the long interchange of confidences that followed their union, Lance was moved to tell Jessie of the woman he had seen in the moonlight, the night before. "Strange, that she should have made me think of you and of the old Wharton story, isn't it ? Who do you suppose she could have been ?"

"I can't imagine," said Jessie. "Perhaps you had a moonstroke ; isn't there such a thing ? Or, perhaps it was a ghost."

When they came in to tea they found the colonel carefully dozing over the market columns of his newspaper. "May I go and get the ring ?" whispered Lance, who had owned to her the secret of his hopeful purchase.

Jessie gave a silent assent. He returned quickly, and slipped the emblem on to her finger.

"Mr. Lance has been telling me the most wonderful things!" said Jessie to her father, as they sat at table. "All about flowers and legends and ghosts."

She was holding up a cup at that instant, for the servant to take, and the colonel noticed the sparkle of the new ring on her hand. His eyes threw back an answering sparkle; he gazed fondly at his daughter for an instant, and then, with forgiving kindness, at Lance.

"Miss Jessie refers to an old family history," the young man hastily explained. "I mean the Wyldes and Whartons. It wouldn't seem so wonderful to you, sir."

The colonel threw himself back in his chair, with raised eyebrows. "The Wyldes!" he exclaimed. "You never told me you knew *my* family history. How does it happen? Or is it, perhaps, only a coincidence of name? By George, it strikes me as *very* wonderful!"

As Lance, in his turn, showed equal astonishment, it became necessary for him to ask questions; and, by a rapid interchange of replies, they arrived at an extraordinary revelation. The colonel raked out from his library a dingy and ruinous old "family tree," by which ocular demonstration was given of his descent from a branch of the identical Surrey Wyldes that the Gertrude of Lance's story belonged to. Puzzling out the different lines on the old diagram, which represented a trunk and branches, with here and there a big circle like some impossible fruit or an abnormal knot in the wood of the "tree"—the said knots or circles representing fathers of families—they ascertained that the Miss Wylde whose life-current had long ago blended with that of the Floyds was a first cousin of Gertrude Wylde, who had been Guy Wharton's lady-love.

The colonel glowed with interest and enthusiasm. "I never came upon anything more thrilling," he declared, roundly.

"But you never said a word about the Wyldes," said Jessie, to Lance. "If you had, I could have told you there was some connection between us and them."

"I didn't think of it," he assured her, "because there was a sort of doubt in my mind whether the girl was English or an Indian—as I told you. But I knew the name of Wylde was mixed up with the affair, anyhow; and the more I reflect upon it, the more clearly it comes back to me that Gertrude Wylde was the woman whom Guy Wharton came to this country to find, and who was lost here."

They referred once more to the "family tree," and detected there, surely enough, a small branch terminating suddenly with the names of Matthew Wylde and his daughter Gertrude, accompanied by the inscription: "Emigrated to America, 1587."

The colonel, much excited, now brought forth a faded tome devoted to the history of North Carolina. Turning its pages, he unearthed the record of Raleigh's expedition and the search-party that came after it. But the names of the emigrants, of course, were not given.

"I remember," said he, musingly, "that I read of this incident, years ago, and was struck with it. But I should never have imagined that it concerned a collateral branch of my own ancestry. How singular! The Floyds immigrated to this country long after that time, and yet here am I, their representative, who have spent my life in this spot, so near where Gertrude Wylde disappeared from civilization—and I never knew of it!"

The discovery supplied them with a theme for meditation and remark, that lasted the rest of the evening.

Jessie bestirred herself, in the midst of a revery which had enveloped all three, after they had talked for some time, saying : " How much it's like the flowers ! We're all one great family—at least, *nearly* one."

" Yes," echoed Lance, " nearly one !"

She blushed, and rose to say good-night.

After she had gone, the colonel came to Lance and, drawing his arm around him, said : " God bless you, my boy—and her. I see how it is, and I'm satisfied."

" So am I," said Lance ; " except that no man is good enough for her."

What a night that was ! Did ever darkness close round a pair more happy than Lance and Jessie ? The great heavens seemed to Lance the only canopy that overhung his slumbers ; for the thoughts and images that filled his dreaming brain rose beyond the barriers of roof and wall, and included a vast realm of peaceful joy, in which the stars burned ever mildly. He had taken a spray of the yellow jessamine with him to his room. He fancied that its fragrance repeated to him all night long, in untranslatable sweetness, the name so like its own and now so dear to him : " Jessie—Jessie—Jessie." And the knowledge that she was a late comer in the line of the woman whom his ancestor had loved, contributed still another element to his trance of silent rejoicing.

Yet, through the whole delicious maze of happiness, he was aware of a surmise which had not presented itself while he had been awake. It was this : since Jessie had the Wylde blood in her veins, and the woman whom he had met by the shore so strongly suggested a resemblance to Jessie, might there not be some hidden bond between them, dating from the lost Gertrude ?

CHAPTER VII.

THE RACES, AND THE MOTTO.

IT so happened that Lance, up to this point in his sojourn with the Floyds, had never, to his knowledge, seen Adela Reefe, although she had come once or twice to the house while he was there. On a single occasion he had ridden with Jessie to the cottage at the headland, and had met "the De Vine boys." Becoming interested in Sylvester and his ambitions, he had stopped to see him at other times in the course of his excursions roundabout, and had also received one or two visits from him at Fairleigh Park. He had, to be sure, heard something of Adela Reefe ; but the fact that he lacked the smallest idea as to what she looked like was the absent link in his knowledge, which made it impossible to guess who the mysterious girl of the night encounter might be. In fact, he never so much as thought of Adela, and he gave up the riddle as one not likely to be solved. But an event was now approaching which brought him sudden enlightenment.

The date of the races to be held at Newbern had been fixed —somewhat early in the season, it is true—for a time shortly after the occurrences which I have already described ; and this affair was the excuse for a general rally of inhabitants from the surrounding districts. Colonel Floyd meant to attend it, with a large part of his household, and Lance, as a matter of course, was going with him.

Dennis De Vine had also looked forward to the festival as the excuse for a great holiday. It had been his intention to take Aunty Losh, Adela, and Sylv in his dug-out sloop, and sail a hundred miles up the Neuse River, to the scene of the merrymaking. But the quarrel with Sylv, which had come so near to a fatal result, threw a cloud over him, and for a time threatened to mar the pleasure of this prospect.

The day after that incident Dennis disappeared from the cabin, and was not seen there again until evening. He was supposed to be out fishing, and did, I believe, actually pass his time in sailing outside the network of sandy spits and islands, as if engaged in trolling for bluefish ; but when he returned he brought but few trophies of the hook. I know that during the afternoon he beached his boat on the inner shore beyond Ocracoke, and took to wandering disconsolately along the dreary dunes. The hour of sunset approached as he found himself near the old graveyard of Portsmouth. It was a rough, melancholy, neglected spot ; and the thick-sown graves lay so near the racing tides that the land which held the dead was gradually crumbling away, and delivered to the sea, from time to time, its mournful burden of forgotten humanity.

Dennis, while trudging unconsciously hither, had been lost in mingled reflections upon the quarrel—alternately grateful for his escape from crime, and remorseful for the passionate temper which had almost swept him on, without premeditation, to the consummation of a terrible deed. All at once he became aware that he stood at the edge of this grim and pathetic graveyard. A shudder ran through him.

"To think," he muttered, "that I was nigh on to bringin' Sylv to such a place as this ! And then how would I ha' felt ? Oh, God, forgive me ! We die soon ' enough, the best way we can fix it. Why should one man want to kill another ?"

Near the water the ground was ragged and worn away, where the chafing of the tides had carried it off piecemeal ; and from the gaunt earth several coffins projected, which were soon to fall a prey to the waves. Dennis gazed upon them with a fascinated horror, and as he looked it seemed to him that in the mouldering receptacle of death nearest to him he could see something bright shining through the crevices of the boarding that, warped by long inhumation, leaned partly open. For a moment the wild fancy presented itself that impossible wealth, in the shape of sparkling jewels, had been buried with the unknown inmate of the coffin. He bent a little closer to examine it. At that instant the bank beneath crumbled slightly—some of the sandy soil slipped into the water—and a fresh breeze, sweeping in from the sea, shook the side-plank so that it fell, disclosing the dusty and shapeless contents. Sweat started to the brow of Dennis ; he beheld there a row of toads, sitting inert and hideous inside the coffin, with glittering eyes.

No more awful example of the ghastiliness of burial could have confronted him than that. The sight redoubled the agony he was already suffering, and with a staggering motion he turned to retrace his steps.

Dennis was not a reflective man ; perhaps he had never before meditated very deeply on the transitoriness of life, and the thousand ways in which oblivion is forever clutching at us, obliterating the few poor traces of our existence that are left when we depart from this world. But the conjunction of circumstances, bringing such a sight to him at that precise moment, wrought powerfully on his mind. " If I could only change !" he said to himself, as he plodded back to his boat. " If I could only be better !"

Yet he was by no means certain that he could improve.

Throughout the next few days he devoted himself to Sylv with a careful tenderness that was almost pathetic. He offered to do him little services ; he tried to exhibit an interest in Sylv's reading ; he was anxious not to have Sylv expose himself to any undue fatigues or risks or dangers. He would not let him go out in the boat.

"'Pears like you thought you was married a'ready and Sylv was your baby," Aunty Losh observed, with kindly sarcasm, noticing his unwonted solicitude. "But I'm glad on't, Dennie. Bein' as you're older'n him, it ar' right, and I'm glad on't." And thereupon she again betook herself to "paddling" snuff, with a pleasant sense of duty performed.

Sylv understood his brother's contrition, but did his best to banish all remembrance of their saturnine controversy in the wood. "How 'bout Beaufort," he asked, as the time approached for making the final arrangements ; "have you seen Deely ?"

Now, the truth was that neither of them had seen Deely for several days ; she had stayed at home punctiliously, dreading to meet Sylvester by chance, and dreading still more to see Dennis, after what she had overheard.

"No," said Dennis ; "but I will see her."

Accordingly he went over to the so-called Doctor Reefe's house at Hunting Quarters, the next day. Adela was at home, but she came out of the house to receive him, and did not ask him in.

"I'm not going," she said at first, facing him with a reserved majesty like that of some wild princess.

"Why not ?" he inquired, his eyes still downcast.

"Because I'm afraid. Something might happen."

Dennis shot a swift, indignant glance at her. "What'd happen, I'd like to know ?"

"I didn't mean anything," said Adela. "I'm not going; that's what." She saw that she had been too abrupt, and she was determined not to disclose that she knew anything of the altercation.

But Dennis besought her in every way he could think of. "I won't talk to you so, like I did last time," he said, penitently. "I know I'm a rough kind o' fellow. I ain't got no temper—or mebbe I got too much. But I'm sorry for what I done, and sorry for mor'n what you know, Deely. I'll promise to be good if ye'll go."

And so, at last, she consented.

Old Reefe regarded the races as a matter of business, being in the habit, I regret to say, of selling considerable quantities of his untrustworthy herb-medicines on these occasions. He was peculiar and of a solitary turn, and had his own way of going to Newbern. He started three or four days in advance, on foot, and did more or less peddling in the sparsely settled country through which he passed. This arrangement was also quite satisfactory to Dennis. His sloop was made out of two large hollowed cypress logs—as is the custom in those latitudes, where the hard knocks that boats must endure on the shoals soon wear out any lighter craft—and the accommodations aboard were limited ; there was really no room for " ole man Reefe."

To people leading so plain and secluded a life as that of the shore, you may imagine what a change and what an outlook of wild excitement this extensive trip to Newbern afforded. Adela was always interested in the boat ; Dennis had given her lessons in sailing, and often let her take the helm. Once on board, her old delight returned ; doubts and troubles vanished, and it was soon a gay party that sat beneath the sail, now briskly speed-

ing midway up the five-mile-wide current, now tacking
from side to side.

An informal, impromptu sort of fair clustered around
the races, embracing booths and stalls for the sale of
various trumpery, with perhaps a circus in a tent, or
merely a nomadic little "show," consisting chiefly of
over-colored pictures, that hung upon the canvas wall,
flapping and trembling in the breeze as if frightened by
their own mendacity.   Then, as I have said, "Doctor"
Reefe went about, lean and sombre, with grayish hair
straggling round his dark cheeks, to hawk his "great
Indian remedies," although it did not appear that there
were any Indians to be remedied.   Adela, who possessed
a knack for making ornamental baskets and bead-work,
likewise availed herself of the brief season to sell some of
her pretty wares, in a modest and desultory way.

Lance, Jessie, and Colonel Floyd occupied themselves
at first with looking at the trotters and watching the
false starts, the true starts, the judges incessantly ringing
a bell in the most confusing way, and the fine, steady
rush of the horses around the track, with small sulkies
and eager drivers apparently glued to their haunches.
But after a time, when a number of heats had been run,
there was an intermission, and Lance and Jessie began
to stroll about in the crowd, examining the limited
means of entertainment, while the colonel talked with
some of his cronies among the horse-owners.   Blacks and
whites were slowly sauntering from point to point,
chiefly in separate groups, and our friends kept on the
edge of the white crowd.   There was a fresh odor of
bruised grass in the air, from the treading of many feet,
and the beating of a drum sounded from the small tent
where an outrageous effigy of the Great Giant of Tartary
alternately swelled out threateningly and crumpled itself

up ineffectually, as the gusts of wind came and went that
fluttered the streamers above him.

Here and there a game of some sort was in progress,
though without enlisting much energy from the partici-
pants, except in one instance. The exception was due
to a newly introduced sport—that of "egg-jumping"—
the point of which was that each contestant, in trying to
make the longest jump, should carry an egg in either
hand. The natural tendency to close the fingers at the
moment of leaping was relied on to make jumpers crush
the eggs ; and most of them came to grief in that way,
for a failure to bring either egg intact through the experiment ruined the competitor's chance for that time.
The enterprising individual who presided over this game
had put up several cheap prizes, among which was a
brilliant neckerchief for feminine adornment, and charged
each person who entered the sum of five cents, the low
rate being due to the fact that the eggs consumed were
no longer marketable ; and their condition was supposed
to increase the dismay of the defeated.

The men toed a chalk line on the grass, and jumped
from it successively. The line never lacked for the
boots of some ambitious contestant ready to make his
attempt; and as Lance reached the spot with his companion, the stalwart form of Dennis De Vine was discovered there, gathering itself together for a saltatory
effort. He had set his heart on winning the neckerchief for Adela ; but, with the eyes of the spectators
upon him, he was conscious of being in an absurd position, and his greatest difficulty seemed to be to suppress
a smile that was broadening on his lips. Twice or thrice
he seemed on the point of jumping, but each time he
paused to give way to a bashful guffaw and stamp his
boots on the ground with humorous emphasis. Finally

he nerved himself, and, readjusting the fragile burdens in either fist, made his spring. For an instant the sunlight showed brightly on his ruddy cheeks and red hair as he flew from the line, rising a few inches from the sod. Then he landed suddenly, several feet away, slipped, and went down, with the yelks gushing in yellow spurts from the shells. A roar of laughter rose from the crowd.

Dennis looked a little angry, but hastened to rub off the egg-yelks on the grass, and, producing another five cents, took his stand at the line again. He waited for one or two companions in misfortune to repeat his failure; but there was no awkward merriment about him, this time. He was too intent upon success. Holding the new eggs firmly and lightly, swinging his arms and then keeping them well up as he started, he made his second energetic venture; and when his feet struck the turf he raised the two small white objects triumphantly. They were unbroken.

He was rewarded with plaudits and shouts of approbation—the length of the jump was respectable—and, with a reluctant flourish of the kerchief, the proprietor of the game awarded him that prize.

" Good for you, Dennie !" cried a deep and rather musical voice near Lance.

He turned, and recognized Sylv. " Why, how are you ?" he asked, cordially.

He would have stepped toward him and shaken hands, but Sylv merely took off his hat, bowing, and gave no sign of expecting further advances. The truth was, he was afraid of Jessie, whose notions of caste made her think it proper to keep these folk at a distance in public places.

" Come," she said to her lover ; " let us be going back to the racecourse."

"I wanted to speak a moment with De Vine," Lance objected, mildly. "I intend to make him part of my schemes; don't you see?"

"Oh, well, not here; not now," said Jessie. "He's not your friend, if he *is* to be your workman. And this is hardly the place."

"Very well," he assented, though not wholly pleased.

But by this time Dennis had elbowed his way through the press of onlookers, bearing his prize like a victorious banner, and Jessie all at once became interested in seeing what he would do with it. "Look!" she exclaimed, abandoning her position of careful reserve. "He's going to give it to his sweetheart—Adela Reefe. Don't you remember my telling you about her? She's really a handsome girl—very handsome. And that reminds me —I *must* buy one of her baskets or boxes. She'd be dreadfully disappointed if I didn't."

The result was that Jessie impulsively carried him off in pursuit of Dennis, whom Sylv also followed.

Old Reefe, mounted on a box under the spreading branches of a tree, not far away, was dispensing his medicaments with an impressively stoical air, now and then addressing the bystanders in a curiously grave manner, quite at variance with the usual volubility of nostrum-dealers; and near him Adela was moving to and fro with a bundle of her handiwork on her arm, waiting for purchasers, but never soliciting them. Aunty Losh smoked her pipe serenely in the background, beneath the shade of the trees.

Lance and Jessie witnessed the pleasant little scene that was enacted, of Dennie's presenting the scarf loyally to his lady-love, and her unfeigned satisfaction in receiving it, while Sylv stood apart for a moment, and then came up to take a share in describing his brother's achievement. They all three broke into smiles and laughter at the recital.

But Lance stood motionless with astonishment. "Is *that* Adela Reefe?" he inquired.

"Certainly," Jessie assured him. "Why shouldn't she be?"

Lance was too much surprised to answer. It appeared to him certain, at the very first glance, that this was the same young woman who had of late been so often in his mind; and, as she looked so much like his recollection of her, the resemblance to Jessie which he had before imagined also struck him now. But he could not as yet be quite sure that it existed. He waited until they came nearer before making up his mind on this point.

Meanwhile Jessie pressed forward, and he with her. She greeted Adela with smiles, nodded with the affability of a natural superior to Dennis, and congratulated them both on his success, in a way that made them feel that she had bestowed a favor. She then began to examine Adela's stock-in-trade, holding up the different articles that took her fancy, turning them this way and that, and bringing out their meek decorative value by the sunniness of the light from her own eyes. "This is pretty. *That's* remarkably good!" she said, like a connoisseur inspecting rare bric-à-brac. "Oh, I *must* have this box of bark and moss! And that belt—just see how quaint it is, Ned."

Lance quietly received each piece that she selected, and kept every one; so that when she had done choosing and he had paid for them, Adela conceived that it would be unnecessary to sell anything more that day.

The belt which Lance was called upon to admire especially was made of simple undressed leather, but it was embroidered with a design in varicolored beads, so

original and ingenious that the thing became positively
charming.   Through the pattern there ran a series of
angular lines that suggested an inscription ; as this,
however, seemed to be only a whim of the designer, and
was illegible, it fell into the general plan of ornament,
with an effect like that of hieroglyphics.   Miss Jessie's
cavalier glanced at it hastily, as they moved away, and
was decidedly pleased with the acquisition.   But he had
no time to consider it, and he was, moreover, exceedingly occupied with the result of the closer scrutiny he
had given to Adela.

It had confirmed his idea that there was a degree of
likeness in her features to Jessie's ; and the fact so impressed him, that he forgot to seize the chance which
had offered of a chat with Sylv.   He said to the young
man only : " I want to see you soon, De Vine, about an
important matter.   Come up to the manor when you
can."

It was impossible to keep the subject out of his mind,
as he returned to the racecourse with Jessie ; and it recurred again and again that night, which he passed, with
the Floyds, in the house of friends at Newbern.   A
whole rout of bewildering surmises and baffled guesses
beset him.   If Adela really looked at all like his Jessie,
why, he asked himself, had not others discovered it ?
Why hadn't Jessie herself remarked the fact ?   But
, then, on the other hand, the thing was so unlikely, and
the positions of the two women were so far apart, that
no one here would be apt to notice or for a moment
consider such a supposition.

It was not until they were once more at Fairleigh Park
that he looked a second time at the belt which they had
bought from Adela. Sitting with Jessie and her father,
in the evening, when they were talking over their experi-

ence on the rail and at the races, he glanced over the various purchases which had been made, most of them of a more ambitious sort ; but when they came to the belt, he studied it with a good deal of care, feeling an interest both in its novelty and in the maker.

Did he dream, or was this another illusion ? The angular pattern in the midst of the design, which he had before noticed, unexpectedly assumed a meaning to his eyes. The more sharply he scanned it, the less he doubted his senses, for the beaded lines took with increasing clearness the forms of letters ; and, on tracing these out, one after another, he saw that they composed a series of words arranged in coherent order—briefly, a motto.

I am not afraid of being old-fashioned. Therefore I shall ask my reader if he ever came upon any sight— ever was smitten, either in thought or in reading, by any feeling that set a thousand flame-points tingling around his brain, and sent irresistible waves of cold, nervous thrill down his spine. By this I do not mean a thrill of horror, but of supreme and overwhelming emotion that instantly suggests your being in the grasp of some more than human power—the power of endless, ideal forces, directed upon the human organism from without, as the harper's hand is directed with omnipotent sweep upon the strings of his instrument. If my reader, as aforesaid, has had such experience, he will understand the strange, exalting shock of wonder and awe that vibrated through Lance's system when he discerned in the wording on the belt :

"I journey whither I cannot see.
'Tis strange that I can merry be."

The old motto of Wharton Hall, in Surrey, England, was perfectly familiar to him, because he had visited the place with his father, on one of their journeys abroad, and having noted down the lines, which still remained engraven on the wall, he had committed them to memory. And here was the last half of that quatrain, obscurely inscribed—as if the embroiderer had hardly understood their full significance—on the handiwork of Adela Reefe. Could there be anything more astounding than this? Did Adela know the origin of those verses? And if she did, what momentous secret did the fact involve?

The next moment, naturally enough, a simple and matter-of-fact solution occurred to him. Adela might have learned the motto from the Floyds.

"Do you see how it reads?" he asked, holding up the bead-work so that Jessie could survey the whole pattern.

"No," said she.

He pointed out the letters with his finger, and gradually spelled the inscription through, until she caught its purport.

"How very odd!" she exclaimed, at the end. But the look with which she accompanied the remark showed that the verses touched no chord of memory or knowledge in her mind. "Where do you suppose the girl got the idea?" she concluded.

The quivering sensation which Lance had felt, at first, renewed itself. He laid the belt down, and, as he did so, his hands trembled.

"Do *you* know anything about this motto?" he said, appealing to the colonel.

But the colonel was also a blank on the subject.

Lance, therefore, was reduced to telling them where he had seen it. In doing this he was quite methodical, but he could not conceal the peculiar agitation which affected him.

Both the colonel and his daughter were much impressed by his strange disclosure, and were utterly at a loss to account for the reappearance of the traditional rhymes in a way so unlooked for ; but they did not take the mystery so much to heart as Lance did.

"It's not only extraordinary, but incredible," he affirmed. "I must see that girl and ask her about it."

CHAPTER VIII.

ADELA'S LEGEND.

JESSIE was not much inclined to give heed to her lover's curiosity about Adela, and his desire to consult her respecting the enigma which had so piqued him. But he continued so persistent, that she was obliged to humor him ; and before a week passed he persuaded her to ride with him to Hunting Quarters and search out the mysterious maiden.

Both Adela and her father were at home, the latter being engaged, when the visitors entered, with some jugs and bottles, in which were stored his marvellous decoctions. Promptly desisting from his work, he invited the young pair to seat themselves ; and Adela, who was just then stitching at some of her semi-savage contrivances, also rose to offer welcome.

The interior of the house at Hunting Quarters was rude enough. The room in which these four people met was badly lighted from two small windows facing toward Core Sound, one of which was open, so that the dull booming of the sea continually entered, supplying an uncouth refrain to their conversation. On one side was a large hearth ; on the other, a door leading to the remaining part of the house—what there was of it. The furniture was scanty : a table, a bench, a couple of stools, some shelves holding bottles, boxes, a few books and various cooking utensils as well as dishes. The lack of sufficient seats for guests was supplied by several blocks of wood sawed off from the stumps of trees ; and to these primitive perches old Reefe and his daughter resorted, in order to make room for their callers.

Jessie presented an excuse for coming, to the effect that Aunt Sally was desirous of having a bottle of Doctor Reefe's famous specific ; but, when this business was over, she turned the conversation to Adela's work.

"Mr. Lance is ever so much pleased with those things you let us have," she said. "And I can assure you he takes the greatest interest in some of them. I think he wants to ask you how you sew the beads, and how you make those moss-boxes."

Adela laughed. "I don't know," she said. "I've done it so long—ever since I was a tiny girl. Ain't it so, dad ?"

Old Reefe, thus referred to, gave a nod, without saying anything. But Lance took advantage of the cue Jessie had given him to go into particulars with Adela as to her mode of manufacture and the several beauties of the articles she produced. Finally he came around to the subject of the belt and the pattern woven upon it. "Have you got any more of those ?" he asked.

"No," said Adela ; "it was the last—the one you took. I can make another, if you want. I've got it all in my head."

"And the rhyme, too ?" Lance inquired, eagerly.

"What? What's that?" Adela appeared a little dazed.

"I mean the words," he explained. "Didn't you know there were words in it?"

"Oh, that part along the middle," said the girl. Her gray eyes took on a far-off, dreamy expression. "Yes; they are words."

Lance controlled his excitement, which still seemed to him causeless and rather annoying. "I wonder if I read them right?" he hazarded. "Would you like to see how they looked to me?"

He drew out a bit of paper on which he had written them, and showed it to her. The action seemed to rouse her taciturn father slightly. But Adela gazed at the paper, and said, with an incredulous laugh: "Oh, no, they don't look like that!"

"Can you read?" Lance demanded.

"Yes, a little; but they don't look like that."

"Well, at any rate, they mean something," he retorted; "and this is what they mean."

He read the rhyme aloud, and their eyes met.

"Yes," she admitted; "I suppose that's how it goes;" and she crooned the distich over, as if singing to herself.

"But what I want to know," he continued, "is how you got it. How did you come to know it?"

Adela remained silent; but her father spoke, after a pause, in a serious, hollow voice. "It is very old," he said. "It is a great charm. We have always known it."

"How do you mean—'you'?"

"Our people," replied the old man, gravely.

"But not all the people around here," Lance interposed. "Miss Jessie doesn't know it."

Reefe made a gesture of dissent that approached the disdainful. "No," he exclaimed, with a sort of gutteral grunt after the word; "*she* don't know—of course."

"But *I* have known it well," Lance said. "I saw it years ago in England."

"You?" cried Reefe, with the first indication of marked feeling that he had betrayed during the interview. "Who are you, then?"

"Oh, I'm a humble citizen named Lance!" said the young man, quietly. "But I know that motto; it has been in our family for a long time."

The old man seemed to withdraw suddenly into himself. "It is a great charm," he repeated, slowly. "Wonderful! It keeps off harm and trouble. My father gave it to me."

"Where did he find it?" Lance inquired.

"He found it far, far back," Reefe responded. But his tone was so vague, and his expression grew so introspective, that Lance half imagined that the old face was growing still older—immeasurably more ancient—as he gazed upon it, and that the speaker was removing himself, by some occult spell, into a distant past.

"You spoke of our people," he said, at length. "Did you mean your family?"

"Where we came from. Our people—over there," the herb doctor answered, pointing uncertainly to his right, in a direction, Lance noticed, which signified farther to the North, up the Sound.

"Yes, they always had that charm," Adela now said. "I don't know why. Who can tell? It all comes from the old story of the Indians and the white folks."

Her father appeared to have lapsed into a semi-trance,

or to be dozing ; but Adela looked aroused ; her interest was kindled, and she was evidently prepared to be
communicative.

"Oh, is there a story ?" Jessie cried.   "Why, I
never heard it.   Do tell us, Deely !"

Some judicious urging was required before the girl
would speak ; but, in the end, the inquisitive lovers
succeeded in persuading her, and at last she narrated to
them the legend of her "people," the substance of
which shall here be given, though not precisely in her
language.

A great many years ago—as many as there are buds
on a tree—an old man dwelt in a wigwam beside the
sweet waters, with his only child, a beautiful girl.   They
had come out of the sea together, no man could
remember when ; but, while the other people in the
wigwams were dark and red, these were almost white.
They had been so long in the sea that the foam of the
waves, touching their faces, had made them so white.
And the old man loved his daughter very much.   They
spoke a strange language together, but when others
talked to them, they replied in the words that all understood.

The old man had no name ; but his daughter was
called Ewayeá, which meant Lullaby or Rest-Song.
She, too, loved her father.   They lived for each other ;
and the old man seemed always waiting for something,
uneasy and troubled, but Ewayeá made him rest and
sang him to sleep ; and he slept much, and was happy.
But when he was resting, Ewayeá would go to the top
of a little hill near the wigwam and look far away, seem-
ing also to expect that some one would come.

By and by he came.   His name was Sharp Arrow ;

and he came suddenly, as if some hand had bent a bow and sent him there swiftly. He loved Ewayeá, but at first she did not love him, because she had not waited for him, and he was a red color ; and she told him he must go and stay in the sea and let the foam dash over him, to wash his face and make him white. Then he went away, but when he came back his face was still red ; and the Old-man-without-a-name told him that he could not have his daughter. But Sharp Arrow stayed there, and he flew in and out of the forest, always returning to the maiden with love and with some presents, or bringing food to her father. So at last he struck her heart. It bled for him, and she longed to go with him, to comfort him, and be happy herself. But she said : " Not yet, not yet ! The Old-man-without-a-name would die if I left him now. I must sing him to sleep many times before we go."

Her father saw that she loved Sharp Arrow, and he was very jealous. He looked at the young man with enmity, while his face every day grew harder, more angry, and stern, like iron. Often, too, he spoke to Ewayeá in the strange language, and pointed to the East, as if he would have her go there. But she only shook her head and sighed ; and sometimes she wept.

The summer flew away, and the birds flew away to find it. But those two lovers did not know it had gone, for their hearts were warm, and thoughts of love grew in them, like the leaves of June. The days parted, one from another, and the seasons separated ; but for Ewayeá and her lover there was no separation. They were man and wife. Their two children played in the shade of the forest, and Ewayeá sang lullabies to them. She taught Sharp Arrow charms and spells. She gave him words out of a book. Her children learned the strange language ; and she looked at the trees, the water and the sky, and made them talk as they had not talked till then. And Sharp Arrow promised that her spells should never be forgotten among his people if she should die.

But she never died.

The old man slept a long while ; then at last he woke. And when he woke his face was wrinkled with anger—it was hard like ice in the sweet waters—and when he looked at Sharp Arrow the look seemed to freeze the young man's face, so that hatred stiffened it into a hardness like that of the old man's. Then, one night in winter, the old man came to the door of his wigwam and stood there like a spirit. He beckoned to Sharp Arrow, with one finger upraised ; the moonlight gleamed white on his bitter white face, and behind him there was much white snow. "I am dead," he said to Sharp Arrow, "and you must come with me!"

The look of hate was still in all his features ; and as Sharp Arrow rose to obey the command, his own face reflected that hatred. The moonlight fell on him, too—his face grew white in it—and no one could have told which face was most like the other, then. But he went forward, and followed the old man.

Just at that moment Ewayeá awoke from her sleep beside the children. She stretched out her arms, tried to catch her husband and hold him, and saw him pass away out of her reach ; saw her father, also, standing beyond, and beckoning.

"Father ! father !" she cried, "why do you leave me ? Where are you going ?" And to her husband she cried : " Oh my heart, my heart, come back to me !"

But they gave no heed to her. The old man moved away, noiseless, on feet of air—always turning backward that icy, malignant gaze—and the young man followed, staring fixedly, helplessly upon him, with the same dumb and frozen wrath upon his own countenance.

And so, as if they had been spirits, they passed noiselessly on and on, disappearing in the pale night and the snow, until all that Ewayeá could see in the quarter where they had vanished was the crescent of the sinking moon, like an uplifted, crooked finger, beckoning some one to follow.

Ewayeá hoped that they would come back. At first she wanted to go after them, but when she tried to move she could not : her limbs were as weak and cold as snow, and invisible arms were thrown around her, holding her back. There was nothing for her to do but to wait. When the spring came again she was always waiting and watching. She stayed every day in the same place, looking out and expecting her father and her lover to return ; but still they came not. At last she ceased to speak : she sat there motionless and voiceless on the ground, ever longing for them, but afraid to stir, for fear that they would come back and not find her. The years passed, and her children grew up and departed, carrying with them the spells and charms they had learned. Yes ; they went away and forgot their mother, who sat there so patiently. But she never once called to them, and only waited—waited—waited. They say she is still waiting in that spot. Summer after summer has blossomed above her, and the new leaves have started and rustled with surprise as they caught sight of her, and have whispered one another all day long about the strangeness of her silent presence. The slow autumns, one after another, have wreathed her brow with weird, unnatural flame ; and the snows of many, many winters have crept around her feet and drifted higher until they almost buried her. But she cares nothing for all these changes; does not even turn her head one way or the other, but simply gazes straight forward, expectantly, just as she used to when she went to the top of the little hill looking eastward. In summer, again, come the butterflies and softly touch her cheek with sympathetic wings, as they hover around; the humming-birds flash and tremble near her lips, as if expecting to find honey there; and other birds look curiously with their bright eyes into hers that make no answer, while the squirrels that chatter on the boughs near by, and nibble nuts, seem to wonder that she does not ask to share their food. Still, she gives heed to nothing. She crouches low, and her weary head has drooped; and the leaves and dust have fallen thick upon her from the under-brush that has sprung up so rankly about her; so that sometimes you might think she was not a woman at all, but only a mound of earth. Yet she is not dead. No! The rains and winds, of course, have worn away the expression from her face, until it looks dull and sad and lifeless; but, for all that, she is not dead. Her arms and knees must have grown very tired in the long vigil she has been keeping, and one would suppose they would have crumbled into earth before now. But, you see, the wild vines have reached out from the surround-ing trees to support her; and they have encircled her lovingly, lending their strength, that she may not fail of her purpose.

No; she is not dead. If you could only discover the exact place, you would find her still alive. But we do not know where it is.

All four remained silent for a few moments, after Adela had finished her legend. Lance had listened with

profound attention ; and the shadowy, fantastic outlines
of the narrative were so extraordinary, that he was at
first too much astonished and perplexed to know what to
think or say about it. Clearly enough, that which the
girl had told might be interpreted as a sequel to the history of Gertrude Wylde, after his ancestor, Guy Wharton, had lost trace of her. It was impossible to say just '
what the tradition, now so vague and impossible, had
originally come from. But the blending of the white
and Indian races at which it hinted, the looking eastward, and the idea of endless waiting and expectancy
that ran all through it—did not these things point
plainly toward the old romance with which his family
was connected ?

He did not believe that his imagination alone was responsible for these suggestions, because Adela could not
possibly know what he knew—her story was an inheritance so carefully guarded, that even Jessie had not heard
it until now—and yet here were these salient details that
fitted on so naturally to his own tradition, and supple-
mented it. Then, too, there was the old, transmitted
rhyme. Ah, that was the clew ! It clinched all the
parts of his guess-work together.

"Was Ewayeá one of your people, then ?" he asked,
at length.

Adela looked at him with surprise, as if he were asking about something which had already been explained.

"Why, I thought I said so," she answered. "We
came from her."

Old Reefe, roused perhaps by Lance's voice, opened
his eyes, and, hearing his daughter's statement, nodded a
silent corroboration.

"And that charm," Lance continued—"the one that

you put on the belt—came from her, too? Did she teach it to her children?"

"Yes; that came from her, too," said Adela.

Lance turned toward Jessie in a bewildered way, gazing at her as if he expected her to say or do something which would dispel the phantasm that was growing so like a reality. But Jessie only reflected his amazement in the glance which she gave him in return.

"Isn't this very remarkable?" he said.

"Very," said Jessie. "It's a perfect puzzle. I don't see what to make of it. But, Adela," she went on, addressing the girl, "why have you never told me this before?"

Adela responded only with a reticent smile, and her luminous gray eyes roved from Jessie to Lance and back again without betraying what she thought.

"We don't tell it," muttered her father. "It was our story—only for us."

"But you *have* told it now," Jessie argued. "You've told Mr. Lance, and he is a stranger." Here Jessie blushed, and corrected herself: "Any way, he *was* a stranger to you."

The old man raised his hand to point at Lance; and —by an odd coincidence—his forefinger, separated from the others, was curved with a beckoning emphasis, as if he were himself the Old-man-without-a-name of the legend. "*He* is one of us," he declared.

"I'm not so sure of that!" Lance exclaimed, feeling that the mystery was going almost too far. "I don't see it at all."

"You knew the charm," old Reefe retorted; and his eyes twinkled obscurely, as he fixed them upon his visitor.

"That doesn't prove that I'm one of you," said

Lance, rising, for the situation vexed him; he was becoming indignant. "It only shows that my people in England knew the rhyme long before yours were heard of."

Jessie rose as well. "I don't see what your father is thinking of," she observed, frigidly, to Adela. "Mr. Lance belongs to a very old family."

Something like a sarcastic chuckle seemed to escape from Reefe's bearded lips; but he remained quite impassive. It was impossible to tell whether or not he had made any sound.

"Before I go," Lance began, desperately, "I wish you'd tell me what this legend means. Did you have Indian ancestors, as well as English?"

He fixed his gaze intently and strenuously upon Adela as he spoke.

"I told you all I could," Adela answered, evasively; and began to resume her work upon one of the moss-boxes.

Reefe looked at him, with a trace of defiance now. "We have as good blood as any," he averred. "But we ask you no questions, and I don't see that we've got a call to answer any more. If ye want any yarb medicine—" And there he paused, indicating that he was ready for business.

There could not have been a completer collapse of the climax which Lance had thought to force. He turned away in disgust. "Come, Jessie," he said, "let us go." And Jessie was more than ready to accede.

But before they went he thanked Adela for her story, and bade good-by to her and her father. As he faced them in doing this, he noticed once more the baffling resemblance between Adela and Jessie, which their unlikeness in stature and general bearing rendered all the

more peculiar ; and the gray eyes of the Reefes troubled
him by their enigmatic expression. The conviction was
strong in his mind, that the cause of their silence was
that they really had nothing more definite to tell him
about their ancestry than what they had imparted. Yet
he wished that they had not stopped at this point. Why
did they have gray eyes ? And yet, why should they
not have them ? Save for a slight bronze or coppery hue
in their complexions, they were of the same European
race that Lance and Jessie belonged to.

Nevertheless, their eyes and their strange legend pursued and haunted him long after he and Jessie had
cantered away from the herb-doctor's door.

CHAPTER IX.

LANCE AND SYLVESTER.

So mingled and conflicting were the considerations in
Lance's mind, on leaving the Reefes, that he was not
sure he would want to see Adela again. But his mood
soon changed ; he was not able to evade the importance
which she had assumed for him.

"I hope you are satisfied now," said Jessie, as they
rode homeward together.

"No, I'm not," he answered. " I suspect myself of
being very much *dis*satisfied."

Somehow he did not dare to speak to her, as yet, of
the theory he entertained, that Adela was a descendant
of Gertrude Wylde. And how could he tell her that he
thought they looked alike ?

But within a few days, so incessantly did the notion pursue him, that he was forced to make a limited confession of it. Jessie observed that he was preoccupied and thinking of something which he would not tell her. "Do let me know what it is that troubles you, Ned," she whispered to him, laying her arm gently around his neck one evening on the veranda, when she found him brooding there alone.

Thereupon he made his disclosure, and was rewarded by a rather tumultuous dialogue, in which Jessie demonstrated clearly that she was not pleased with the idea which he presented.

"But how can it be any other way, Jessie?" he demanded, reproachfully. "Everything leads up to this conclusion; and, surely, if Adela Reefe represents to-day the line of that poor girl, Gertrude, who would have been your own cousin if you had been living then, how can we be indifferent to the fact that the same blood is in your veins and hers?"

"I won't have it so!" Jessie returned. "I don't care if it is. And, besides, she has Indian blood; that makes all the difference. It is no longer the same."

Lance bethought him of those reported cases in which the stock of negroes and whites had been blended, and he feared that it would be next to hopeless for him to overcome Jessie's aversion. Still he said: "But that is so far off, child. She is so like us now, that I can't help thinking of her as if she might be a kinswoman of yours —can't help taking an interest in her welfare."

"Never say that to me again!" cried Jessie. "No one in that class shall be considered as a kinswoman of mine. If you are going to give yourself up to such fancies as these, you may as well choose between them and me."

Her tone exasperated Lance, but he controlled himself. "Dearest," he said, "I have given myself up only to you. You know it; don't you?"

Then Jessie showed contrition, and humbly, while the tears rose to her eyes, acknowledged her hastiness; and the little quarrel proved to be only a convenient ground-work for new demonstrations of mutual tenderness. But there remained in Lance's mind a residuum of doubt, lest his betrothed should not fully sympathize with all his impulses, his desire to be true to every one who could justly make a claim upon him. He did not abandon the project, which had unconsciously been taking shape, of somehow including Adela in his schemes of improvement.

While this dubious colloquy was fresh in his thoughts, it chanced that Sylvester De Vine, responding to the invitation he had thrown out at the races, trudged up to the manor to see him. Lance's love affair, and the misty problem concerning Adela, had not prevented him from giving a good deal of meditation to his plans, which he had also talked over with Colonel Floyd, regarding investment in new enterprises. Consequently, he was primed for the interview with Sylv.

At that time the process of making paper from the refuse of Louisiana sugar-cane, commonly called "bagasse," had scarcely been thought of; Lance, at any rate, had never heard it suggested; but it had occurred to him that the glutinous reeds, which grew in such unmeasured abundance along this marshy North Carolina coast, might be utilized in paper-manufacture; and he had annexed the idea to his other pet desire of reclaiming Elbow Crook Swamp. He was anxious to enlist Sylv in both these enterprises, having already ascertained that the young fellow was far more receptive and progressive than Colonel Floyd. What he needed was an assistant who would give time and energy to the preliminary steps and experiments, animated by faith and assisted by due compensation in money.

"Would you undertake to explore the swamp for me, and give me a detailed report?" he asked Sylv.

"It would be very difficult," Sylv answered, "and would take time. I might do it for you, though, by and by."

"Oh, there's no immediate hurry. You can wait a while. I shall probably have to go North during the winter on business and to arrange about mobilizing capital to work with here. I want to find out what is practicable before I do anything serious. But, in the meanwhile, we might start in on a trial of the reed-pulp for paper."

Sylv pulled his tangled beard meditatively, and replied : "That won't help me much with my law studies."

"Yes, it will, indirectly," Lance declared. Then, after reflecting, he added : "I'll tell you what I'll do ! I'll give you some assistance for the present, so that you can go on reading. It won't do you any harm. Afterward, you can undertake my job."

It was not to be wondered at that, from this beginning, they should go on to speak of Adela. "She astonishes me," said Lance. "I did not expect to find any one like her here. It's a pity that she can't have a chance to develop, too."

Sylv cast a sharp glance at the young philanthropist. It may have been that the remark threw a new light for him upon Lance, or upon Adela.

"Yes, it would be a good thing for her," he replied, with moderate enthusiasm. "She's engaged to marry my brother—Dennie."

This was news to Lance, and it took him by surprise. Somehow, his first sensation was one of disappointment, though he could not have explained to himself or any one else why. In Sylv's accent, also, there was a vague hint of despondency, as he made his announcement. Possibly it was the first sign of a sentiment which he had not, up to that time, suspected. The two men dropped into silence for a moment.

"Well," said Lance, with abrupt energy, "that's all right, I suppose. And *I'm* engaged to Miss Jessie. It will be all the pleasanter to have you and Dennie and Adela working with us for a common end."

It was taking a sanguine view, to suppose that such a harmony could be maintained; but it gave Sylv great pleasure, although he saw the difficulties in the way. His face lighted with surprise, which gradually changed to quiet satisfaction.

The two men talked long and earnestly, and by the time Sylv set out for home they had agreed that they would try to persuade Adela to go to school at Newbern, Lance undertaking the expenses.

"I'm not main certain Dennie'll let her," Sylv warned him, as they parted.

".But he ought to be very glad to have her go," Lance replied. He had no misgivings on that score.

Sylv was brimming with eagerness and anticipation for Adela's future as it expanded before his vision, in the light of his friend's generous offer; and it was a new experience to him to be treated as an equal, almost a companion, by one so much above him in position and fortune. Altogether, he felt very happy. His desire for intellectual improvement was so single and controlling, that he was able to extend to another the same congratulation he gave himself; and the prospect just opened for Adela filled him with keen, unselfish delight. As he had told Dennie, his regard for her was simply that of a brother ; and it was only in the opportunity as presented to a sister that he rejoiced. Yet he found, when he came to mention the matter to Dennie, that it threatened to renew in some measure the trouble which had recently come between them.

" I'm glad for *your* luck, Sylv," said Dennie, in a cordial tone. " But 'pears to me you uns might kinder be satisfied with polishin' and rubbin' on your own brains and makin' 'em all smooth and shiny, 'thout interferin' with Deely. 'Pears to me like she ar' good enough the way she ar' now. That's what."

" So she is," Sylv assented. " But it would make her happier, and she'd have a heap more real pleasure in life, if she could be educated. She was very glad to learn to read, you know. Now, this is one chance out of a thousand ; she may never get another."

Dennie, however, was not open to argument. He looked with favor on the scheme of Sylv's receiving money and employment from Lance, partly because it would gratify his brother and partly because it would lighten his own cares and bring him nearer to marriage with Deely ; but if Deely was to be included in the abstract movement for unnecessary culture, he would be as badly off as before.

In spite of Dennie's opposition, Sylv could not relinquish the plan ; and he had the imprudence to broach it with Deely on his own account. She did not manifest any pronounced desire to enter into it, but they talked of it several times, and it was evident that she was considering it.

Dennie heard of these consultations, of course, and reproached his brother. He exerted great force of self-command, and avoided any outbreak of temper ; he was resolved never to be jealous again. But Sylv saw that the subject was a dangerous one, and he promised not to urge it upon Deely any further. Sorrowfully and apologetically he conveyed to Lance the information of this obstacle to Deely's acceptance of his proposal, and said that he feared she could do nothing about it.

It was reserved for Dennie himself to bring about, unwillingly, the consummation of Lance's philanthropic design.

There was to be a wedding-party at a house in the woods, near Hunting Quarters, to which the young people were invited. Dennie came to Reefe's early, in order to escort Deely to the scene of the ceremony ; and on their way to the wedding he spoke of the school idea.

"We ought to be goin' to the parson, 'stead of your goin' to that thar school," he said. He urged her again to fix the time for their marriage.

Deely still demurred. "I'm only nineteen," she answered. "I reckon I won't be too old if I do wait a while."

Dennie was very much put out by her obduracy. "I don't know what to make out'n the way you go on," he complained. "Mebbe you're goin' to that thar school, after all."

" 'Twouldn't be strange if I did," said she, although she had in reality abandoned the thought.

He persisted in urging his wishes ; she continued in a contrary mood ; and Dennie at last refused to talk. They completed their walk to the house of the hymeneal merrymaking in a bitter silence, both very miserable. But Deely possessed the advantage of expressing her unhappiness by means of the greatest gayety, while

Dennie had to fall back upon the more ordinary masculine resource of looking glum and morose.

There was an abundance of corn-whiskey and of
" common doin's," as well as of " chicken fixin's," with
other delicacies, at the supper and dance which followed
the brief formality of the wedding-service. The simple-
hearted and jolly guests proceeded to have a very good
time ; and while the bride and groom remained in one
corner, happy at being ignored, the rest shuffled to and
fro in a lively jig, stamping their heels, indulging in
sundry gratuitous capers, and shouting with laughter.
Dennie, meanwhile, devoted a much closer attention
than was needful to the corn-whiskey, the forcible quality
of which he could have ascertained by a single drink.

It may have been due to his diligence in reducing the
supply of the beverage that, as the hilarity of the others
increased, and as Deely grew more and more excited
with the dance, his depression and gloom deepened
portentously. He had taken no part in the dancing, and
had begun by affecting to watch Deely's energetic share
in it with indifference. But it was impossible for him
to keep up this pretence, and the climax came when he
saw his betrothed giving her hand for the third or fourth
time to Dan Billings, a handsome young fisherman
against whom she knew that Dennie cherished a special
grudge.

Dennie stepped forth upon the floor that trembled
with the heavy tread of the athletic revellers, and, shov-
ing his way between the astonished pairs of youths and
maidens, struck a commanding posture.

" This hyar's enough !" he screamed, confronting
Deely. " It's time to go home ; and I'm goin' to take
ye with me, right now. D'ye hear ?"

The old fiddler, mounted on a box at one side of the

room, stopped the frantic discord he had been sawing
from the strings, and began mechanically to rosin his bow
with a lump of the best virgin-pine rosin.

"I could ha' heard you if you'd stayed over t'other
side," Deely retorted, her dark cheeks flaming angrily;
"if you war goin' to shout out so, what do you want to
come so close ?"

"I say," repeated Dennie, in a more subdued voice,
"I'm goin' along, and I mean for to take you with me.
Dan Billings ain't goin' to dance with you no more this
night."

Upon this Billings, who was a vigorous young fellow,
asserted his rights, and gave Dennie to understand
roundly that no one should dictate to him his choice of
partners, "when the lady was willin'."

A serious result was imminent ; for Billings, elated by
his apparent success with Deely, became increasingly
noisy and bumptious, and retorts flew hotly from one
man to the other, until Billings raised his fist to strike
a blow at Dennie. When it came to that, Deely
stepped between the wranglers, and prevented their
fighting.

"Now *you're* wrong, Dan !" she exclaimed. "You
both ought to be ashamed, making me so much trouble.
But there sha'n't be a fight, whatever. I'm goin' home
this minute, along with Dennie."

The other girls had drawn aside, dumb and frightened,
and the men were disposed in a group around the chief
actors, feeling that they ought to interfere, but restrained
by a respect for the privilege of fighting, which they
might some time wish to exercise on their own account.
Billings relaxed his clinched fingers, quite abashed at
being so abruptly robbed of his dignity as Deely's
champion ; but it took a few moments to cool Dennie's

wrath. He insisted that the fisherman had "told him insults," and must be punished.

"I'm waiting," Deely reminded him. "You said you was going, and now I'm ready."

The bride and groom remained oblivious of all this stir, but the bride's mother came forward, urging Deely not to leave them. The girl, however, would not yield. Every one could see that she was greatly incensed at Dennie's conduct, but there was a decisive calm about her that made persuasion useless. She had, in fact, arrived at a conclusion much more far-reaching, which she lost no time in imparting to Dennie when they had left the house.

"My mind's made up," she said to him, without heat. "I've borne your tantrums as long as I can, and it's no use. By and by it'll get so that I can't have any will or way of my own, and I don't think you'll ever be any better, Dennie, until I'm far away where you can't tease me. Yes; I've made up my mind. I'm goin' to that school."

To Dennis the announcement was like a knell. His burst of temper had left him much quieter and, as usual, rather ashamed; and he felt that Deely's intention of punishing him was quite justifiable. Still, he could not as yet believe that she would carry it out.

"You won't treat me so hard as that," he protested. "Think it over another time, Deely. Everything'd be all right if you'd only marry me."

"I don't want to talk about it," was her answer. "I've decided, now, and I'm goin' away."

In the course of the next few days her lover was forced to recognize that she was in earnest, and her resolve irrevocable. An extra session at the small academy for young ladies which Lance had selected was about to begin ; and, through Sylv, Adela obtained a conference with him on the subject of going thither. Old Reefe put in some objections ; but as Adela was determined he gave way, and the final arrangements were soon made.

The conference just referred to took place near the manor. Lance met Sylv and Adela in the grounds, by appointment, and talked over the details with them. But just as they were bidding him good-by Colonel Floyd came strolling along ; and Lance, in walking back to the house with him, told him, full of enthusiasm, what he had done. The colonel seemed to think it rather strange.

" My dear fellow, what has put this into your head ?" he asked.

" Why, it seems to me the most natural thing in the world," Lance replied. " It grew out of my plans, when I was consulting young De Vine. Besides"—he hesitated an instant—" something leads me to feel a peculiar interest in this young woman."

" Evidently," said the colonel, " or you never would become her benefactor." But he volunteered no criticism further than to say : " I'm not altogether sure, Lance, that you are doing wisely."

" If you think," said his prospective son-in-law, " that there's any good reason why I shouldn't befriend her, I suppose I could abandon the thing, though I've committed myself now."

The colonel devoted a few moments to reflection, under cover of his spectacles. Then he said : " No, I am not clear that there is any sufficient reason. It struck me as odd, and may seem so to others. But then, in your character— You see, you are something of a professed philanthropist, and people will learn to understand it on that ground. Otherwise—" Once more he broke off, and resumed : " You are the next thing to a married man, now, which makes it proper enough for you to take the poor girl under your wing. Perhaps you had better talk with Jessie about it."

Somehow the phrase " poor girl " grated slightly upon Lance's ear. Nor did he relish the prospect of debating with Jessie the wisdom of his proceeding ; but it was plain that he would have to do so. It was true there had been no trace of the clandestine in his undertaking, and he had asked Sylv to bring Adela to the garden only because he considered the whole transaction as a side-issue, in which he was separately concerned ; hence he preferred not to thrust it upon the colonel or his daughter. But it was also true that Jessie's vigorous rejection of his theory about Adela had made him less sure of her approval than he would have liked to be.

By one of the surprises frequent in the moods of women, even though one supposes their views to be settled on a particular point, it turned out that Jessie, when consulted, did not oppose his design.

" I have been thinking over what you said, dear, about educating people," she announced to him, " and perhaps you are right. If you're wrong, you'll find it out by an experiment. So all I have to say is, ' Go ahead.' That's the way you'd like to have me put it, isn't it ?"

Her whole manner was sweet and trustful ; she wanted to make amends to him. But, unless I am mistaken, Lance's effort on behalf of Adela was not entirely to her taste.

Thus, while they endeavored to keep up a good understanding, an entering wedge of doubt and possible division had been put in place.

The day having come for Adela's departure, difficulty arose as to her escort, if she was to have any. Aunty Losh was not precisely the person to introduce her at a

Young Ladies' Academy ; and Dennis also felt himself to be inadequate for that duty. Sylv, as was natural, refrained from offering his services. Neither was it possible for Lance to accompany her. The end of it was that Aunty Losh and Dennis went with her by wagon as far as Beaufort, and there she took the train alone for Newbern. Lance had been to the city and prepared the way for her, so that she might be received by the principal of the school, at the station.

But the time which followed was a dreary period to poor Dennis. Knowing his own faults, and that his loss in Adela's exile had been brought on by himself, he made no remonstrance after he saw that her purpose could not be altered. But his wonted cheeriness and energy forsook him as soon as she had gone ; he performed his daily tasks in a listless and perfunctory way ; he talked little, and did not forget his misery long enough to smile. On the other hand, he abstained from complaint ; but occasionally, when alone with Aunty Losh, he would confer with her briefly about Adela and the change that had occurred. The jealousy that took root with such ease in his uncultivated mind, and sprang up there like a weed at the slightest encouragement, soon began to flourish again on a suspicion that Lance must have some interested motive in helping Adela. Aunty Losh, it must be said, was not a good counsellor. Much as Dennis tried to conceal this new source of trouble, it was perfectly apparent to her ; and, because Dennis was her favorite and she instinctively sided against all innovations, she fanned the flame instead of quenching it.

" I reckon Deely may be your wife one o' these hyar days," she said, when they had been discussing his affairs and Lance's connection with them over a cup of yaupon. " Who would ha' thout you wouldn't been her husband now ? But there's an old sayin' what's in my head, that the man as has got his hand on the back o' the chair is mighty often the one as sits down in it."

Dennis saw the application, and was filled with alarm. Possibly it had its effect in prompting him to seek assistance from Sylv ; but his loneliness, and the harassing thought that Adela might also be lonely, or that something might go amiss in her new surroundings, where he could not be present to help her, had a great deal to do with his impulse. Besides, in contrition both for his jealousy of Sylv and his general disagreeableness toward his betrothed, he fancied that it would be a fine thing to show that he cared for her at a distance, and that he trusted his brother.

"Sylv," said he, one evening, while they were finishing the bestowment of the day's catch in the shed at one side of the cabin, where they kept the fish cool by means of spring water—"Sylv, I'd like right well to have you do somethin' for me."

"Say the word, Dennie," Sylv returned.

"I—I want you to go up thar to the city and stay thar, whar ye can see Deely and make her feel like she had a real, true friend—some one to 'tend on her as I mout, if I was fit—and to help her if she want any help. Dog-gone it ! Mebbe it's foolish, and I reckon she ar' happy enough and won't need nothin', but 'pears like I couldn't stand it, the way 'tis now. I want ye to go, Sylv—for me."

"You ask *me* to do this, Dennie ?" said Sylv. "Why did you think of *my* going ? Why not go yourself ?"

"'Cause I'm not fit for't. An' what's more, she don't want me. She said she war a-goin' away, so's she could be alone, and I could be alone. An' I couldn't do nothin' if I was thar, Sylv."

" I see.   It would be some comfort to you if I were
to go.   If you're sure you want it, Dennie, I reckon I
can manage."

" There ain't no more doubt on it," answered Dennie,
" than when I put my helm down to starboard to get
the east breeze, steerin' north'ard.   There ain't no one
else I can count on, Sylv, 'less it be you.   An', Sylv, I
—I trust you ; I got faith in you !"

He held out his rough hand, and Sylv grasped it
firmly.   There were tears in Dennie's eyes, seeing
which Sylv pressed his brother's weather-beaten palm
the harder.

" All right, Dennie.   I won't fail you."

And so the compact was made.

Sylv was absolutely honest in what he said.   He knew
but one ambition, and the gaining of any woman's love
had never formed a part of it.   Why was it, then, that
his spirits rose so at the thought of being near Adela
once more ?

CHAPTER X.

THE LIKENESS.

You remember how little Lance had seen of Adela
Reefe, and that he knew her scarcely at all.   But this
makes it the stranger, and rendered it at the time all the
more unaccountable to him, that, on her removal from
his neighborhood, he should have been afflicted with a
sense of vacancy, and should have suffered from the
melancholy which   one might expect to feel when

suddenly separated from a dear friend. Was he not engaged to Jessie, and thoroughly contented in his love? Moreover, Adela had not entered into his life as an important factor. Yet, now that she was gone, he perceived how quickly and completely the web of surmises which he had thrown around her had taken him also into its tangles. Her identity and destiny had engaged his thoughts far more deeply than he had guessed.

Acting on his offer of assistance, and obeying Dennie's wish, Sylv presently came to him to suggest that he would like to go to Newbern to pursue his studies.

"But I have just made arrangements," Lance told him, "to put up a small building where we can experiment with reed-pulp; and I expected you to assist me."

Not without embarrassment, Sylv made known the special reason proposed by Dennie for his going. Lance thought the plan a rather curious one, and allowed himself a queer, vicarious jealousy on Dennie's account, at the notion of his being so far from Adela when his brother should be in the same town with her. But he had promised to help Sylv; so he consented to send him to Newbern and maintain him there for a while, the cost to be returned in future services.

"Perhaps Dennie will take a hand with me in the pulp experiments," he reflected.

Thus it came to pass that a shed was built in the woods not far from the manor, where a boiler and a small beater and washer were placed, convenient to the limited water supply from a "run" or creek. An experienced vatman was sent for from the North; Dennie was engaged to collect and haul reeds, and aid in other ways when he could. All this involved a good deal of expense, and the colonel watched the work with suppressed horror at the young man's extravagance. But the experiments went on, and Lance became enthusiastic over the details of drying the reeds, getting the mixture of caustic alkali just right for boiling, and trying rags in various proportions.   Finally he was able to produce from the vat a few sheets of tolerably good hand-made paper, on which he fancied that he could see already inscribed a record of the profits that were to be his.

It took many weeks, however, to accomplish that much.   At first Jessie entered into the new enterprise with great interest, and made it doubly charming to him; but after a while, finding that it consumed her lover's time and distracted his attention from her, she began to regard the fascinating shed, with its boiler and engine and rude apparatus, as a dangerous rival.   Nothing daunted by such symptoms of her discontent as he observed, Lance continued his application with a fervor that seemed to her little less than fanatical.   Meanwhile he saw Dennie very often, and was constantly in receipt of news about Adela from him.

Indeed, since neither Aunty Losh nor Dennie had ever become enslaved to the luxury of reading, it was necessary for Lance to interpret Adela's letters to them. These epistles, in the beginning, were somewhat slight and informal.   They would begin thus : " I write to inform you that I am enjoying good health.   I hope you are the same."   But as she went on with her studies, and as the various particulars of her new life appealed more decidedly to her attention, her style became more familiar and cordial ; she described what happened at the school, day by day, and often lit up her account of events with flashes of humor that, to Lance, were delightful.   She hit off some of the absurdities of modern routine education with a surprising sharpness of perception, and was greatly amused at the old theologian who attended to the religious instruction of the girls. He had shown her some books of Hebrew, the characters in which reminded her of her own invented patterns in silk and beads. But withal it transpired from what she wrote, that she made astounding progress in her lessons. She quickly outstripped her classmates in their work, and was promoted to a higher grade. Lance wondered whether this were due to the stored-up energy of a nature that was in some respects primitive, or whether it came from inherited aptitude—an aptitude derived partly, through the dim centuries, from Gertrude Wylde. Several times she alluded to Lance, and sent to him reserved messages of friendly thanks for his kindness; but perhaps she would not have written so familiarly on other topics if she had known that he was to see her letters. The truth was, it had not occurred to her that her betrothed and his aunt would apply to Lance to decipher her letters. And Lance, embarrassed by these references to himself, refrained from disclosing them.

Inevitably, from the supervision which thus fell to his lot over everything Adela did or said or thought, so far as her letters formed a record, it ensued that his interest in her increased. I am afraid he watched those letters with an alertness not to be excused, for some trace of a thoughtfulness respecting him, equal to his own toward her; and when she addressed to him directly a short communication, to tell him how she was getting on, and how grateful she was for his assistance, it was in a mood closely akin to disappointment that he read it through without having detected a word that could be construed as indicating even a commencement of friendship.

Now and again he contemplated turning the letters over to Jessie, and felt a desire to talk with her about the progress of his pupil. But he fancied that she would receive the confidence coldly, and he forbore to say anything, except in the most general terms. Why, in the mean time, he should expect anything more from Adela than a formal recognition of indebtedness, was a riddle to him ; but nevertheless he knew that he was unsatisfied.

It should be understood that his peculiar state of mind was not at any one time clearly apparent to him ; he merely caught glimpses of it. His preoccupation with the paper manufacture all the while kept his attention busy, and it was but dimly that he perceived what was going on in other regards. But when his experiments had reached their culmination, and he had decided to build a mill and begin operations, it became necessary for him to go North. He resolved to run up to Newbern, first, and see Adela Reefe, before bidding good-by to Jessie. This intention he was about to confide to Jessie, when one morning she unexpectedly presented herself at the engine-shed, at the moment when he was perusing a recent letter from his charge.

"So I've found you at last !" cried Jessie, standing by the sill of the open shed-door, wrapped in a light shawl, with a broad hat bent archly over her head, and looking wonderfully pretty. She caught sight of the letter. "Aha !" she said. "I thought you came here to work. But it's only make-believe, I see. Well, I've a great mind to write you letters myself and send them down to you here to read."

"Oh, it's only a letter from Adela Reefe," Lance answered. "Dennie De Vine brought it ; he's just gone away again. Would you like to see it ?"

The vatman was occupied at the other end of the shed. Jessie took the letter and glanced at it ; then returned it to her lover, indifferently. "Deely seems to be quite contented," she observed. "When are you going to finish, Ned?"

"Finish? You mean what I'm doing here? Why, I can go with you now, if you want."

"I wish you would, then. I feel just like having a little walk and talk. You're going away so soon, it's only fair I should see something of you."

"I know that, dearest," said Lance, "and I'm afraid I've spent too much time over this business. It's only fair to me, too, that we should be together."

They sauntered away in company, and strolled through the woods. "I have been thinking," he told her, "that I ought to start in two or three days. But I must see Adela and Sylv first. I don't want to go North without knowing just how they seem up there, in their new life."

A change came over Jessie's manner. "You mustn't go!" she said, with sudden vehemence. "It isn't right, Ned."

"Not right, my dear. Why?" Lance bent his earnest, clean-cut features to look down at her more searchingly.

But Jessie lowered her eyes, and would not meet his glance. "Oh, I have watched you," she said, "and you are often talking with Dennie; you talk about that girl, I am sure. And now she is writing to you. Don't you think you have done enough for her, without going to see her?"

"Perhaps so," said Lance, his energetic mind arrested by a sudden discontent, and by a wonder as to whether he had unconsciously fallen into error. "But surely you don't allow yourself to be troubled about it, do you?"

" Why, no," Jessie answered. " It would be foolish to do that. Why should I? Only, it may be that you don't think what you're doing, Ned. She is not our *friend*, and she never can be. I have agreed that you should be her benefactor if you want to. But think how it might seem for you to go up there and call on her. Isn't it too much?"

" I will do as you think best, my dear," Lance assented.

" Thank you," said Jessie, at once growing radiant.

They passed on through the sun-flecked gallery of the spicy woods, chatting on various topics, and were outwardly quite content. But Lance could not banish the idea that he had been deprived of something which was his right; and Jessie, for her part, was not nearly so serene as she appeared to be. A subtle intuition had warned her that Lance was wrapped up in his care for Adela to an extent which he himself was not able to measure. The circumstance weighed upon her with increasing force; and many times at night she had been awakened by her own tears, only to fret out the solitary hours with vain questionings and attempts at reassurance. Her trouble seemed needless and absurd; but somehow Adela Keefe came flitting across her dreams, and even darkened her waking moments, like a shadow revived from the past, that had the power to blot out the vivid and sunny present.

That evening the lovers looked over some old miniatures of former Floyds and of the Wyldes, from whom the colonel traced his inheritance. In every one of the female faces Lance instinctively hunted for traits that should account for Jessie's features; but he could not find any. Not only was he baffled in the search, but when he retired to rest the old puzzle as to the

similiarity between Jessie's face and Adela's grew upon
him, as more complicated and less easy to shake off than
ever.

A few nights afterward his hands clasped Jessie's
cheeks as he bade her farewell, on his departure for
Beaufort, where he was to take a coast-wise steamer for
New York.

It was late October. There was a chill in the air.
The leaves of the deciduous trees had turned, and were
already falling. The pines were rusty in places, their
needles showered to the ground in great numbers; the
snow-goose had already been heard piping in the air, on
its southward flight; and the waves of the Sound and
the sea, as they broke upon the shore, seemed to shiver
with a knowledge of approaching winter. But Jessie
stood with her lover on the veranda, in the darkness;
and her face rested so yieldingly in his palms that Lance
half imagined he could carry it away with him. There
in the night it was like a picture painted long ago and
dimmed by time, yet shining out through the obscurity
with its youth and loveliness and passion still intact.
No; he could not carry it bodily away with him, but
he could take it in his heart; and so he did, holding it
there long after the farewell kiss had left his lips.

But after he reached New York, and during the long
months of winter, the magic of fancy played strange
tricks with the image he had brought in his heart.
Strive as he would, he could not prevent it from waver-
ing and flickering, as it were, and occasionally taking on
a darker hue, so that he seemed at times to be contem-
plating Adela, instead of Jessie.

One of the first things he did was to hunt up some old
memoranda in which the tradition concerning Guy
Wharton was definitely set down. This cleared up his

recollection of it ; and his next act was to write to a lawyer of his acquaintance in England, who knew something about the Wharton history, asking him to use his best endeavors to get some authentic likeness of Gertrude Wylde.

Unfolding to Hedson, his father's old partner, the paper-mill project, and finding it received with favor, he next exerted himself to form a small syndicate for purchasing and reclaiming the swamp-lands, since that undertaking would require more capital than he cared to venture. But the swamp was not the Treasury of the United States, nor was it a fantasy of such vast dimensions as the Panama Canal ; so the syndicate could not be formed. For capital, despite all the cant about its conservatism, is really moved by extremes : it is allured either by a dead certainty or by an equally defunct impossibility. Elbow Crook Swamp was a something between the two.

"Wait until spring," Hedson advised. "Then you will have time to explore ; and, besides, I may get down there myself to take a look !"

Hedson enjoyed the harmless pride of believing that anything at which Hedson had " taken a look," and was able to speak well of, must necessarily glitter like gold to his brother bondholders.

This affair and others detained Lance a long time. His mind was fixed on settling in North Carolina, at least for the first years of his married life, and he was anxious to get all his investments in good order before making the change. At Christmas he took a flying trip to Fairleigh Park, and enjoyed a brief season of jollity and of companionship with Jessie ; but he was soon back again among the snowy streets. He had seen Sylv, but would not permit himself an interview with Adela. On his return Hedson informed him that he was about to sail for England, being called thither by business, to be absent a couple of months. Lance had received no news from his legal friend in London, and did not indeed expect anything valuable from that source ; the records of the Surrey Wyldes were doubtless too scattered to be traceable, and it was scarcely possible that any vestige of Gertrude's features would have been retained among the possessions of the Whartons. But, not wishing to forego any chance, he petitioned Hedson to see the solicitor and co-operate with him. The acute perception of the American man of business might perhaps aid the careful British lawyer in getting at something, even in so sentimental an inquiry. Lance would have gone himself, so active was his interest in the question, had it not been for his reluctance to place the ocean between himself and Jessie.

Toward the end of February Hedson sent him a half-page letter, which ended with the words : " Think I have got something for you." Exasperating silence followed this communication. But, in latter March, Hedson landed at New York, and brought Lance a drawing. " It's from an old picture," he said. " Had the devil's own time getting it ; but I bored everybody concerned, until they couldn't stand it any longer, and had to help me ferret it out."

" And you're sure this was Gertrude Wylde ?" asked Lance.

" Why, my boy, you don't think I'd say so if I wasn't sure, do you ? Besides, look at this curious monogram on the back. It seems to be two Gs and two Ws intertwined. You see, G. W. alone would stand for either Gertrude Wylde or Guy Wharton—a singular coincidence. The fact that the letters are repeated seems to

show that Wharton had noticed this and resolved that his
initials should be linked with hers, which were the same,
so that in that way at least they might be united. It's a
mark of identity. But why do you ask ?'' he added.
'' Is there anything wrong about it ?''

Lance was excited, evidently. The drawing shook in
his hand. '' No,'' he said ; '' nothing wrong. Quite
the contrary. It's exactly like her in some ways.''

'' You don't *look* crazy, Lance ; but how can you
possibly know whether it's like or not ?''

'' Oh, I mean—I forgot ; you never saw Adela—Miss
Jessie, I mean.''

'' No,'' said Hedson.   '' I take, now.   Like *her*, eh ?''

Lance nodded silently.   To him the picture resembled
Adela more than Jessie.

<hr>

CHAPTER XI.

LANCE RETURNS.

APRIL, coming to thaw the ice on Northern streams,
and to mould the first buds that started out timidly as a
young artist's efforts at creation, also dissolved the spell
of solitude which had so long encompassed Jessie.

Lance was ready to build the paper-mill, and had
written that he would take the rail southward as soon as
possible. It had been agreed at Christmas-time that
the wedding should come off in May or June. Activity
began in the turpentine plantation ; the trees were
'' boxed'' and '' tapped ;'' the sap commenced to flow.
The air grew milder, the stars shone with a more hazy

lustre in the night heavens, and birds renewed their notes in the thickets about the manor, or flew with transient greetings over the lonely land, on their mission of heralding the return of spring to higher latitudes. But Jessie could not rid herself of the mournfulness and the partial lethargy that had so long clung to her. She knew that Lance was coming, and her heart throbbed the more warmly : she waited eagerly to feel his arms clasped round her. Yet a lingering fear persuaded her that the happiness might still be deferred or, in the end, frustrated.

It was in such a mood that she leaned, one evening, on the railing of the old veranda, vaguely musing and inclined to sadness. There was no certainty as to the hour of Lance's advent, for he had not named a time, and into that far-off nook where she lived the lightning of the telegraph never penetrated. But of late Jessie had adopted a custom of straying out upon the veranda, as if she expected to see Lance approaching.

Suddenly she heard the click and crunch of unwonted wheels upon the drive near the house. She started up and listened, in a tremor of incredulous delight. The sounds drew nearer ; presently a light flashed across the moist branches of the shade-trees, and the next moment she beheld the lanterns of a carriage, dimly illuminating its battered varnish, the smoking backs of two horses and the muffled torso of a sable driver. Then Lance's young, energetic face appeared in the square of the carriage-door, faintly roseate with the light from the house. He was fumbling at the door-handle before the wheels stopped turning.

The sable driver subsided completely into the depths of his sableness, as the two figures clasped each other at the top of the steps.

" Ah, Ned, I have waited for you so long !"

" And so have I for you, dear."

" Do you know, I felt almost as if I were that poor Gertrude, waiting and waiting still ?"

" You *are*, dearest—you are *my* Gertrude !"

And then the colonel, always discreet, allowed himself to be seen in the hallway, prepared to welcome the wanderer.

Lance barely restrained himself until the next day before seeking an opportunity to tell Jessie about the drawing which Hedson had brought from England.

" You've written me next to nothing about Adela Reefe," he said to her.   " But I suppose you have kept on taking charge of her letters for Dennie."

" Oh yes," said Jessie ; " he brought them all the way up to me.   Poor fellow !"

" Why do you call him that ?"

" It seems so severe for him, having her stay away at such a distance, and for so long.   He's dreadfully in love with her."

" Yes, I know he is," Lance confessed.   " Those times when I was with him so much, and you hardly liked it, I was talking with him about her and trying to console him.   He let me into his confidence, and told me how he was afraid he had driven her from him and should never get her back.   But Sylv used to send an encouraging message, now and then.   Has he sent any more ?"

" Sylv has hardly written at all," said Jessie.

Lance mused aloud : " That's strange."

" Yes," responded his sweetheart, in a tone as if she were about to say more ; but she did not go on.

At this point Lance thought it best to bring forward his little surprise.   Excusing himself, he went to his room and came back with the drawing. "By the way," he began, reseating himself, "I wonder if Adela has changed much in looks, under the influence of education. It would be curious to see her, wouldn't it?"

"I saw her," said Jessie, "just before she went back, after you left us, at Christmas."

"Well, then, you can tell. What do you think of this?" And her lover produced the portrait.

Jessie stared at it in some astonishment. "Where under the sun did. that come from?" she exclaimed. "Was it done for you?"

"What do you think of it?" he repeated.

"It isn't perfect," was the answer; "but still, I should know it, I think. Why, Ned, are you cheating me? It isn't meant for Adela, is it? You naughty boy, I could almost think it was an attempt to show how *I* shall look when I'm stouter! It's a joke."

"Then you think it's like you?" he inquired. "Does it strike you?"

"I won't say another word, until you tell me *what* it is."

"It is a picture of Gertrude Wylde," Lance returned.

Then there was silence for a moment. Jessie took the drawing and looked at it intently. Her voice was low, and quivered with a sort of frightened tremor when she next spoke. "Why didn't you tell me at first, Ned? And what did you mean by speaking as if it were Adela Reefe? It *is* like her; and it is like me, too. Oh, what is this secret? What is the meaning of it all?"

"As well as I can make it out," said Lance, "the meaning is that Adela is a direct descendant of Gertrude Wylde, and a kinswoman of yours. The only thing remaining, in my mind, is to find out whether her father or his family came from Croatan. If that is proved—"

" And if that is proved, what then ?"

" I know of nothing to follow, except that we should recognize her as a relative."

" Never !" cried Jessie. " This is a mere dream. It's impossible to prove her descent from our stock. I can have nothing to do with her."

Her vehemence was such that another man might have suspected some underlying motive of feminine jealousy. But Lance merely laughed. " Oh, there's no legal claim involved," said he, lightly. " Of course, 1 don't expect that anything tremendous is going to happen, even if she does turn out to be of your blood. But suppose we appoint your father arbitrator as to this portrait ?"

Jessie consented, and they referred the picture to Colonel Floyd.

" If this is a well-authenticated reproduction," said the colonel, deploying his finest hand-book manner, " the appearances would seem to indicate some connection. 'Pon my soul, I never noticed any resemblance till now ; but while the similarity to our Jessie is perceptible, it is not nearly so pronounced as the likeness to this Adela Reefe. Is it possible that an inherited type of countenance should last so long, under such conditions ? Very singular ; very strange !"

He did not evince enthusiasm, and he paced the room restlessly.

" What we want is to go and see old Mr. Reefe," suggested Lance, " and ask him about Croatan."

The colonel fell in with this proposition ; and on the morrow they rode down to Hunting Quarters. It was not an easy matter to draw Reefe into conversation ; but they at last succeeded in pinning him down to facts, and, without discovering their purpose, he assured them that, to the best of his knowledge, his predecessors had lived in the region of Croatan, until the time of his father, who crossed Pamlico Sound and settled near Hunting Quarters. To make a clean breast of it, he also admitted that his stock probably contained Indian blood; but of this he was rather proud than otherwise.

"It is settled," said Lance, when he came to tell Jessie the result of the inquiry. "There can be no reasonable doubt now. I must go up and let Adela and Sylv know about it at once."

Jessie leaned back in her chair and fixed her mild gray eyes upon him. She had never looked more captivating than at that instant, the side-part in her hair giving an accent of dainty self-reliance to her whole pose and demeanor. "Let me ask you a question," she said.

"Willingly."

"About poor Dennie. Has it ever occurred to you, Ned, that you may be doing him a great injury by sending Adela off in this way, and throwing her with Sylv?"

"No, of course not," answered Lance, somewhat nettled. "Would I have been a party to it if I had thought so?" But the mention of Sylv in this sort of way caused him an inward shudder. If there were any peril of Dennie's losing Adela, why should it be Sylv who should win her?

"I think you are helping to separate them," Jessie continued, "and you ought to reflect, and stop. Besides, why should you go on so, mixing yourself up in her affairs?"

"I'm not. I ought at least to see her and tell her my discovery."

Jessie suddenly rose. "I *hate* that woman!" she cried, sharply. And, at the same instant, Lance saw his engagement ring flashing upon her finger.

" You shall not hate her," he declared, with passion. " She is your kinswoman—one of us. It isn't right that you should say that, and I won't endure it."

" Never mind whether you will endure it or not," Jessie retorted. " She has occupied enough of your attention already."

" My dear child," Lance remonstrated, " it's impossible that you should be jealous of that girl ! But what else can you mean ? What do you demand ?"

" I think that you ought to just drop her, from this time on," said Jessie, closing her lips decisively.

There are scientific thinkers who tell us that the will is not a cause, but merely a state of consciousness resulting from previous conditions of the nerves and the emotions. However this may be, Lance's will asserted itself in strong opposition to Jessie's. The probability that Adela was a lineal descendant of Gertrude Wylde appealed strongly to his imagination. Now that his theory seemed so well established, he was resolved to have her kinship acknowledged ; and, further, he experienced a strong attraction toward her, the stress of which he did not fully comprehend. He himself represented the man who had loved Gertrude, who had vainly searched for and lost her. Was it not fair that he should have some hand in the destiny of the girl thus reclaimed, after the lapse of centuries, from the oblivion which had overtaken Gertrude's life ?

" I will not drop her," he said, unyieldingly. " And, what's more, Jessie, I am going to see her, and shall stand by her."

CHAPTER XII.

SYLV'S TROUBLE.

EXACTLY what was to be the issue of Lance's sentiment respecting Adela, it would have been hard to say. No fatal breach had as yet been made in his relations with Jessie ; yet they parted, after the difference which I have just detailed, with a coldness that promised ill ; and, for the first time, Lance met the issue that had for weeks past unobtrusively put itself in his way. If Jessie would persist in being so narrow, so unsympathetic, what was to come ? And if any trouble from this source should divide them, what was there left to him ? Facing this alternative, Lance was forced to perceive that the interest which he had allowed himself to feel in Adela had, unawares, grown into a dangerous emotion. In one way it seemed absurd. In another, it was tragical. Did he actually, in view of the rupture which now seemed likely to occur between himself and Jessie, contemplate such a possibility as giving his life up to Adela ? If he were to do that, the question of treachery to his humble friend, Dennis De Vine, would be involved. Nevertheless, some unseen power seemed to propel him toward an erratic solution of this sort. He wondered whether at last the yearning of his ancestor, long ago, was fated to meet fulfilment by his own union with the latest offspring of Gertrude Wylde. No ! he would not think of it : he refused to surrender himself to such fantasies. And still he could not escape their importuning.

He was involved in a struggle. He did not know

what to make of it ; but he resolved to maintain his own dignity, first, by going to see Adela, and then, after that, everything concerning Jessie and himself might be righted. Meanwhile he kept one idea firmly before him, which was, to remain true to Jessie so long as she would let him do so without sacrificing Adela.

But before he had time to carry out his determination of seeing Adela, an unlooked-for incident occurred, which altered the situation materially.

The last bell for the day had sounded at the "academy" where Adela pursued her studies, or rather was pursued by them, for they followed her steps from morning to night in a race with which it was hard to keep even, notwithstanding her prowess. The bell signified freedom for a brief period. When it sounded she was allowed to go out for a walk, the usual discipline of the school having been relaxed in her favor, to admit of her taking her recreation in Sylv's company. Sylv was duly accredited as Dennie's ambassador, to look after Adela's welfare ; hence it was considered very proper that he should see her every day. In this way he had taken a great many walks with her.

When the bell rang, therefore, he met her at the gate of the garden surrounding the academy, and they strolled away together. Had Lance seen them at that moment, he would have been surprised by the noticeable change which had come over them both. Adela had now been at school some ten months—nearly a year—and her steady application, with the loss of that out-door life to which she had been accustomed, had subdued the color in her cheeks, though it had not made them pale. The delicate brown tinge was always there. But the stiff black hair that had formerly blown so carelessly about her head was demurely combed and orderly, now, and a serene, womanly thoughtfulness had somehow drifted into the lines of her face, making its wild beauty sweeter.

Sylv, too, had acquired a more polished air. It was not a gawky polish. His clothes were very plain, but he appeared at ease in them; and although his tangled beard was reduced to comparative trimness, it hinted nothing of the incipient dandy. On the whole, they were a very serious and simple pair, who would have looked extremely "countrified" in Richmond, and still more so in New York. But they had altered very much since the days on the shore.

Had Lance seen them then, he would have been surprised—and perhaps displeased—by another thing. This was, that as they moved down the road leading away from the town, they looked so like a pair of lovers.

Ah, while they had been growing so neat and orderly on the surface, and had come to show marks of the educational mould, had they possibly undergone another change of an opposite kind, within? Were their hearts as well regulated, as calm, as their dress and their faces?

Through the long period of their sojourn together, they had lived upon hopes, interests, ambitions common to both. Adela had been fired with zeal for her new occupation; they had talked over their daily successes or reverses every afternoon; and though I have not said much about Sylv's natural refinement, and his quiet, persuasive quality, these two things—combined with constant association—had exercised a great influence upon Adela. Imperceptibly she had grown into a life which belonged to them alone, apart from every one else.

"How did you get along to-day?" asked Sylv.

"All right," said Adela. "But the algebra was hard. It seems as if I couldn't think of anything but squares and roots and coefficients. It appears to me like

I'll have to extract the square root of my head right soon ; and if I do, there won't be anything left.''

" You're getting tired, I reckon," Sylv suggested. " Maybe you ought not to work so much. How would it suit you, Deely, to go home for a few days and rest ?''

" Oh, vacation's coming in a few weeks," she answered, wearily. "It ain't that, Sylv. I ain't tired with the work ; but it's because my life seems so queer, and I don't know what I want. I don't want to stay here, or to go home. I'm afraid I'll never be happy any more.''

They were now in a quiet spot outside of the town. Some willows grew beside the road, which was here carried over a small bridge that covered the gurgling flow of a brook. Sylv stopped short, and eyed her meditatively.

" Not happy ?'' he questioned. " Why not, Deely ? Wouldn't you be if you were with Dennie again ?''

Adela paused, too. " I can't tell," she said. " I don't know what is the matter with me, but I don't seem to be satisfied with anything, Sylv. I never can go back to what I was, but I don't see that I can go forward, either.''

" But Dennie loves you just the same," said Sylv, rather falteringly.

The girl clasped her hands and gazed absently in front of her. " I know he does," she said, in an inert way. " I know it well enough.''

" And you know he has been trying to learn to read, just to please you, and so as to keep up with you as well as he can.''

" Yes.'' But still her face did not lighten. The gathering sadness deepened upon it, if anything. " Oh, why did I come here !'' she suddenly cried, despairingly. "If Mr. Lance had not sent me! Ah, what was the use?"

Sylv regarded her compassionately, but he was himself undergoing an anguish that it seemed impossible to withstand.

"Come," he said, soothingly, "let's go down yonder among the trees and talk about it. We'll see if there isn't some way of making you happy. I reckon the time has come for a change, and we ought to see what is needed."

She yielded, as though he were entitled to lead her. Taking his hand, she walked with him down on to the young grass at the side of the highway, and in among the trees alongside the "run." In the retired nook that they came to they seated themselves, while the spring breeze murmured through the light leaves above them, unsuspicious of any woe in the minds of these two young persons.

"I was angry with Dennie," said Adela, speaking low, "and that was why I left him to come here. But he has been so good, and so patient."

"Yes, that he has!" Sylv corroborated, fervently. "Why don't you go back to him?"

The gaze which Sylv fixed upon her, in asking this question, was very unlike that of an impartial and philosophic adviser. His eyes burned with a rapacious though restrained fire. Yet his tone was composed.

Adela broke into moaning. "Why do you ask me that?" she exclaimed. "Oh, don't you *know* how hard it is to go back? Do you think it can ever be the same? I don't want that kind of life any more : I am for something different now. You see, all this studying and thinking and reading has given me a new idea, and there's no one to take a share in it. When I go back

and marry Dennie that part of me will be alone.
What am I to do ; oh, what *am* I to do ?"

Her distress was so acute that she gave way to tears,
which she helplessly tried .to press back with a hand at
her eyes.

"Don't cry, Decly," said Sylv, taking her other
hand. "You're tired out, and you're troubling yourself, but you don't need to. By and by you'll be
happy ; never fear !"

Adela clung to his hand instinctively. "You're a
kind fellow, Sylv," said she, ceasing to sob. "I know
you wish me well. But it's all over with me. I ought
not to think of anything but Dennie. If I can make
him happy, why—I ought—to be satisfied." But the
stifled tone in which she uttered the words showed how
far she fell short of that duty.

Sylv longed to speak more tenderly to her. The
touch of her trusting hand in his was maddening. He
would have laid down his life, at that instant, to comfort
her ; and if he was ready to sacrifice his own, what
mattered the life and happiness of any other ? But
there was only one way in which he felt sure that he
could secure lasting comfort to her, so far as one man
might ; and that way he dared not propose. Why had
he not foreseen this difficulty and this peril in time to
evade them ? He had imagined that his whole life
depended on books, and here he found that it was nothing as compared with a woman. He had indulged in
the tranquil belief that he was a disinterested student ;
but now he awoke to the fact that he was a reckless
lover !

"Decly," he exclaimed, rising, but still keeping her
hand in his, "if you don't love Dennie enough to go
back to him, you must not do it !"

" And break his heart ?" she asked, looking up at him with an effort at reproach.

" I speak to you as his brother," answered Sylv—" his brother, whom he sent here of his own accord to watch over you ; and I say that it would be wrong. You would not be happy yourself, and you would find it impossible to make him happy."

Adela drew her hand away. " But I have promised him ! And I will keep my promise."

As she spoke she rose erect : he could hear her close her teeth with a grating sound.

" I don't intend to argue about it," he said. " You are free to settle everything your own way. It appeared to me like I must tell you my opinion. That's the end of it, Deely." He paused. " I got a letter from Mr. Lance ; says he's got back, and is coming up to see you. But *I* am going away to-morrow."

Adela started violently. " *You* going away !" Then she trembled toward him and laid her hands on his shoulders. " Oh no, no ! Don't leave me now, Sylv. Don't go away !"

" I must," he replied. " I've got through. I've done all I can. I must go back to work for Mr. Lance."

Adela's hands still rested on his arms. He could hardly move them otherwise than to enfold and sustain her. Unable to support herself, she drooped and sank toward him for an instant.

" Dear—dear—sister," he almost groaned, " don't despair ! Don't give way ! I wish I could save you from suffering."

She recovered herself and stood upright before him, looking into his eyes. She trembled, and he longed to embrace her once more, holding her to his heart for as long as he should live. But neither of them made any movement toward such a renewal of her dependence upon him. Steadily, yet with a kind of doubt and fear, they gazed at one another ; and the whole story of their hearts was made clear. But not one word of passion was uttered.

"I must leave—must leave to-morrow," Sylv repeated, as they started simultaneously to go back to the school ; "and I think I will send Dennie up here." Instead of advancing this proposition with the courage he wanted to show, he made it sound like the knell of all their hopes. Nerving himself, he added : "Shall I tell him you've forgiven him ?"

This time, by a prodigious effort, he spoke bravely ; yet his eyes, without his knowledge, seemed to beg her to come to the aid of his failing fortitude.

"Shall I tell him ?"

"Yes."

"And that you're ready to go with him now ?" The faltering look had vanished. A white, still light of triumph rested on his paling face.

"Yes," said Adela again, with trembling lips.

———

CHAPTER XIII.

LANCE AND ADELA.

SYLV was on the point of beginning his journey, when Lance walked into his boarding-place with a hearty salutation.

"Isn't this very sudden ?" he asked, with pronounced astonishment at Sylv's new move.

"It looks so to you," said the young man. "But I've been thinking it over a long time. It isn't best for me to stay here."

Lance saw that something was held in reserve, but could not conjecture what. "Suit yourself, Sylv," he returned. "If you're satisfied, I ought to be."

"Besides," said Sylv, with the air of having already given one reason, "I ought to do some of that work I promised for you."

"It *would* be an advantage to begin exploring the swamp before warm weather comes on," Lance agreed.

"Well, sir, I'm ready to go at it right straight off," said the other.

There was a disproportionate grimness in his tone and manner, Lance imagined. The declaration had apparently cost him an effort.

"Lord bless me, Sylv," he exclaimed, abruptly, "how thin and pale you've grown! I didn't fairly notice it until this moment. It evidently won't do you any harm to have a change."

"No, sir. I have not been feeling well."

"All right. Wait till the afternoon train, and I'll go back to Beaufort with you. I only want to see Adela for a while. Will you come along?"

He did not really want Sylv to accompany him; and perhaps this was manifest in his way of speaking. Yet he was somewhat surprised when the young man, turning aside and pretending to adjust some of the articles in the forlorn miniature trunk he had been packing, said: "No, thank you, Mr. Lance. I said good-by to her last night."

"It's just as well, that way," said Lance, nervously. "I have something important to tell her, and it will be better to see her alone."

Sylv straightened up, and glanced at him almost fiercely. A suspicion occurred to him. "Something important?" he asked. But he did not dare to demand particulars.

Nor did it reassure him much, either, to have Lance
answer, "Yes; I'll tell you about it afterward."

For his part, Lance, in noticing Sylv's abstracted be-
havior, recalled what Jessie had said as to throwing the
young fellow so much with Adela, and wondered
whether there was any confirmation of her fear in the
constraint which had overtaken his *protégé*. But he
was so anxious to see Adela, that he did not stop to reflect on that point more than a moment.

Ushered by the matronly principal of the academy
into its scrupulously dusted but threadbare parlor, he
awaited the girl's advent with a good deal of trepidation.
The window-blinds were closed, and the interior was per-
vaded by a mock twilight. When Adela at last made
her appearance, her figure, from the opposite side of the
room, looked so dim and uncertain that Lance was
strongly reminded of the first time he ever saw her—the
time that she rose out of the earth, as it were, and again
crumbled back into it.

"Miss Reefe!" he said, scarcely above a murmur.

"Oh, Mr. Lance! Sylv told me you were coming."
And she approached him through the dimness of the
room, groping, one might say.

They shook hands formally, and to Lance's distraught
fancy it seemed as if her fingers withdrew themselves
with the recoil of absolute dislike from the touch of his
own.

"You're not glad to see me, I'm afraid," he began,
boldly.

"Oh yes—yes I am. What makes you think so?"

" I can hardly tell, but I think I should know if you were. It is so dark here I can barely see you. Shall I open a shutter ?" He made a movement to do so.

" It is light enough for me," Adela answered ; and he at once desisted from his purpose. " Won't you sit down ?" she asked.

He accepted the invitation.

They conversed for a few moments about her studies and about what he himself had been doing since they last met. But at length he said : " You never would be able to guess, Adela, why I have come to see you to-day. You told me a very interesting story once—do you remember ?—about your people. That was a legend ; but now I have a true story to tell *you*, which is connected with yours. Would you like to hear it ?"

" I always like stories better than anything," said the girl. " Do tell it to me."

Thereupon Lance narrated the tale with which we are familiar, adding the details of the picture, the first clew which he had caught in her resemblance to Jessie, and the extraordinary coincidence of the old rhyme from Wharton Hall. Adela listed intently, without interposing a syllable ; but he could hear her breath coming and going, and occasionally she sighed. She was seated in a chair near his own ; but, though his eyes were growing used to the gloom of the apartment, he felt her presence more by the warm irradiation of her vitality through the air than by actual vision. From time to time there was an audible flurry of light feet and flitting skirts in the passageway without, or in the rooms above, indicating the movement of young women from one point to another of the scanty scholastic edifice ; and once a desk-bell rang punctiliously from a distance. But otherwise they were uninterrupted. As Lance proceeded with his story, the dimness of the light and the random brushing of the breeze against the shutters aided a species of hallucination that laid hold of him. While he retraced the mazes and the by-paths of the tradition that led back so far into the forests and the obscurity of an earlier epoch, the gloom of the wilderness itself seemed to surround him ; the leaves of an unknown forest-land muttered and rustled in his ears ; he felt like an explorer ; he was making his way, he could fancy, toward the goal of his long striving and his harassed desire. Should he not meet, at the end of his wanderings, the object of his search ?

When he had finished the story he said : " *You* have Indian blood in your veins, Adela. "

Her voice permeated the dusk slowly and hesitatingly: " Yes. But how do you know ? "

" I have seen your father, and he has told me. " Lance rose and stepped toward the window. " Gertrude Wylde was your ancestress, " he declared, " and she was the same woman as Ewayeá in your legend. It is I who have discovered this, and I have brought you, at last, out of all that mystery ! "

Flinging the shutters open he stood there, looking toward her. Adela at the same instant left her seat and placed herself before him. Then, for the first time, he could see the change that had crept over her features.

" Good God ! " he cried. " What has happened ? "

Adela spread her hands out in timid deprecation. " I don't know, " she said. " What do you mean ? "

" You are so much more—you have grown so like Jessie since I saw you, " Lance returned, wellnigh gasping. " If it were not for that darker tint— "

" Mr. Lance, " she interrupted, " what can you be

thinking of? Why do you talk so excitedly, and why did you come here to tell me this?"

"Because," he said, "I have been intensely interested in the problem. I believe you belong to the line of Gertrude Wylde. If you do, you represent the woman whom my ancestor loved, and you are closely related to Jessie Floyd. Do you suppose it makes any difference to me that Indians came into that line? No; I see in you the lineal descendant of Gertrude, and a kinswoman of the Floyds. I wish to have it clearly understood that you and they are of one family. You must take the place that belongs to you."

"What place?" Adela sighed. "Can you tell what place mine is?"

"Of course I can. Haven't I said what I thought?" But while Lance uttered these words, he noticed how sad and wan she looked, and he also felt the difficulty of bringing her within the circle of life to which he belonged.

"You have made a great mistake," she replied. "I am only Adela Reefe, and I cannot be anything else. Did Sylv tell you? I am going away from here. I shall not stay any longer, for I promised to be Dennie's wife, and I am going to marry him as soon as he comes for me."

"To be Dennie's wife!" exclaimed Lance, instinctively treating the idea as though he had not heard of it before. "Yes; yes; I suppose you are to be. But why should that prevent your being one of us? You will be a kinswoman, a cousin, just the same."

Adela gathered herself up, and spoke with resolution. "I don't know if you are right," she said, "but any way, Mr. Lance, if I *am* a kinswoman and a cousin, do you think Miss Jessie will want to have me for one?"

The best that Lance could do was to parry this direct thrust. "If you are so," he answered, "what difference can her wish make?"

"I will tell you, easy enough," Adela retorted, proudly. "It is just that I won't have anything to do with people who don't want me for one of them. If I had ever supposed that coming up here to school would make it seem as if I wanted to do that, I wouldn't have come. Oh, I didn't know all this when I came! No, no! And I'm sorry I did it. I tried to be grateful to you, Mr. Lance, and I do thank you for your good meaning; but I'm sorry I came."

"Adela," he said, rather coldly, "I can't let you talk in this way. You are proud and angry, and don't know what you're saying. Remember that, whatever happens, I stand by you."

"I don't want any one to stand by me," she returned. "I am all alone, and I will stay so. Suppose you had never come here, Mr. Lance; who would have guessed that I had anything to do with that old English family? I could not have guessed it myself, even. I know you've tried to help me, and now you want to make something different of me from what I always was before. But I'm going back to marry Dennie, and the best thing you can do is to leave me where you found me, and forget all about me. I shall just be Dennie's wife; that's all. I don't ask to be anything else."

It may seem to you unreal that Lance should have been so much exercised regarding Adela's happiness and her future, especially since he was bound to Jessie Floyd by the most sacred promises. Unreal it is, I grant, to people who live by the tinkle of the horse-car, the tick of the clock, and the reading of the newspaper. But this individual, impracticable man—so like many other men

who, in dissimilar circumstances, conceive themselves to
be prodigiously practical—was bent upon an idea.   And
he was determined to carry out his idea.   He cared more
for his theory than he did for himself or for any one besides.   It was his ambition to be impartial—to secure the
recognition of all rights which he thought were in need
of vindication.   And so far did he carry that desire, that
he was really somewhat bewildered by it; in consequence whereof he held himself ready, at this especial
moment, to sacrifice one great obligation to a lesser
obligation.

"I'm not going to be satisfied with this result," he
said.   "I am determined that it shall not be in vain that
I have sought you out and found you.   Listen to me,
Adela!   It is a question of justice—in fact, of simple
humanity—and I'm bound to have justice done.   You
may go back to Hunting Quarters, if you like, any day,
and marry Dennie; but you ought not to ask to be
dropped out of our lives.   I wish to see you put where
you belong.   If you have changed your mind, and do
not want to marry Dennie, only tell me so.   Your
happiness is at stake, and it shall be preserved at all
hazards."

"How can you preserve it better than I can?" Adela
demanded.

Lance delayed his answer, inwardly trembling.   It may
be that we ought not to inquire into the wild and erratic
impulses that assailed him at that instant; but, amid
their dizzying influence, he held fast to the ideal of
honesty on all sides.

"Very likely I can't," he replied, calmly.   "But I
wish to say that, if anything should go wrong, if any
trouble should come to you, I may be counted on as your
friend—no matter who opposes."

Adela melted at once into frank dependence. " Oh, Mr. Lance," she said, " I have sorrows, like other people, and I don't know what they will bring at last ; so if you *will* help me when I need help, I shall be glad ! But please don't think about me now ; only let me go— let me go !"

And with this sorry climax the interview ended, Lance retiring with an inexplicable sense of defeated endeavor. In some way, which he was not able to analyze as yet, his dream had been exploded. The unravelling of the mystery of Gertrude Wylde had been to him a romance of the most fascinating kind ; but now that the romance had culminated, no one seemed to know what to do with it. Apparently he had followed a will-o'-the-wisp, when he expected any good to attend his success in ferreting out Adela's identity ; for it had put him at odds with Jessie, and it brought no pleasure to Adela herself.

CHAPTER XIV.

DENNIE'S TROUBLE.

WITH heavy hearts both Lance and Sylv accomplished their journey to Beaufort late that afternoon ; and on the way Lance explained to his companion the new light in which Adela must be regarded.

Sylv, however, said little, and appeared anxious to reach home, where he could consult with Dennie.

He found his brother busily engaged in completing a ditch across the neck of the headland, which he had

finally, in deference to the wishes of Aunty Losh, under-
taken to dig, to the end that her live-stock might be kept
from straying over to the mainland. "I am fearsome o'
the tides," said Dennie, as he had said long ago ; "but
aunty wants this hyar for to be done, and so I am doin'
on it."

The docile, plodding industry of his brother smote upon
Sylv with a singular reproach. He could not throw off
the conviction that he himself had been essentially idle in
his devotion to book-learning, while Dennie had remained
so faithful to the dull duties at home.

"Dennie," he said, "I got some good news for you."

"Ye mean that ar ?" queried Dennie, halting in his
toil, with his shovel in the loose ground. "I ain't had
no good news for a long sight, Sylv. What mout it be ?"

"Deely's coming back to you."

Dennie stood stock still and wiped the sweat from his
brow. Then he touched his grimy knuckles to his eyelids ; but, without betraying emotion in any other way,
except by the softening of his voice, he said : "I'm glad
on't, Sylv. Ar' she a-comin' back because she want to ?"

"Yes ; oh yes ! There couldn't be any other reason,
could there, Dennie ?"

"Well, I warn't right sure," said Dennie. "No ; I
reckon they aren't no other reason." Seizing the shovel,
he made a few more plunges with it into the soil. "Well,
I'm right glad on't, Sylv. When ar' she comin' ?"

"Now, I'll tell you how it is," Sylv returned, assuming
an expository manner. "Deely thinks you've been a
right good boy, and she allows she was impatient with
you. But, then, you were impatient too. She's made
up her mind to let go the rest of her school term, and she's
waiting for you now up at the city. All you've got to
do is to go there and get her."

Dennie abandoned his work for the moment, and gazed at his brother affectionately. "Thank ye kindly, Sylv. Ye been a good brother to me. Oh, it don't 'pear true! I don't make out how it's so; but I waited and sarved kind o'patient, Sylv, and all to once it comes out squar'. Deely's been fair to me, old man, and so ha' you been. Wall, it's more'n I desarve."

With the guilty knowledge of a hidden love for Adela in his heart, Sylv would rather have faced the threatening muzzle of his brother's gun, as it had once been pointed at him, than to have stood up before the glance of trust and affection which Dennie now directed toward him. But, thank Heaven, his conscience was clean. He had not betrayed the trust. He had preserved his honor, and had left Adela free.

"Don't think about what you deserve," he said, "but just you go and do what she expects you to. You go up there and fetch her back."

"Did she ask ye to tell me that, Sylv?"

"Yes."

"Then I'll do it! But I ar' got to dig this hyar ditch first off, don't you see I have? 'Cause I tole aunty I would, and she'd be a heap sight put out if I didn't. But ye'll go up to the city with me, won't ye, Sylv? I'd feel lonesome and quar' ef ye didn't."

"I'm right sorry, Dennie; but I can't. I've got to do some work for Mr. Lance, and I ought not to go back."

However, when Dennie was ready to take his departure Sylv came to him with a sealed letter. "I can't go with you, Dennie," he repeated; "but there's a few words I wanted to say to Deely, and you might as well carry them, I thought."

Dennie conscientiously dumped the missive into his

hat; and, with a last joyous whisk of his red beard, took leave of his brother.

His impatience to see Adela caused him to spurn the faithful dug-out as a means of travel, and he went by rail. In the long months of separation from his sweetheart he had succeeded in carrying out a great self-improvement. The hope of making himself worthy to recover her was the mainstay of his gallant persistence in this work, and it had wrought a wonderful effect. He was still the same Dennie—his temperament could not be remodelled—but from being irascible, hot-headed, untrustworthy, he had come to exercise a self-control that made him seem uncommonly gentle. What he gained in that direction he had to hold by untiring vigilance and firm will; but a succession of victories convinced him that now, when the reward was held out to him, he could prove his fitness to receive it.

A driving rain poured down upon North Carolina as he left the coast. The sea showed its white teeth at Hatteras and all along the sandy spits and islands that fringe that shore. Every one said that still uglier weather was likely to come soon. But to Dennie the drenching showers and the hurly-burly of the winds only enhanced the gladness in his heart. He basked in the delicious glow of cosiness which children feel when snugly housed from pelting storms that they can watch at ease. The slow-paced cars seemed to him to glide ahead with wonderful swiftness—his own happy anticipation lent speed to the wheels—and the humming rails echoed and rang again with one continual song of hope, hope, hope.

How many fond, encouraging things he would say to Adela! How bright he would make the prospect for her! He would show her, beyond question, that she need never undergo any trials or troubles which he could prevent.

It was not so easy to do all this, at first, as he had imagined it would be. On meeting, they were both rather
quiet. Dennie took her hand bashfully: he discovered
all at once that he was in the presence of a superior being.
The muscles of his right arm, also, appeared to succumb
to a peculiar disorder, and would not act when he wanted
to throw that arm around her waist. Good Lord! was
he afraid? Had he been afraid to clasp her in his arm a
year before? But gradually this paralytic attack wore
itself out: he sat down beside her, and presently his right
hand was visible to his own eyes, resting easily at a point
on the right side of her belt.

"I'm glad to be with ye again, Deely," he said, carefully eliminating as much of the gruffness as he could
from his strong out-of-doors voice.

But the hearty gruffness that remained was, somehow,
very agreeable to Adela. "Dear old Dennie," she said,
in a gentle, musing way, as if she were speaking of him
to some third person.

"And ye're glad, too, be ye, Deely?" he asked, gazing at her indulgently, but with some vestiges of anxious
doubt.

"Yes, Dennie, I'm glad to be with you; you're so
good now. And I like to see you happy."

"That's a puss," said the big fellow, but instantly felt
astonishment at his own familiarity. Finding, too, that
he was instinctively patting her with his hand, he promptly stopped, because it struck him that his hand was too
rough, and he might hurt or crush her. He drew it softly
away to a more normal position. "Why, they tell me,"
he resumed, "that ye're a great lady now—a sort o'
prin*cess*, or su'thin' that way. I didn't know for sure
ye'd want to see me or have me hangin' round ye no
more."

And then he laughed at the deceptiveness and the wild humor of his own speech.

"Oh, Dennie," she implored, "don't talk about that! What difference does it make?"

"Ye needn't bat yer eyes," he replied. "I ain't 'shamed on it, if ye ain't. Why Sylv, he said how ye war just as good as Miss Jessie, 'cause ye war born away back out'n the same family; leastways, some one else did the bornin' for ye, them ar times. But I—well, *I* allays thought ye war a heap sight better'n Miss Jessie or any one else."

"I know that, Dennie. You always loved me true. Oh, it was wrong for me to come away from you so!"

Adela leaned her head upon him, and began to sob slightly. This proceeding was so totally unlooked for, that Dennie was amazed.

"Thar, thar," he said, "ye'd oughtn't for to cry when I come back to ye. No; ye had the right on't, Deely. I warn't fit, then, and I wouldn't ha' been a fip better ef ye hadn't ha' left me be. It ar' all right, I tell ye. But fust, when I saw ye just now, thinks I, ye've changed so, and ye look so sort o' ironed up all careful, ye won't care nothin' for a old rough boy like Dennie no more. But if ye're goin' to cry, Deely, why, I want for to stop ye; and I do think it war all right, your leavin' me."

"Oh no, no," she reaffirmed, still weeping. "I did you a great wrong, Dennie!"

Dennie's face became apprehensive for a moment; but that look quickly dissolved, and he permitted himself a subdued laugh. "It ar' enough to make a man laugh," he said, in excuse, "to think o' my forgivin' ye; but if ye feel ye done wrong, why, I'll say I forgive ye, Deely. I do forgive ye, right free."

She had made the only confession she could. Indeed,

what was there to reveal, except that in her long companionship with Sylv she had learned to love him, before she comprehended what was happening, and that she had honestly, at a fearful cost, stifled that love so far as might be, in order to remain true to the man she had promised to wed? But to tell this would in itself be to dishonor her vow.

She looked up to Dennie with streaming eyes, and her hand sought his. "Thank you, thank you!" she murmured. "I have suffered a great deal here, Dennie— away from you. I know you have suffered too. But you are generous and kind ; and now I hope we can forget all the pain."

Dennie, in listening to her, was strongly impressed with the feeling that he was hearing something read from a book, so sharp was the contrast between her utterance and his. But the contents of the supposititious book were very soothing and acceptable. He turned quickly to her, and for the first time since his arrival they embraced each other with thorough self-forgetfulness.

"But, Deely," he said, "I ain't like ye ar'. I ain't got l'arnin' the way ye have now. Don't ye reckon that ar'll disapp'int ye?"

"No ; not a bit," she answered, warmly ; "you'll be kind and good to me, Dennie, and I will be a good wife to you. All I want is for you to take me away from here. Take me home!"

There was an almost desperate energy in her voice. The truth was, Dennie's presence acted upon her as a restorative, and awakened many memories of the simple and happier time when they had played together and grown up together and carried on their courtship by the shore. Despite her love for Sylv—or perhaps in consequence of it—she threw herself upon Dennie's protection with an eagerness she would not have believed possible until she met him face to face. His big figure, his glowing cheeks, his heavy hands and rough accent—all brought to her a whiff of the salt air in which she had been born and bred. Her secret misery was dulled by his trusting companionship; she was lulled into reveries of some existence of comparative peace, in which she would be able to fulfil her ideal of duty and find her recompense in so doing.

"Take ye home, dear girl! Why, that's what I'm wantin' to do," he rejoined, tenderly. And, fired by the thought, he went on to tell her where they would make the home; how Sylv and he were going to take part in Lance's wide-reaching plans; how he would perhaps have something to do with the paper-mill or the market gardens that were to replace the swamp; and how happy she and he could be.

Adela entered eagerly into all these glowing particulars. A new life opened before her, which she believed would be beautified with all sorts of unexpected happiness; and she was filled with thanksgiving because she had clung resolutely to her plighted troth.

"We'll go to-morrow!" cried Dennie, with enthusiasm. "D'ye think ye can make out to be ready, Deely?"

"I could be ready to-day," she replied, "if there's a train."

Dennie, wonderful to relate, had provided himself with a time-table, though the "summer arrangement" of the railroad to Beaufort was not complicated. He resorted to his hat to find it. But as he plucked the printed slip from its place in the inner band of the hat his eye lighted on Sylv's letter. Until that moment he had entirely forgotten that he was a usurper of the postal function.

"Dog-gone it !" he exclaimed, "I come mighty near not givin' you this. It's from Sylv."

Adela stripped away the yellow envelope with startled haste ; and on a poor sheet of blue-ruled note-paper she read these words :

"DEAR DEELY : I did not mean to write anything, but the feeling comes over me that I ought to say good-by to you and Dennie. I have decided that my life here has been a failure, and I am going away. I shall not come back. Mr. Lance thinks I have gone to do something for him, but it is no use to look for me, because no one can find me.

"I love you and Dennie, and want you to be happy together. Remember that, and do not mourn over me any more than if I had died. You know we cannot help dying. If I could do any good by staying I would ; but I am certain it is better for me to go.

"Tell Dennie I trust him to make you happy. I believe in him and love him. Good-by. SYLV."

Dennie awaited the result of her reading in dumb expectancy, and saw the look of horror in her face, but could not account for it.

Adela shrieked aloud. "Oh, he is dead !" she cried. "He meant to kill himself ! Help, Dennie, help ! What are we to do ?"

She stretched out her hand, with the letter in it ; but Dennie only shook his head, in helpless bewilderment.

"I can't read it," he said, piteously. "I don't know enough, Deely. That ar writin'— Deely, what ails ye ? What's he said there ?"

The mistress of the academy came running in, alarmed by the girl's outcry.

"Sylv is going to kill himself," Adela repeated. "He says he's going away; but I know—oh, I know what he means! See, Dennie; that's what he says." And again she held the letter toward him, distractedly. "He says good-by to you and me. Can we go to-day? Is there any train?"

Dennie offered the mistress his time-table, which to him was merely an illegible curiosity—a memento of his unprecedented journey.

Without looking at it, however, she drew out her watch with a sharp tug at the silken guard that held it. "Yes, you have time," she announced, "if you hurry. I'll bring your things, Miss Reefe."

She disappeared.

"Tell me 'bout it, Deely," said Dennie, fumbling hopelessly with the letter, which he had now taken into his sunburned hands.

Adela set foot upon her agitation, and rapidly read the letter over to him.

Dennie appeared to be stunned. "Suicide?" he said. "What for? Hev you got any right for to think that ar?" His tone was indignant. "What call ar' he got to kill hisself? Sylv—our Sylv, I tell ye. My brother!"

"Because he hadn't anything left to live for! He was miserable," Adela answered, with vengeful emphasis. "It is Mr. Lance did it—sending me here. No! I did it, because I would not tell him what I felt. I wanted to be true to you."

The truth burst upon Dennie like a flood, and his fierce temper rose to meet it. For an instant a blinding light flashed dazzlingly by across everything that surrounded him; he grew giddy, and Adela had no more important existence in his eyes than the table and the chairs around him, or the lifeless walls of the room. His single desire was, in his rage, to destroy something, to create havoc and ruin, answering to the ruin of his own hopes. But the next instant he felt as if he were among the pines, with his gun aimed at Sylv ; and the thought that Sylv at this very instant might be lying dead somewhere brought a ghastly picture before his eyes. The whirl of maddening light passed away, and he stood humiliated, mournful, calm, motionless.

"Then it's true at last !" he said, hoarsely. "You loved that man—my brother—and he loved you."

For a moment Adela could not speak. Her lips moved, without sound. At last she answered : "Yes. But I never told him, and he said nothing to me. 'Twas only after we came here."

Dennie replied in a voice that made her think of the muffled breaking of the waves on the distant coast. "I was fearsome of it, Deely, but I swore I wouldn't think on't. It ar' best I know it now. We'll go and look for —for Sylv. If he ar' alive, I'll bring you to him."

———

CHAPTER XV.

ELBOW-CROOK SWAMP.

WITHOUT notice Hedson had appeared on the scene ; he was hospitably received by Colonel Floyd, and asked Lance to show him over the ground in which the as yet unborn syndicate was expected to invest.

Accompanied by Sylv they were occupied in a general survey of the swamp, from the outside, at the time when

Dennie was talking with Adela in Newbern. "Yes, yes; fine country for a cemetery," said the hale but sceptical Hedson. "To come down to bed-rock on this thing," he added, turning to Lance, "the expense of paring off the natural growth and filling in here would be enormous, to say nothing of what the lawyers call 'supplementary proceedings.' You know what that means, don't you, Mr. De Vine?" Here he included Sylv in the favored list of those for whom his remarks were intended.

The upshot of the exploratory drive was that Hedson gave a semi-adverse judgment; notwithstanding which he began to consult with himself inaudibly as to the best mode of going to work to buy some of the waste land in question on his private account.

Sylv showed an unmistakble eagerness to begin his task of investigating the interior of the swamp, and before he parted from Lance for the day he took him aside and told him that he should be in the swamp by daylight of the next morning.

Hedson and the colonel found plenty to talk about that evening, and Lance was left alone with Jessie.

The conversation that passed between these two was somewhat ruffled. Jessie found fault with her lover because he had gone to Newbern against her will, and Lance assured her that his eccentric interest in Adela Reefe was now appeased: he had done all that he wished to, in disclosing to her the probable relationship with the Floyds, and would henceforth leave her affairs, for the most part, alone. But Jessie was not content with that declaration.

"If she comes back here to live, as you say she is about to do," she asked, "what do you expect?"

"Simply that we shall receive her as one of us," said Lance. "I have befriended her and the De Vine boys,

and I intend to keep on.   They are inevitably a part of
my system and my plans now."

"Then you are going to overturn everything," Jessie
asserted.

In short, silly though it was, they quarrelled more
seriously than they had done hitherto.

Jessie, there is reason to believe, was very unhappy in
consequence, and passed a wretched night.   And Lance
scarcely slept a wink.   He lay restless on his bed, turning
and tossing, until it seemed to him that he veered this
way or that with the varying gusts of the tempestuous
wind that hourly grew more turbulent, until Fairleigh
Manor shook in its angry clutch.

"How the wind roars!" he growled aloud, starting
from a half doze ; and after vainly waiting a while longer
for repose he got up, dressed himself, and went out.

The earliest gray of daybreak was visible in the east-
ern sky, but the atmosphere was so surcharged with storm
that he fancied he could hear the seething of the angry
ocean in the blasts that whirled around him, though he
was not within ten miles of the open sea.

An hour after he had left the manor a worn-out wagon
from Beaufort drew up in front of the door, and Dennie
alighted.   Dennie raised such a clamor at the door that
at last the inmates began to arouse themselves.   Jessie
was the first to respond to the summons.   She gathered
hastily from Dennie the object of his untimely call, and
learned that Adela was with him in the wagon.   They
were looking for Sylv ; had been detained at Beaufort,
and were only just arrived ; so they had come at once to
the manor to ask Lance if he knew anything of Sylv's
whereabouts, since Lance had been mentioned in the
letter of farewell.   But, a servant being sent to Lance's
room, it was discovered that he was not at home ; and

Dennie forthwith started to drive to the shore, hoping that he might get some clew from Aunty Losh.

Imagine Jessie's wonder and anxiety when she found that Lance had disappeared ! Her conscience had already stung her for the absurdity of her quarrel with him ; but now that he was out of reach, and that Dennie had brought to her the apprehension of something tragic impending over Sylvester, her excitement rose to fever-height. Daylight broadened while she sat up, nervous and speculating, amid the noises of the disturbed household ; and the wind-storm increased in violence every moment, keeping pace with her terror and her perplexity. Filled with forebodings, and finding it impossible to remain inactive, she completed her toilet, had one of the stable-hands called, and, leaving word for her father that she had gone to the headland in quest of Lance, she started to drive through the plantations.

Hunting Quarters being the nearer point, Dennie dropped the reins when the jaded team which he drove brought him to a fork in the roadway, and told Adela to drive to her father's house. He himself set out on a full run for Aunty Losh's, and never paused until he reached the cabin-door.

Aunty Losh reported that Sylv had risen before dawn and gone toward Elbow-Crook Swamp, saying that he had something to do there for Mr. Lance.

The storm raged more furiously than ever. The ocean could be heard thundering at the outer bulwarks of the coast irresistibly. The great billows were actually at that moment surging far beyond their wonted limits and shaking the very roots of the low hills out by Hatteras, though Dennie could not see them there. He could guess the tumult that was in progress at Ocracoke and lower ; the air was full of mist and flying spray ; the sea was literally pulling down the outer sand-heaps, eating into them, doing its best to tear open a new inlet; and the waters of the Sound were furrowed, foaming, and uncontrollable. Yet Dennie could not delay. He began at once to retrace his course, heading for the swamp, for he had several miles to go. It was only for an instant, as he crossed the planks over the ditch he had so recently made, that he observed how the water from the Sound was boiling through the artificial channel.

He went on in headlong haste.

Before he had been twenty minutes out of sight Jessie drove up to within a few rods of the ditch, and sped across the intervening space. Her coachman warned her not to go thither. "You'll be blown away, missy," he cried, despairingly. "Dis yer am a hurricane, and de hosses can't stan' it much longer."

But, if she heard him, she paid no attention. In a few moments she had crossed the narrow planks, which, bedded though they were in the earth, trembled at the assaults of the wind. She had no more than vanished among the trees around the cabin when the tide, rushing in renewed volumes through the ditch, swept away the frail bridge as if it had been straw. The banks began to crumble; and the coachman, barely able to guide his horses, whipped up and drove away as well as he could, in search of aid.

Dennie got over the ground with marvellous rapidity, taking the shortest line for the swamp. The wind was blowing inland, and bore him along with it; so, when he had gone two thirds of the way, it seemed to him that but a few minutes had elapsed. He was on the regular road, now; but it was providential, nevertheless, that he should encounter in that spot another man. He hailed him loudly, amid the howling of the wind; and the man, turning round, proved to be Lance ! He, too, was on his way to the swamp. Going forth aimlessly, he had made up his mind to join Sylv, if he could find him, in the proposed expedition. Alarmed by the prodigious force of the tempest, however, he would have turned back and endeavored to regain the manor, if he had not met Dennie.

A few hasty words gave him knowledge of the threatened catastrophe ; and the two men joined forces in the forlorn attempt to find Sylv and prevent his self-destruction.

Dennie knew where a boat could be had to launch upon the devious river that ran through the swamp ; and, fortunately, it turned out that Sylv had not taken this boat for himself.

Together they entered the gloomy jungle. They not only plunged into the desperate undertaking of trying to save the life of another man, who had resorted to this convenient cover with the evident purpose of never emerging thence, but they also engaged in a struggle which, for themselves, was very like a life-and-death matter.

For some time they could not use their boat. They were obliged to drag it through a tangled mass of roots and vines and treacherous brake, until they could reach the stream. The exertion they made was almost super-human, and would have been impossible to them except under the terrible incentive that drew them on. Only when they were afloat, and paddling warily along the dubious and unfamiliar current, did they understand how their labor had sapped their strength. And only then, also, did they perceive that they had passed from a world of uproar and elemental upheaving into a realm as secluded and quiet as a tomb.

The mighty winds, it is true, rumbled through the tops of the trees under which they were buried ; but the dense mass of boughs and springing verdure that walled in the secret places of the swamp, as with a hundred separate walls, would not permit that wild commotion of the outer air to reach them. Birds had fled hither from the hurricane, and even dared to chirp in the lonely and forsaken thickets of this uncouth wilderness. Day was spreading above the thick canopy of boughs, and was pouring its light all round the vast area of the swamp at its edges ; but here, within, there reigned a perpetual and awful twilight. The slow, brown stream ran on ahead, turning here and there, opening into blind creeks, sprawling through the dusk like some great snaky thing with a hundred sinuous arms and feelers ; but it was rather by instinct and touch than by any other means that the two men in the canoe traced the main body of the slimy current. No landmarks were to be counted on there : the points of the compass were obliterated.

The swamp was the home of oblivion. They moved through it as through a place set apart for those who are condemned to a death in life.

From time to time they shouted aloud. Having no weapons with them, they could make no other signal. They called to Sylv, with a hope that he might answer to them from the next bend in the stream, or from some adjoining depth of bough and bramble. Yet always the same dead silence swallowed up the sound of their voices, and no human response came back. The raw air, the shade, the moisture of the oozing current, gradually invaded them with a chill that seemed to run through their very bones ; but it was with a more deadly chill that they gazed into one another's eyes, and thought, without saying it, that perhaps they were even then pushing their way over the liquid grave in which Sylv might have sought relief.

How long they urged that ghostly chase it would not be easy to say: they could form no judgment of the time. But at last Dennie caught sight of what appeared to be a ruddy flame on a low island in the muddy flood, some distance in advance. Neither of the paddlers was quite positive that it was a real flame, but they put new vigor into their strokes, and hallooed again. Once more, no answer.

Still, the flame grew more distinct. The canoe swept rapidly forward and rubbed against the roots and sediment of the tiny island. No other boat was moored there, but the fire flickered and spurted up more vividly. Beside it they beheld Sylv, haggard, inert, and seemingly unconscious of their approach.

"Sylv! Sylv!" cried Dennie.

"What are you doing here?" Lance demanded.

Sylv shrank back, then started to his feet; the flame-light—looking so garish in that gloomy place—thrown upward on to his wan cheeks in such wise as to make them seem more hollow than they were in fact.

"I came here to die," he answered, without emotion. "Why did you follow me? It would have been over before long."

They heard the booming of the storm-wind in the trees overhead, like the groan of some remote unknown multitude of sufferers; and it chimed in well with the lonely reverberation of his voice.

"It is over now!" Lance exclaimed. "Don't you see that we won't let you die? It was mad of you to think of such a thing, Sylv!"

Dennie drew close to his brother swiftly, and put his arm around him, as though to guard him from an unseen enemy.

"Sylv," he said, "it ar' all fixed and done. Deely loves ye—she have told me—and I see that I ain't the one for her. I'm clean done with all that ar foolishness, Sylv, and I told her she'd got to marry ye, anyhow. Steady away now, Sylv. D'ye listen to me?"

The burly, red-bearded brother slid his hands down the arms of the slender, dark-haired one, and held him as if he feared that he might still break away and escape.

Lance, looking on, thought he had never seen anything more tender, more brave and manly, than Dennie's expression and attitude. He had never, he thought, heard finer sweetness in a man's voice than came from Dennie's lips.

Sylv broke down. "Dennie, boy," he cried; and then paused, choking. "Dear old Dennie!" (His brother winced at that unconscious repetition of Adela's phrase.) "I never thought this would come! I was true when I said I did not love her. I couldn't know what it would be like, then. But, you see, I tried to get out of the way. Oh, why didn't you let me die here!"

The morbid mood which had impelled him to the resource of slow suicide, by starvation in the swamp, could not at once be dispelled; but by dint of soothing words and of reminders that they must lose no time in getting back to the outer world, the two allies prevailed over Sylv's melancholy.

"Where's your boat?" asked Lance.

"I set it adrift," was the answer.

A fresh peril was thus intruded upon them; for the canoe would hold three persons only with the greatest precautions.

" You uns go, and then one can come back for me,"
Dennie suggested.

But Lance would not risk leaving him alone. It was
decided, therefore, that they should all embark and make
their way to safety, if possible. The hazard and suspense
of the situation, however, roused Sylv up thoroughly.
All his finer qualities reasserted themselves, and he became the guiding spirit in the endeavor of the party to
extricate itself. He whom the others had come to recall
to life was now eager to lead them out of the dilemma
in which they had placed themselves on his account. But
in the anxiety of the moment he forgot one thing. The
flame which he had kindled, like a torch in the gloomy
vaults of death, was left burning ; and they had paddled
some distance before they remembered their neglect.

Meanwhile the lonely beacon, unwatched, had shot out
an experimental tongue to try sundry dry vine-stems hard
by. The stems responded with a brisk crackle. The
flames scaled the side of a tree almost instantly, and ran
along the boughs. Thence they transferred themselves
with ease to another tree. Thus, in a few minutes, the
blaze spread from the island into the rest of the dense
wood, and became a conflagration.

The smoke blew lazily toward the occupants of the
canoe ; then a lurid glow shone along the murky water.
They saw their danger, and paddled with might and
main ; but the danger of upsetting the overloaded craft
handicapped them and retarded their progress.

Soon the glow came nearer and burst into actual fire.
The whole swamp seemed to be roofed with writhing
flame. The heat was frightful : birds flew away madly
through the labyrinth ; the shadowy shapes of wild creatures scurried through the tangle, and scared serpents
slipped out from their lairs, trailing across the sluggish

stream.   All the while the fire pursued the three human
fugitives with what seemed a vindictive intelligence : the
long draperies of gray moss caught the sparks, flashing them on in vivid festoons, and wrapping the forest in a
magnificent combustion.

Blinded, stifled, and dizzy, the canoeists were at last
obliged to abandon their narrow bark and push their way
through the fearful maze on shore.   Luckily, however,
when they were driven to this extreme they had come
nearly to the edge of the wilderness.

Each struggling for himself, Lance and Sylv suddenly
achieved safety : they set foot upon the solid ground,
and felt the fierce wind from the sea.   But at that juncture Dennie, who was behind them, stumbled, and was
caught in the mire.   The hissing mass of flame advanced
upon him, and Sylv, seeing his danger, turned to help
him.

Lance tried to hold Sylv back.   He fought with him,
in his desire to prevent what he thought a certain sacrifice of two lives instead of one.   But Sylv, nerved by an
ecstatic force, sprang away from him and reached his
brother's side.   How it was done neither Lance nor Sylv
could say afterward ; but the attempt succeeded, and
Sylv dragged Dennie out of danger, though not un-
scathed.   The intense heat had blistered their faces and
hands even in the few moments that it had to work upon
them ; and Dennie, hurt by the fall of a heavy branch
which had struck his leg, lay in the road, unable to rise.

CHAPTER XVI.

"I LIVE, HOW LONG I TROW NOT."

ONE might well have supposed that the period of final destruction had come on that eventful day. Wind, fire, and sea all combined to make it a memorable one. For, while Lance and the De Vines were going through their adventures in Elbow-Crook Swamp, the incoming tides, fomented by the winds, not only swept away the paltry planking that joined Aunty Losh's headland to the main shore, but also proceeded to crunch up and dissolve a large portion of her real estate.

The freakish inroads of the sea on the North Carolina coast are scarcely subjects for exaggeration, because they themselves outdo fancy. The ocean thereabouts has an occasional fit of map-making. Not content with changing the soundings as it pleases, it sometimes closes up an old inlet, at a single mad flurry, or insists upon opening a new avenue in any place that may suit its convenience. And so, at this particular crisis, having thundered at the outer gates and found no admission, it sent a heavy tide into the Sound, and played havoc there. The green waters, ordinarily manageable enough, converted themselves into cataracts. They heaved, frothed, billowed and raged, until Aunty Losh's demesne, once an innocent promontory, became a very perilous and uncomfortable island.

The watery ditch turned into a rushing tideway ; then it became a deep channel ; and lastly it widened into an angry reach of turbulent waves, which could be crossed only by boat. All this transformation, be it remembered, was accomplished in a few hours.

Meanwhile, Aunty Losh and Jessie cowered in the little cabin on the dwindling territory, and expected every moment to be swallowed up by the surges that lashed so wildly around them.

But the retreating coachman had known what he was about. He had gone at once to Hunting Quarters, where he had found Adela, who was herself distracted with anxiety for Sylv, and therefore in a perfect mood for venturing upon the wildest scheme of rescue that could be imagined. It so chanced that the dug-out was harbored in a cove which the girl could reach. The rude sloop clung there, thumping heavily on the bottom, and lurching now and then against the shore, with an impact that would have smashed any other sort of craft at short notice. But this was precisely what she was made for, and so she endured the strain.

Adela prepared to take her out to the now isolated cabin, and bring off the inmates. Old Reefe remonstrated. He said it was certain death to go ; that no boat could live in such a wind on a short, shallow sea ; and that his daughter must wait until the storm abated.

"No," cried Adela ; "I am going, whether it's death or not ! How do you know what will happen to them out there if I wait ? The cabin itself may be swept away, and poor old aunty in it. Then, Dennie is there, and—and perhaps Sylv." For one instant, as she uttered this name, her voice sank. "If they had any boat, 'twould be another thing. But they're cut off—they can't help themselves—and I'm going."

The brave girl hardly believed that she could make the trip in safety, but she thanked her stars that Dennie had brought her up to handle a tiller —and the rest she left to Providence.

The water was swashing up close to the door of the

little hut, and Aunty Losh and Jessie sat within, holding on to each other in silence when, through the deep, prolonged roar of the tempest, they fancied that they heard a shout—a woman's shout. Simultaneously with it there came a thud, like the dropping of some heavy weight upon the ground just outside of the house. "Lord be praised!" Aunty Losh exclaimed. "Thar ain't nothin' could do that ar but the ole dug-out. Open the do', Miss Jessie."

Jessie considered this as a command to invite dissolution into their fragile shelter; but she obeyed.

In a few moments they were on board the sloop, bouncing and reeling through the violent waves. By this time Colonel Floyd, having also received the alarm, reached the spot on horseback. Waiting with old Reefe on the shore, he noted every motion of the plunging sail, which was let out barely enough to give the dug-out headway. Adela stood at the helm, strong and masterful as a man, but with a quick, feminine eye for every chance or change of the terrific gale, and with a touch that responded instantly to her observation. She ignored her two passengers absolutely.

But when, after several escapes from foundering and a weary battle of tacking from one point to another, the sloop rounded, with her heavy prow, into the cove and touched the land, the girl dropped down in the stern, exhausted.

There had been no time for delay or inquiry, and indeed it would have been impossible to talk in the overpowering bluster of the storm, while fighting a way through it; but Adela had been very much astonished both by Jessie's presence at the cabin, and by the absence of Dennie. She now tried to learn from Aunty Losh what had become of him; but the poor old woman's mind

was in such confusion from fright and from the suddenness of her rescue that she could not furnish much enlightenment. As for Jessie, she had gone to the headland without any knowledge of Lance's actual whereabouts, but thinking it probable that her lover would be
there, since she had heard something vaguely about his
arrangements with Sylv. It was now noon, and the suspense in which she remained about Lance, joined to
Adela's fearful dread concerning Sylv, would not permit
them to rest. The colonel, who had been thrown into a
wild excitement by the failure both of his daughter and
of Lance to return to the house, hugged Jessie close to his
heart with silent prayers of thanksgiving, and wrung
Adela's hand with gratitude, while the tears ran down his
cheeks. The carriage had followed him with fresh horses,
bringing dry wraps, food, and restoratives; and the
colonel insisted that the best thing to be done was for
the three women to get in and go at once to the manor
with him.

Meanwhile Sylv and Lance, helping the disabled Dennie between them, had arrived at the house, and were
taking care of the sufferer.

I need not detail the recitals and explanations that followed. I will say only that Jessie treated Adela like a
sister that day, and ever afterward. It was strange,
mysterious, yet beautiful, to Lance's eyes, to see them
together; one of them the latest offspring of Gertrude
Wylde, rescued from oblivion—coaxed back, as it were,
from the forest shadows and the red race to her own race
and kin—the other a descendant of Gertrude's cousin,
to-day rescued by her kinswoman from the engulfing
waters of the Sound. The whims and prejudices that
had hampered Jessie before were now totally dissolved;
and Lance's dream was realized, after all. The wild

thought which had crossed his mind, of devoting his life to Adela, proved to be simply a perversion of the ardent desire which he had felt, that she ought to be included somehow in the lines of relationshp and love prescribed by her ancestry. His allegiance to Jessie, never really shaken, was perfect and enduring. But these results would never have come about had not the actors in the curious drama remained, through all their troubles, sound and sincere of heart. They had, every one, risen somewhat higher than they were when their relations began. Each had advanced in his or her own way. Sylv strove upward by means of intellectual effort and by will ; Dennie attained to as lofty a standard of conduct through the working out of instinct and passion. But in whatever manner they had proceeded, all were true.

The wild storm went down that night, though the rolling sea and the curling breakers of the Sound continued to heave for hours, throwing out in the darkness broad lines and crests of phosphorescence that made them look like fluid white fire. Then the rain came, in torrents ; and it was well that it came, for the danger to the inflammable pine-plantations, from the conflagration in Elbow Crook, had become alarming. Not even the sullen fierceness of that furnace—in which the swamp-woods, with all their intricacies of flickering boughs, like some gigantic red coral work, were melting down—could withstand the providential rain-streams. The fire faded away as if by magic ; and the next day, when Hedson went out, with scores of other gazers, to look at the expanse of charred *débris* where the woods had been, he remarked tersely (but in an undertone) to Lance : "That property is now worth just one hundred per cent more for our purpose than it was day before yesterday. The clearing has been done free of charge."

By the middle of the summer the county awoke to the
fact that a syndicate of Northern capitalists had purchased
the tract and were going to develop it into a prodigious
vegetable garden.   The reed-pulp paper-mill went up;
there was an immense quantity of ditching and levelling
carried on in the swamp.   Little houses began to make
their appearance; new dwellers came to live in them;
and a school and church were found to be necessary.
There is now a flourishing community in that place; and
while Lance, I am glad to say, has made a good deal of
money, his pleasure has grown largely from the knowledge that he has brought about improvements which
others also enjoy.   Sylv acts as his chief adviser and
confidential agent.

Dennie's accident left him somewhat lame, but he has
still found it possible to be of service in some of Lance's
undertakings.   He prefers, however, to retain a degree
of independence by living on the island with Aunty Losh,
and following more or less his old employment in a
superior dug-out schooner, which has replaced the sloop.
On the island he has remained ever since the marriage
of Sylv and Adela and their installation in a pretty house
which was built for them, near enough to the manor to
make it convenient for the children of Jessie and Adela
to meet often when they shall grow a little older.

One slight question came up, I must admit, as to who
had the best right to appropriate the old Wharton Hall
motto.   Sylv acknowledged that it belonged primarily to
Lance, by inheritance from Guy Wharton; but, then, had
it not been handed down to Adela as well?   The point
was settled without dispute; for Sylv's house was built
before Lance was ready to remodel the manor, and when
the plans were submitted to Lance he proposed—with Jessie's permission—that he should be allowed to contribute

as his gift a tablet for the hall, on which were to be shown (not cut in, but raised in bold relief) the lines beginning

"I live, how long I trow not."

Dennie has no new house and no old motto. I cannot suppose that he is altogether a contented man ; but I believe he is happy in having taken the right course.

"My old heart do ache for ye, Dennie," said Aunty Losh to him, about the time of the wedding. "There ain't much on't left at my time o' life ; but what there be of heart in me do ache, for sure. But ye done right, boy. 'Tain't no use tryin' to drive a woman. It's mighty like when ye tryin' to make a passel o' hens come into the house ; and ye chase 'em up and say, 'Shoo !' and gits 'em a'most to the do'; and then they jist run straight past it. No ; ye can't drive a woman, Dennie, if she's sot her mind ag'in it. That's what."

Dennie looked up from the tackle he was mending, and smiled. "Wal, aunty," he said, "you and me make out to git along pretty squar' together, don't we ? I don't want for to drive ye, and ye can't look to drive me, neither. *I* don't complain."

The last three words will do for his motto ; and they make a sufficiently honorable one.

MAJOR BARRINGTON'S MARRIAGE.

I.

MAJOR BARRINGTON before the acquisition of his military title was a rather shapely gentleman, with a fine, carrot-tinted complexion and strong, reddish whiskers, corresponding well with it, and branching out on either side of his chin with a valiant air.

Nor did his appearance greatly alter, immediately after passing from the condition of plain citizen to that of a defender of his country. His chin (which was shaven, and had a pretty little dent in the bottom of it) came for a time more prominently before the public, being carried somewhat higher in the air; but otherwise you would hardly have known what a great man he was.

It happened thus: The War of the Rebellion had been going on for about a year, and Mr. Zadoc S. Barrington was a boarder in the respectable but shabby mansion of one Mrs. Douce, in East Thirtieth Street, New York—a short, pale, dusty-looking woman, who had under her threadbare wing a maiden relative, Natalia by name. Natalia was alternately visitor and boarder, according as her slender income gave out or held out, and the consequence of this variable status was an equally variable disposition on the part of the aunt toward the niece. Mrs. Douce had naturally a dry heat of temper,

which was possibly the source of that pulverous look
about the face already noticed ; and it was only by turning on periodical smiles, like the spray from a watering-
cart, that she was able to allay the gritty particles of her
irritability in the presence of paying boarders. It was
to be expected, therefore, that during Natalia's impecu-
nious seasons her aunt should relapse into unmitigated
dustiness, and puff her discontent, so to speak, in dreary
little gusts at the forlorn maiden.

Being forlorn, was it strange that Natalia should look
to Barrington for sympathy ? Not at all. By degrees
he thus came—without any movement on his own part—
to take an important place in her daily experience. A
variety of little hopes and illusions, of which her life
had been pretty well divested before, and which she
alone could not have revived, sprung up spontaneously
under the most casual glance of Zadoc S. For example,
though she had no appetite for Mrs. Douce's feeble din-
ners, she could get up a fictitious enjoyment of them by
looking at the robust Barrington, whose bold coloring
and hearty appearance deceived her as to the real measure of his relish for that dreary cookery.

Barrington was not dangerously youthful, but neither
was Natalia. Financially he was not prosperous, but she
was decidedly not so. Heaven only knows how, during
the years of his residence in New York, he had con-
trived to subsist. It was not on any scientific principle
of survival that he persisted ; but rather on the principle
of the fallen sparrow. Still, he was a portly sparrow,
and must have needed a good deal to keep him on his
feet. But he remained on his feet—he never soared.
And yet, such as he was, Natalia—let us confess it with
a becoming amount of maiden timidity—yes, Natalia
had begun to love him.

II.

But she did not tell her love. She let concealment feed upon her cheek—which, to be accurate, was not damask, but rather of the quality of sarsnet. However, before her appearance had had time to suffer by this process, an unexpected proceeding on the part of Barrington led her to reveal her sentiment—to surprise and, one might say, surround him. Did capture follow? Let us see.

At this period his affairs were very low. He was a prospective patentee, a filer of caveats for little inventions, which no one could have been hired to infringe, the most ingenious point of which was their perfect adaptability for not making money. He was also by turns an agent for books, subscription engravings, sewing-machines, and what not. He did everything but succeed. Finally he conceived the idea of a new vegetable lamp-oil that could be made from floating oily matter to be found in any swamp. He had made close computation of the swampy land in the whole State of New York, which could be bought for a trifle, and turned into sources of boundless wealth. For a time he fed the flame of hope with this visionary fluid ; but a serious lamp explosion, resulting from one of his experiments, deprived him at once of half his whiskers and all his expectations. There was indeed one resource left him, the nature of which we may discover presently ; but he hesitated to avail himself of it, because it might compromise his independence. In fact, a certain steady effort to be a man and to keep his self-respect, in spite of his many failures, was Barrington's finest trait, and always gave me a liking for him, notwithstanding his weakness.

By the time his singed whiskers had regained their pristine vigor, and when the war had passed through its first year, there drove up to Mrs. Douce's door, one day, an express wagon with a trunk in it. The startling thing about this was that the trunk (which was made of sole-leather) was quite new, and had painted on it, with terrific distinctness, this legend :

CAPT. Z. S. BARRINGTON, U. S. A.

The painted end of the trunk happened to be nearest the house. Now, Mrs. Douce was at that very moment in her reception-room on the ground floor—a sort of little bin or wine-cooler of a room, where (having nothing better to cool) she kept callers, and sometimes herself—and from there she spied the appalling arrival. She did not know, which was the fact, that Barrington, tired of his sparrow's life on the pavements of the metropolis, had been in correspondence with friends at Washington, who had secured him the promise of a commission on his applying for it. He had not at once made such application, but had gone off with much high beating of the heart, and ordered the trunk, as a preliminary, feeling perhaps that the final step would be easier to take after committing himself thus far.

Mrs. Douce, I say, not knowing this, opened the door for the expressman in a great flurry of excitement. "Now, indeed," thought she, melodramatically, "I begin to feel what war is!"

Then she ran up-stairs herself, to inform Barrington that the trunk had come. But he was equal to the emergency. With an unshaken demeanor the hero rose from the table at which he had been conducting a busy and wholly useless correspondence, and looked at Mrs. Douce with a magnificent calm, which gave her a strange sensation of having penetrated some great general's headquarters. Then he proceeded down-stairs to parley with the expressman, who for a moment seemed to take the place of a flag-of-truce bearer, or some kind of military ambassador.

As Barrington descended he heard Natalia in the drawing-room conducting to its close an extensive piece of music, with a copious rumbling of low notes and a twittering of high ones, which was apparently reluctant to be brought to a close at all. The sound touched his heart, somehow; but he went on. It also touched Mrs. Douce, who had followed; but she did *not* go on.

III.

SHE stopped in the narrow passage, just by a niche containing a tall and bilious-complexioned alabaster vase, with scraggly arms, which had always impressed her as giving the house a great advantage over other boarding-houses. (That vase, by the way, had levied its tax in many a bill.) But now it seemed gloomily symbolic; everything had begun to seem unnatural and suggestive since that trunk appeared. She fancied the vase was like a "storied urn," containing the ashes of some valiant warrior who should no more wield the humble breakfast-knife at her devastated table. Overcome with emotion, she passed on and pushed open the drawing-room door.

"Natalia," she exclaimed, impressively, "guess what has happened !" As the expressman, with fate-like footsteps, tramped up-stairs, carrying the trunk on his shoulder, Barrington, who came after him, noticed that the rumbling and twittering of the piano had ceased, and that his landlady had disappeared. The two women were, in fact, conversing in agitated whispers on the other side of the closed parlor door.

"Well, never did I think to lose *him !*" exclaimed Mrs. Douce.

"Poor aunt !" said Natalia ; "and so late in the season, too."

"It isn't that so much," interrupted the other, severely ; "but it hurts me that he should have been so sudden and so secret."

"Perhaps he thought we—" Natalia paused, and blushed. "But why *should* he think we'd urge him to stay ?"

"Hark ! is he coming down again ?" said her aunt. No ; it was merely the expressman. He thumped his way down to the street door. They heard the wagon drive off, and for a moment afterward they held their breath, as if a battle had been raging near them, and the heavy current of the fight had now swept by, leaving them in suspense, lest it should return. Then the dignified step of Barrington resounded on the staircase. He came to the door, and opened it. "I ought," he began, stepping in with a smile, "to explain matters a little."

Mrs. Douce's mood was like that of elderly matrons at the wedding of a young friend. She hardly knew whether to laugh or cry. "Oh," she returned, in the breathless, short-of-supplies manner usual with her in awkward situations, "oh—no—explanation is needed,

Mr. Barrington !" and, after a short pause, simpering, "I'm sure."

Natalia, meanwhile, stood in a shrinking, drooping attitude near the battered rosewood piece of furniture from which she had been drawing music, and looked a good deal like one of those young ladies in old colored prints who devote themselves to standing mournfully under weeping willows, among headstones.

"Well, you see," proceeded Barrington, who took Mrs. Douce's denial at its worth, "I didn't say anything, because—well, it wasn't quite settled."

"Then you're not *sure* of going to the war ?" Natalia burst forth, with pathetic eagerness. (Barrington noticed that her heightened color was becoming to her.)

"Sure ?" answered he, cruelly ; "oh, yes ; humanly speaking, I suppose it's sure enough. I—good gracious ! —I only—"

These incoherent phrases were drawn out by the effect his statement had produced. Natalia's eyelids fell at his words. She was trying to repress a tendency to sob. By the time the hero had discovered this a tear had found its way into sight beneath her eyelashes.

"There !" cried Mrs. Douce, sternly. "Any one might have known it. *We* aren't made of sole-leather, Mr. Barrington. [He said to himself it was lucky she had told him this.] Common humanity and friendship ought to have shown you what this suddenness would lead to."

"I can't help it," murmured her niece, referring to the tears now hurrying down her face, and misled by the matron's angry tone and her own confusion into the idea that *she* was being scolded. (She was at this time without money.)

"Of course you can't, dear," said the aunt, sooth-

ingly.   "As if any one with any considerateness, or
average humanity, I may say, would suppose you could !
I am not the woman to blame you for giving way under
the circumstances, Natalia.   It only shows you've got a
heart, while *some* people—Mr. Barrington, excuse me,
but I must speak out."   However, she didn't speak out
any further, but wound up with : " Anyway, it can't be
worse than it is [though nobody had intimated that it
could be].   You've decided to leave me.   Well, that's
what I must expect, I suppose."   And she dropped into
a chair, and patted her thumbs together, as if there were
some crushing sarcasm in the action, which satisfied her
wounded feelings.

Barrington succumbed to remorse.   Besides, Natalia's
unhappiness aroused his sympathy, and he became angry
—without knowing whether he had a right to be so—at
Mrs. Douce's taking the part of a comforter.   He
fancied he could do this even better than she.   " Of
course," he said, stiffly, " I don't expect to leave you
without compensation for not giving notice.   I shall pay
you for two or three weeks extra."

He felt a dreadful sinking of the pocket as he spoke ;
but dignity required the sacrifice.   The landlady did not
respond for an instant ; her eyes wandered about with a
pained, prophetic air.   " What have I done," she cried,
" to bring this upon me ?   Mr. Barrington, have I ever
asked you more than we agreed upon ?   *Have* I treated
my family meanly ?   You have been in this house two
years, and I know you can't point to anything.   What
have I done to be insulted so ?" she demanded of the
faded window-curtains.

A moment of silence followed this outburst ; then she
swept out of the room, with a thin rustle of her black
dress, and left the prospective captain and Natalia alone.

IV.

MISS DOUCE put away her handkerchief in a business-like manner, and looked at Barrington with soft appeal. "Ah, why didn't you tell?"

"Tell? My dear Miss Douce, I had no idea—"

"Thoughtless man, not to foresee!"

"I didn't suppose your aunt would be so much annoyed."

"Oh, I didn't mean *that!*" said Natalia, growing judiciously pettish.

"What then?"

"Not *her*," said the maiden, significantly.

"Really, Miss Douce," said Barrington, "you have surprised me—I had no idea—"

"Don't, for pity's sake, tell me again that you had no idea!" exclaimed Natalia.

"I beg your pardon, I meant to say something."

"What good can it do to say anything, when you have done your best to break our hearts?" she demanded. And here she brought out the handkerchief again, and began to look dangerously tearful.

"Goodness!" said the unfortunate man. "I'm sure I didn't mean to. I would a good deal rather stay at home than have you feel this way."

"You have caused me great suffering, whether you meant to or not," declared Miss Douce, with a quaver in her voice. Then, replying to his devotion : "Will you give up going, to prove your words? Will you stay at home?"

Barrington felt the glory upon his horizon beginning to fade. He braced himself by a chair with one hand ;

with the other he took Natalia's. "Do you ask this as a personal favor?" he said.

Miss Douce was weeping slightly again. "I don't want you to go," she answered, shyly, turning away her head. "Yes, for my sake, stay!"

At this crisis Rawsden, one of the junior boarders, who had just returned from business and had been met at the reception-bin by Mrs. Douce with news of the dread trunk, passed up-stairs and caught a glimpse of the tableau, from the hall. "Aha," he muttered (for he was a cynical youth)—"Hector and Andromache!" And then he glided on and up to his remote chamber.

Zadoc S. still hesitated a moment. "I shall not go immediately, in any case," he said, gently. "I shall be here some days yet."

"But why go at all?" urged the Andromache. "Is it irrevocable?"

"No," he answered, unguardedly. "I—I haven't got my commission yet. I'm only expecting it."

There was a sudden revulsion of feeling on this announcement. Barrington became aware that his position was not so heroic as it had been, and Natalia began to blush violently at having betrayed her feelings on a sham emergency. But, as it happened, neither of them thought of getting out of the trouble by laughing.

"You see, now, why I kept it to myself," he proceeded, awkwardly, after some delay.

Miss Douce had released her hand, and now rose abruptly. "Oh, yes," she said; "I suppose it was all very foolish of me—but—you will forgive me?"

"I assure you, I feel honored," cried Zadoc, warmly, "by your solicitude. And, if I dared—if you would allow me—"

Let me here confess that I haven't the slightest notion

what Barrington, in that moment of impulse, was going to say. But explanation is made unnecessary by the fact that Miss Douce didn't allow him to finish.

"Don't say any more," she begged. "It is too painful. I must go and find my aunt, Mr. Barrington, to tell her there's a hope of your staying. For if your commission *shouldn't* come—"

"I should wait, of course," he responded, captivated by her glance.

Naturally, after this, he went up to the room which Mrs. Douce's fancy had transformed into a headquarters, and wrote to his Washington friends not to get the commission. Of course, too, Mrs. Douce came gently rapping at his door, in the evening, with a face as solemn as an obituary notice, and with his bill in her pocket, whereon she had obediently registered the item of compensatory payment, which she had so scornfully rejected in the afternoon. Quite of course he said, with dignity: "You may leave the bill, but I have decided not to go." And then, by sequence, she affirmed—her face irradiated with joy—that she had brought the bill very reluctantly, in the first place, and, if he would excuse her, she thought she would *not* leave it.

As a further matter of course, Miss Natalia, being informed of the abandonment of warlike measures, pretended not to care anything about the episode, and to feel that it was rather an impertinence than otherwise to bring it to her notice.

On the other hand, little Rawsden had been cracking his joke about Hector, etc., to a Miss Sneef, a rather pretty young boarder, whom he honored by confiding to her his more successful sarcasms; and, when she imparted to him, next day, the news of Barrington's capitulation, he had the presence of mind to smile pallidly

and look as if he had known all about it from an early
period of his existence. Without changing his tone, he
muttered, dryly : "Antony and Cleopatra !"

V. .

THE two parties most concerned said nothing about it
to each other for days. But the interval was not unem-
ployed. Mrs. Douce, having now discovered her niece's
inclination (if she had not known it before), was allured
by a calculation, based on the fact that Barrington had
always managed to pay his bills, and on the hope that if
Natalia were to become Mrs. Barrington two permanent
paying boarders might be secured, with possibly, in
time, a half price besides. "One of these days, after
all," she said to Barrington, whom she took an early
opportunity of seeing alone, "you will be going off and
leaving me, I fear."

"Oh, no," said he ; "I've really given up the war !"

"But there are other things than war."

"Other things to carry me away, do you mean ? Or
other disasters ?"

"Well, not exactly disasters," said Mrs. Douce,
hastily ; "I mean marriage."

"You don't call that a disaster, then ?" Barrington
inquired, wickedly. "But what on earth has put this
into your head ?"

"It's much easier to get into my head than war. If
you could think of such an unnatural thing as going to
war, you might easily decide to marry," was the landlady's equivocal conclusion.

" What, I ?" exclaimed Barrington, trying not to grow
red, but doing so. " I see I've made you suspicious."

At this juncture a faint ghostly voice was heard rising
from the basement, where the cook had long been buried,
to the third-story banister, where they were talking.
" Mrs. Douce, Mrs. Douce !"   And Mrs. Douce, giving
him an arch look, observed, with a dry laugh : " I don't
know what you're plotting."   Then she obeyed the
voice.

Whether this talk was the cause, or whether it was
owing to the interest which Miss Natalia Douce's be-
havior with regard to the military trunk excited, Barrington's attention was more closely directed to her now,
and he observed in her from day to day a deepening
melancholy.   She became listless, and fell into reveries.
She played more than usual on the piano in the dowdy
parlor, behind the bilious-looking but aristocratic vase ;
but there was less rumbling and twittering in her music
than formerly, and there were more pensive strains.   She
played " Make me no Gaudy Chaplet" and nocturnes
by sundry composers ; she sang " The Three Fishers."
All this was the more interesting, in that there was no
apparent personal application in the music she choose,
since no one had insisted upon her accepting a gaudy
chaplet, and she was not wedded as yet to a fisherman.
But one evening Barrington, coming down a few minutes before dinner, entered the parlor as she was wrench-
ing from the key-board the last phrases of a funeral
march in the " Songs without Words."   He listened
attentively until she had finished ; then, after a moment's reflection, called out from the arm-chair he had
taken : " But why do you play such mournful things,
nowadays, Miss Natalia, especially before dinner ?   No
wonder you have no appetite."

Natalia didn't answer, but got up in silence and made for the door.   On the way, however, she turned toward him with a look of indignation and a terrible flash of the eye.   The next instant she was gone.   She did not appear at dinner.

"What do you suppose is the matter with your niece?" Barrington blandly asked the aunt, at table. "I made a casual remark about her playing, just now, and she left the room without a word."

Mrs. Douce did not answer the question until the next day, when she came to Barrington's room.   "I've found out all about it, now," she said.   "The idea of asking me what was the matter, when you had been speaking to her in that way!"

"Good Lord!" cried Barrington, nettled.   "What way?   It was innocent enough; and I really don't like those tunes."

"After all that has happened!" continued the landlady, casting up her eyes.

"Well, *what* has happened?" he demanded.

"Why, your thinking of going to the war—and—and Natalia's feeling badly, and—well, you understand, though I can't explain myself, you've put me out so with your abruptness."

"It's always my abruptness or my suddenness," complained Barrington.   "No; I *don't* understand you."

Mrs. Douce's dusty face hardened and dried till it became a very desert of physiognomy.   "Well," she said, "you are not a boy, and I—well, I am old enough, I suppose," with a catch of the breath, "to be your mother.   So we may as well speak plainly.   You see that Natalia is deeply interested in you; you consented for her sake to give up going to the front; and now you coolly abandon her.   Not content with that, you begin to taunt her with her melancholy. I little expected this, Mr. Barrington. I little expected it."

"Oh, you're unjust!" said Zadoc S.

"At least, you'll admit you've wounded her feelings and ought to apologize," was the rejoinder.

"Perhaps so," he confessed, feeling sorry for Natalia.

"Go and see her," urged his landlady, gently, though still with something of the desert atmosphere in her voice. "Speak to her about it."

"I will."

"But, remember there's only one thing can make your conduct consistent and restore her happiness."

"You mean," said Barrington, exploring the dent in his chin with his forefinger—"you mean, propose?" Then, as if this were quite out of the question, he shook his head vigorously, smiling. "Of course not that; but I don't see what else you can mean."

"Nothing else," said the voice of the desert.

"It's impossible," he rejoined, quietly.

"You *must*," responded the voice.

Then Barrington delivered a crushing blow. "I have promised to marry some one else," he said, with great composure.

To Mrs. Douce's gasping, broken, indignant queries he replied that the lady's name was Magill, and that she was a widow possessed of ample means. There had long been an understanding between them, he declared, but he had been unwilling to marry without an independent property of his own. Unable to acquire this, he had hoped at least to gain distinction in the army. That hope he had sacrificed out of pure sympathy for Miss Natalia Douce's distress; and now he had concluded to marry without further delay.

VI.

I PASS over the period of internal convulsion in the
Douce hearts, widowed and maiden, which followed
Barrington's disclosure.   For a time their disconcert-
ment was so obvious that Rawsden had it all his own way
in making contemptuous remarks about them to Miss
Sneef ; and to judge from the conversation of these two
singular young people, you would have supposed that
nothing could give them such exquisite delight as to prove
that all human beings are unspeakably false and absurd,
and that if they could but have succeeded in showing
each other—Miss Sneef on her part, and Rawsden on his
—how they two were the falsest and absurdest of all,
their happiness would have been complete.

But Natalia soon rallied from the shock of Barrington's engagement to Mrs. Magill, at least far enough to
begin an exasperating warfare of innuendo, which,
though it stabbed her own heart as well, brought a balm
of revenge to her own wounds, but left Barrington quivering under the petty blows.   She made frequent allusions
to that neglected trunk belonging to the non-existent
Captain Barrington, U. S. A. ; affected to believe that
he kept in it a complete set of defunct accoutrements,
which she begged him to put on some time and show to
the " family ;" and in general taunted him most unfairly
with his abandonment of his whilom noble resolve to
seek the martial field.

Before long the entire " family " of boarders had
joined more or less actively in this guerilla attack ; and
the worst of it was, that they always kept just beyond
the pseudo-captain's range.   He couldn't retort upon

them without losing his dignity.   At last he hit upon a
masterly defence.   One day he said to Natalia, carelessly,
at the table : " Oh, as to my uniform that you've been
asking about, I'll show it to you to-night !   I am going
to drill."

The effect was gratifying.   Natalia grew pale at the
thought that her cruel sneers had actually driven Barrington (whom she continued to adore in spite of his de-
sertion) back to the cannon's mouth, so to speak.   The
other boarders were also deeply impressed, in their several degrees.   These emotions were considerably modi-
fied, yet not wholly effaced, when the military aspirant
finally appeared in his trappings ; for he did not wear
the United States uniform.   He was clothed in the
splendors of a militia major.   He revealed to the little
group of fellow-boarders, who had assembled with a sort
of hushed solemnity to inspect him, that for some time
he had been getting up a new, independent cavalry company, of which he was now the commander.

" And you're all organized ?" asked one gentleman,
gazing at the major as if he were an entire company in
himself.

" Yes ; first drill to-night," said Barrington, with a
business-like air, lighting a cigar, and looking quite
terrific.

" Thought a company was commanded by a captain,
and not a major," observed Rawsden, rescuing himself
from a secret feeling almost of admiration, and becoming
cynical again, just in time to retain the approval of Miss
Sneef, who gave him a sagacious glance.

" Yes, that's the common way," said the officer, with
superior indifference ; " but in consideration of my zeal
and expense in getting up the company, which is very
large, I rank as Major of the National Guard of the

State." Then, with striking precision, he executed a brilliant retreat from the parlor, slammed the street-door, as he went out below, with a report like a cannon, and left the awe-struck boarders to spend a miserably peaceful evening, in a state of deep humility, while he reaped the first honors of his new career.

———

VII.

THERE was much question among them as to where he had got the money for this great undertaking ; but Mrs. Douce shrewdly suspected that the widow's gold had something to do with it. She was right. Mrs. Magill's money had gilded the major's uniform and the spurs whereby he was now hoping to leap into the saddle of fame.

Still, there was no immediate sign of the threatened marriage for some time after this. Barrington took part in sundry parades, and he and his company were freely mentioned in the papers. But the widow remained so entirely in the background that Natalia almost believed she was a myth ; and there was no change in Zadoc's military life, except that the letters U. S. A. on the trunk were replaced with N. Y. S. N. G. Then came the tremendous day when Barrington's cavalry were ordered out, with other militia, to resist the rebel invasion of Pennsylvania. I will spare the reader the hardships of that campaign. It is enough that the gallant major should have undergone them ; and, to tell the truth, he was not slow to make the most thereof. He never went into a fight, and hardly so much as heard the snapping of a cap or the drawing of a sabre while his company was at the front ; for they were kept marching and counter-marching, for strategic purposes, guarding supply-trains or small batches of prisoners ; but he was a hero, for all that, when he returned. He had been obliged to forego shaving during his fortnight's absence, and this gave him a suitably battered and realistic look. I'm sorry to say he was in no hurry about shaving after he came back. He deliberately made capital of that stubby growth on his chin and upper lip, and it lent great effect to his tales of suffering with mud and rains, and beds of hard wood in barns, and to the agony he expressed at not having met the craven foe.

Rawsden and Miss Sneef attempted to turn these narratives to ridicule, but the effort failed signally. Barrington was a success. He had always been trying to be one, on some solid basis or other. Now he had become so on no basis at all.

VIII.

MRS. MAGILL was satisfied with her investment, but she wished now to make it permanent. In short, she thought in time that the major should fulfil his promise of marriage. It is scarcely necessary to say that, meanwhile, his resplendent military renown had redoubled his fascinations for the pensive Natalia ; and that maiden's faithful admiration and devout sympathy with him in the dangers to which he had lately been exposed had begun to make an impression on his simple, pompous and sanguine middle-aged heart. In all this time the two women who divided his affections and interests had not

once met.   Being charged with their rival influences, it
almost seemed as if the major, while uniting them in his
mind, had possessed a sort of chemical power of keeping
them apart.   But now he became extremely anxious to
bring them into each other's society.   The pretext he
found was that of private theatricals.   He proposed to
Mrs. Magill that an entertainment in this line should be
gotten up at the drill-room of the company, which was a
sort of riding-school arena, easily transformed into a
theatre.   She consented at length, but only on the understanding that this was to be Barrington's last grand
frolic before settling down to married life.

"Yes," said Barrington, in vague terms; "I sha'n't
want to remain single any longer."   But he was a good
deal alarmed to find himself wondering, at that very
moment, which lady it was that he intended to marry.

Mrs. Magill and Natalia were made acquainted, and
among them the three soon completed their plans for the
performance.   The piece selected was Boucicault's
farce, "Wanted—a Widow."   The major had pressed
Mrs. Magill to take a part, but, with a becoming distaste
for publicity, she declined, and Natalia was induced to
play in her stead.   Considering the title of the farce,
the widow's abstention was certainly judicious; but I
think she would have been better pleased to see Natalia
in the rôle of Lady Blanche Mountjoy, rather than that of
the successful widow, Mrs. Lovebird.   Lady Blanche
was taken by Miss Sneef, who, being young and pretty,
yet withal sceptical by nature, made a success of the
part.   Mrs. Magill, whose eyes began to survey Natalia
in the appalling light of a rival, after the first interview,
took care to be present at all the rehearsals, as you may
believe; and a little real drama, for which no rehearsal
was needed, began to move within the fictions one.

IX.

Mrs. Magill was a short and rather fleshy person, with a bland countenance, in which the experiences of her forty years—good and bad alike—had agreed to get under shelter of a placid and non-committal tinge of pink, there to make what pretence they could of not being experiences at all. There was the same discreet, uncommunicative look about her hair, which she wore stamped down along her forehead, with the severe simplicity of a butter-pat. Natalia's face, on the contrary, showed whatever she had been through. Thus, the widow and the unmarried woman trenched on each other's provinces, and promptly took a dislike one to another.

The farce in hand, as all my readers may not remember, turns upon the fact that *Henry Revel* (Barrington), having been jilted by a lady who became *Mrs. Lovebird*, has taken to reckless courses, and finally becomes a heavy debtor, in hiding from the sheriff. In this dilemma he gayly advertises for a rich widow, " with immediate possessions," and his whereabouts thus come to the knowledge of *Amy Lovebird*, now widowed, who deserted him originally only to marry a rich man who could save her father from ruin. She seeks Harry at once, in order to explain and to draw him back to herself. When he receives her response to his advertisement, however, pride and resentment make him unwilling to profit by her wealth. Meanwhile, *Amy's* friend, *Lady Blanche*, plans a stratagem to test him, so that it may appear whether he receives his former flame's advances out of mercenary policy, or with the old-time affection.

She persuades Amy to appear before him as if in great poverty, while she herself (*Lady Blanche*) writes him a letter, stating her fortune and a fictitious age, and requesting a meeting to consider the matrimonial project. When Harry meets Amy and hears this made-up story of her poverty, although his early love remains unabated, he decides to see the other widow, Lady Blanche, whose letter he has just received, to marry her, and to use the money thus acquired for the relief of *Mrs. Lovebird*. This decision, of course, makes him appear for a time false to *Amy ;* and the motive of the piece is, accordingly, that of the hero's struggle between the powers of love and of money. Since he finally marries *Mrs. Lovebird*, the superficial moral of the play was favorable to Mrs. Magill, considered with reference to Barrington's vacillations, because the major's affair with her antedated the first springing up of a sentiment for Natalia, and, moreover, she was rich. So the widow had no fear as to the moral influence of the drama upon his mind. But the deeper lesson of this amusing composition is that of fidelity to love without money ; so, as a matter of fact, it had a powerful effect in attaching the major to Natalia. At first he thought little about it. But, as the rehearsals went on, he found that theatricals, being an art, and having the magic of art, sometimes give one a strange, new interest in the real person, exhibited under subtly novel circumstances ; and he began to think it would be pleasant to follow up his imaginary devotion to Natalia with a real passion.

X.

In proportion as this feeling of the major's grew, Mrs. Magill tired of seeing him perpetually going through the farce with Natalia, and coming out as her tried and trusted lover. She resolved to hasten the date of the performance, perhaps also hoping, furtively, that Natalia wouldn't be ready, and would therefore fail disgracefully.

On his part, Barrington, to whom the new partiality for Natalia had made the rehearsals increasingly pleasant, found also that the conflict between this and his promise to Mrs. Magill brought in an element of painfulness. He became exceedingly blue, and even treated the widow morosely.

"Zadie," said she, one evening, as they walked home from the drill-room, "what ails you? I thought you were going to get so much amusement out of these theatricals."

"I wish I'd never gone into them !" he answered, gloomily.

"How unkind to say that, after the condition we made about them !" This allusion didn't improve his temper.

"I don't forget my promise, though I *am* sorry," he said, dubiously.

"Sorry about the promise, you mean ?" asked the widow, with an archness that failed for want of a street-lamp to light it up.

"You wouldn't like it if I should says yes," he retorted.

"Oh, if you're sorry," she exclaimed, haughtily, "we'll give up the"—here the major became attentive and eager—"the theatricals altogether !" she concluded.

"The theatricals," muttered he, disappointed ; "I thought you were going to say— But no ! We'll play the farce out, and, when it's done, we'll have the wedding.   Does that satisfy you ?"

"It's very wrong of you to talk of it that way," said Mrs. Magill, too sagacious to lose her temper.   "But I know you'll regret it."   And so, holding him firmly by the arm, she carried him off to the door, where they parted.

XI.

At length, the evening of the performance came, and all the independent cavalry, and their friends, assembled to look at it.   Rawsden was unusually cynical that day, and came near disabling Miss Sneef for her part by the number and variety of his pessimistic remarks.   But this was due merely to his own inward trepidation on her behalf ; and it was with a strange whirl of by no means cynical emotion, raging underneath his calm dress-coat and well-starched shirt-bosom, that he left her at the dressing-room, and took his own place in the audience. As for Barrington, the contradiction of moods into which he had fallen excited him to great energy, and he consequently achieved a brilliant success in the first part of the piece.   Mrs. Magill sat refulgent and diamond-flashing in her place, drinking in the praise of the major, which was murmured on all sides ; these bright moments compensated her for all the pain of the rehearsals.   But between the first and second scenes the curtain fell, to allow the arranging of a new "set."   The shadow of

that descending curtain was destined to darken seriously
the widow's fair prospect.

Just as the audience were getting impatient for the
second scene, an audible disturbance arose on the stage,
in the midst of which the green cloth was rolled up,
revealing a pictured street.   No one "came on," however ; and as a moment elapsed, and the disturbance increased, Mrs. Magill suspected something wrong.   Then
Natalia burst out on the astonished spectators, through
the right entrance, with a distracted air, crying out, with
apparent unconsciousness of the lifted curtain, "What!
Major Barrington has cut his head open ?   Where ?"

Some of the audience began to laugh, several ladies
screamed, and the cavalrymen were divided between a
wish to comfort their frightened guests and the duty of
running to their commander's aid, when Barrington appeared from the sides, moving mechanically, and with a
distinct wound on his forehead.   At this sight Natalia,
who had but half crossed the stage, paused, screamed
sharply and spread out her hands, seeking support.
Meanwhile the stage-manager had got the curtain started
down, and it dropped silently upon the unexpected
tableaux.

By the time it had touched the boards Mrs. Douce had
reached the dressing-room.   She now stood leaning over
her niece, who had fainted, and was lying in a chair.
Mrs. Magill, being of inferior velocity, was much longer
in making her way to the stage through the crowd of
excited people now hurrying to and fro.   A hack had
already been ordered for Barrington, who was sitting behind the street in Lady Blanche's drawing-room, with
his head bound up, and looking rather pale.   The hero
of a hundred failures, he had at last managed to get a
genuine hurt.

" Oh, horrible, horrible !" cried Mrs. Magill. " Speak to me, Zadie ; how did it happen ? Can no one tell me ?"

" We were just getting up Lady Blanche's chandelier in great style," exclaimed the manager, " when Major Barrington came along, and—"

" No more, no more, for mercy's sake !" entreated the widow, with a shudder.

" Yes," continued the manager, with severe accuracy ; " he hit his head against it."

" Mrs. Douce," cried Mrs. Magill, " run out and get my things for me—at once—please."

" I'm sorry," said the landlady, rather sharply, " but I can't leave Natalia." Here some one came forward, and said the hack had arrived.

" You see," protested the widow, " I *must* have my things." But Mrs. Douce devoted herself to Natalia, obliviously.

Barrington had by this time been got on his feet, and was walking slowly toward the stage-door, the arm of a fellow-officer under his own.

" Major," cried the exasperated widow, " stop !" And, as she spoke, she stepped in front of him.

Barrington did stop ; but he looked feebly peevish, and in a tone of disgust said, plainly, " Do let me alone, can't you ?" There could be no doubt as to his words.

The conflict over his remains, which seemed likely a moment before to become obstinate received a check in this utterance from, as it were, the very dead. Mrs. Magill fell back in horror, and the major was triumphantly borne away with Natalia.

XII.

THE farce was never finished ; but the assembled company set about the dance which had been planned to succeed it.   Rawsden and Miss Sneef enjoyed this very much, in their superior way, and, in fact, the break-down of the histrionic effort made those youthful misan-thropists thoroughly hilarious.   The events of the next few days, after the " caving in" of the Major's head (as Rawsden described it), furnished him with still further material for entertainment.

Mrs. Magill resumed the field early the next morning, seeking to visit her poor major.   This Mrs. Douce pre-vented her from doing by powerful and imaginative de-scriptions of Barrington's condition, and citations from medical authority.

Mrs. Magill then proposed to hire a room in the house.   But Mrs. Douce solemnly averred she had no room to spare.   Still, the next day Mrs. Magill came, with a carriage full of things, including light bedding, to occupy the enemy's country, and declared she would bivouac in the parlor.

" But the parlor belongs to my boarders," said Mrs. Douce.   " Use of parlor included, those are the terms."

" Then I'll take the reception-room."

" The door is very narrow," said Mrs. Douce, scruti-nizing the massive form of the invader so insinuatingly as to make the non-committal pink in Mrs. Magill's cheeks give place to an angry red.

Mrs. Magill turned, and called out of the open door to the carriage-driver to bring in the bedding, etc. " Recollect," she said, severely, to Mrs. Douce, " he is my husband that is to be."

The landlady looked inquiringly at the driver, and then, as if correcting her impression, said : " Oh, the major ? That makes no difference. Those things shall not come in ! Besides, it isn't at all certain that he is."

" Not certain ? How can you dare ?"

" He says so himself."

" Then he's out of his mind," said Mrs. Magill, calmly.

" He *was*," replied Mrs. Douce.

" I won't converse with you," said Mrs. Magill.

" Then please order your man not to bring in those things."

But Mrs. Magill refusing, "*I* will tell him," announced Mrs. Douce, stepping out to do so.

Mrs. Magill, with great presence of mind, instantly shut the spring-lock door and began to walk up-stairs. There was a furious rattling at the door-handle, from the outside, followed by violent ringing. But no one came to open, until the widow had gained the first landing. Mrs. Douce, being admitted at last, swiftly mounted after her. It was a fearful chase ; but there was no way of heading off the intruder now.

They went up another flight. But Mrs. Douce overreached her opponent by calling out, in a loud voice : " You can't see him, Mrs. Magill ! *Mrs. Magill !* Mrs. Magill !"

Immediately after this they heard the lock working in Barrington's door. The major was safe in his intrenchments.

Nothing daunted, however, Mrs. Magill strode forward and knocked. There was no answer except a slight cough, probably caused by the officer's sudden exertion in locking his door. " Major," said the widow, in a gentle tone, " do you hear me ?" Echoless silence received her words. She began again, with a considerably increased alertness of voice : "Major ! Are you engaged or not ?"

"Very much so," answered Zadoc from within, and with a startlingly robust and comfortable voice for an invalid.

"I mean, to me," explained Mrs. Magill, with annoyance. "Mrs. Douce, here, has the face to declare that you are not. I wish the question answered in her presence. Are you engaged to be married ?"

"I am sorry not to be able to open the door," responded the evasive Barrington. "It fatigues me to talk in this way, so I hope you'll be satisfied with my answering this one question."

"Well," said the widow, more affably, "say you are—"

"I *are* engaged to be married," promptly struck in the major, with untimely jocoseness.

"*Am*, you mean," Mrs. Magill corrected. But silence had resumed its reign on the other side of the door.

"Very well, that will do," she concluded, somewhat as a prose Portia finishing a cross-examination in a modern law-court might have done. She shot upon Mrs. Douce a glance of scorn, saying, "I shall come again to-morrow," and then proudly departed.

XIII.

But she did not come on the morrow. Barrington sent her a note, which effectually prevented her doing so.

"Dear madam," it said, "our remarkable—not exactly interview, but conversation, this morning, may have misled you. My reference to an engagement of marriage was to another than the one you had in mind— in point of fact, my very recent engagement to marry Miss Natalia Douce.

"You will pardon the mental reservation in my reply, when you reflect that I made it out of regard to your feelings. Those feelings I am sorry to disturb in any way, and I believe you will see that it is the truest consideration for them that leads me to give up the design we once cherished. Our understanding, too, was that when the farce was finished we would marry. The farce was never finished ; the condition was not fulfilled ; and therefore our agreement is dissolved. I have just sent in my resignation to the company, and shall dispose of the horse according as you may desire. The uniform I will retain (since it would not fit any one else), as also the respect for you, which has long been entertained by
"Your friend,
"ZADOC S. BARRINGTON."

To this note the major never got any reply. In due time, therefore, his marriage with Natalia, being unimpeded, took place very quietly, and, after going off for a small wedding journey, the husband and wife came back to a pair of Mrs. Douce's small rooms, and began to live in them.

Yes ; this corpulent, middle-aged sparrow of a major had decided in favor of idealism—prosaic though the form in which it was presented to him—as against money and ease without honest affection. He threw aside the only success he had ever achieved, which was due to the opulent siren, Mrs. Magill, and fell back to his old shabby independence, with a poverty-stricken little wife

to share it.   I don't say it was good political economy;
I dare say it was very bad sociology; and perhaps I
ought to show how some dire catastrophe came upon him
in consequence.   The only obstacle in the way is, that it
didn't.   He remained reasonably happy ever after.

By this it is not to be understood that he prospered
materially.   As a matter of fact, he had a terribly hard
time.   There were the old struggles, the old uncertain-
ties of fortune to be faced, with new anxieties added.
His own opinions and his wife's were at times far from
being in unison.

After a time, too, he found himself a father; and,
though I don't doubt his little infant girl brought him
compensations, he grew visibly older.   His once courageous complexion, which I have described as carrot-
tinted, lapsed slowly toward the hue of turnips when in
a boiled state; and—melancholy change!—his dainty
martial chin, with the dent in the bottom of it, was hidden by a practical red beard, while his hair became proportionately thin on top of his head.   If Mrs. Magill
cared for revenge she probably took it now, in the con-
templation of his hard career and the alterations in his
appearance.   He felt this a little, I know; for, as we
were walking together one day near Worth's monument,
he suddenly changed our course, with a hasty, " May as
well go this way;" and I perceived the wealthy widow
coming toward us.

We were not quick enough to escape her, and Barrington winced at her expression.   Yet I am equally
certain that he never regretted his choice.

Luckily for Rawsden's slight remaining toleration of
mankind, he left Mrs. Douce's before the baby was
added to the other household ornaments.   Now that I
think of it, Miss Sneef had previously left the house, and

Rawsden's critical mood grew upon him so rapidly that he, too, found a change necessary. In fact, he followed Miss Sneef.

Yet he continued to bestow a share of his amused contempt upon Mr. and Mrs. Barrington from a distance.

"Barrington got a taste for the drama that time," he once said to me, recalling the private theatricals, "and he keeps it up well. I think his piece will have a long run."

"What piece?"

"*The Ex-Bachelor and his Baby!*" said the little wretch. "A tragic-comedy—by the whole strength of the company."

I think I should have kicked Rawsden for this, but that something in his manner hinted an inconsistent envy of the major. And he presently went on to say that as for Miss Sneef and himself, although not believing at all in the necessity of sentiment and all that sort of thing, they had concluded—since they didn't seem to be able as yet to get tired of each other—that they would try marriage, and see what that would do for them.

Such was the distorted little tribute of this *nil admirari* youth to the element of real manliness he could not fail to see in Barrington's marriage.

"BAD PEPPERS."

I.

"You see, I want to strike down to Bad Peppers."

These words were pronounced by the third person at my right on the bench. The bench, it must be explained, was covered with red velvet, and situated in the cabin of a steamer. And the steamer was the *Weser*, bound for Bremen.

I could not imagine at the moment what "Bad Peppers" meant; and the remark—uttered at our first dinner on board—came out with such ludicrous distinctness, in the midst of the clatter at table, that I made haste to observe the individual from whom it proceeded. I beheld a rough but impressive head, with cheeks of a settled red, and beetling grizzly hair, looking out over the board in a dogged, half-perplexed, but good-humored way, though the owner of the head was evidently unconscious that he had said anything open to comment. He was a man, I should say, of forty-six; but as I looked at him now in the glare of the skylight above, the simplicity and frankness in his face were so marked, that I could not help imagining the short gray curls turned to golden brown, and feeling the momentary pity that comes over one in looking at an elderly person who reminds one of childhood, yet is hopelessly far removed from it. I felt a little sorry for a man with this kind of a face attempting so large a task as crossing the ocean to Europe, and I was a little amused at the idea, too.

He was talking earnestly to my handsome friend Fearloe, who sat on this side of him; but I observed that he was watched with a certain patronizing scrutiny by a young German opposite.

"Yes, you see I couldn't get rid of this rheumatism anywhere," he continued, "and so I took a friend's advice and started for Europe. They say that Bad Peppers will fix up the worst case you ever saw better than any amount of medicine. Anyway, I'm going to try it."

Peppers as a cure for rheumatism! What could he mean? And if this was to be the remedy, why go to Europe to try it? But he proceeded:

"And that's the reason, you see, why I want to strike right down to Bad Peppers."

The mystery began to grow less opaque. Possibly he might mean by "strike down" that he wished to reduce his diet to the article in question; but I thought it more likely that Bad Peppers was a place which he had made his objective point. I determined to ask Fearloe at the earliest opportunity, and therefore drew him away as soon as dinner was over.

"Who is your new acquaintance?" I inquired.

"He reports himself as Steven Steavens, a wholesale grocer from Philadelphia."

"And he's going to Europe to cure his rheumatism? Europe ought to be flattered, certainly," said I; and I am afraid we both laughed rather scornfully at our unsuspecting fellow-traveller, who was pacing another part of the deck with a fierce meerschaum pipe in his mouth. "But tell me what he means by this Bad Peppers. Is it a place? I'm sure I never heard of one by that name."

"Of course," said Fearloe, "it's a place, but that

isn't the right name.   He means a resort of some
note for invalids in the canton of St. Gall, Switzerland
—Bad Pfeiffers, or Pfeiffers's Baths—south of the Lake
of Constance, and near the Rhine : a very picturesque
spot, too."

"You've been there, then ?"

"Yes," answered Fearloe, who, I may remark by the
way, had been nearly everywhere—out of America. He
was one of those Yankees of the later generations who
are born with a genius for belying their own nationality.
When he was in England, the English would actually
claim him for one of themselves, in the face of positive
denial from his own countrymen ; though I must do him
the justice to say that he made no merit of this, and
never allowed newspaper paragraphs to be written about
it.   In France he was frequently taken for a French-
man ; and in Italy his fine statuesque features and rich
dark beard, with the aid of a good Roman accent, might
easily cause him to pass for a descendant of one of the
old patrician families.   In consequence he was very apt
to be looked upon as a foreigner during his occasional
flights through his native land, and possessed accordingly a remarkable power over the hearts of sundry repub-
lican young women ; for women love to pay homage to
a judicious male superiority, and this is the reason the
daughters of our nation delight in foreign manners,
which assume that grandeur of the male that most Amer-
icans are too polite and timid to assert.   These things
being so, I do not wonder that Fearloe was a litttle conceited on one point—his success in impressing the female
heart.

"You speak so well of the place," I continued, after
a pause, "that I've a great mind to 'strike down' there
myself.   Do you advise it ?"

"By all means, Middleby, after you've seen the Exposition. Paris will be hot, and you will need a change of some sort."

"I hope it won't be a change to rheumatism," I replied, with another laugh. I had not noticed that Steavens had come nearer to us as I spoke; but the word "rheumatism" seemed to attract him, and roused the only association with the Old World which he as yet enjoyed.

"You gentlemen have been to Europe before?" he said, advancing, and taking me in with a half-inquiring nod, as if my acquaintance with so foreign-looking a person as Fearloe was sufficient guarantee of my experience in travelling. "Now I would consider it a favor, gentlemen, if you would come down with me to the smoking-room. We can have a little something to drink, and then we can talk this thing over."

Fearloe smiled condescendingly.

"This thing?" inquired I (perhaps not with the utmost respect, since his sentence struck me as rather too informal for the very beginning of a chance acquaintance). "You mean the Bad—"

"The whole of it," broke in Mr. Steavens. "The European continent—Bad Peppers, Paris, and all the rest of it. You've been there, and know just what a fellow ought to see and do, and now I'm away from my store, I've got a little time to sit down and think over what I'll do. So, if you don't object, gentlemen—"

"Not at all," Fearloe hastened to assure him, being always ready for novel encounters.

"I can't tell you anything about Pfeiffers's Baths," said I, trying to be companionable too, "for I never heard of them before; but whatever I do know is at your service."

As we moved toward the gangway the grocer turned to Fearloe, and asked, in an undertone, "What
does he call it ?   Feiffers ?   That ain't right, is it ?
My friend that set me on going there, he said Peppers.
I thought, first off, he meant they put red peppers in
the water when you bathe ; but he said no, it was the
name of the man that started the place, he guessed."

"You can pronounce it either way," said Fearloe,
magnanimously.

"Well, I prefer Peppers," declared Steavens, with
an air of relief.   "But it's kind of queer, now, that
your friend, Mr. What's-his-name—"

"Middleby," I suggested, claiming my place in the
colloquy.

"—Middleby," he continued, without embarrassment,
transferring the remark to me.   "Ain't it queer, Mr.
Middleby, that you never heard of the place ?   I thought
everybody knew about Bad Peppers."

I was foolish enough to be irritated at this presump-
tion on the part of the childlike grocer, and had a great
mind to hint that he preferred a wrong pronunciation
of the name because peppers were in the line of his
business ; but I contented myself with saying that I
thought there were places in Europe a good deal better known than the baths.

In the smoking-room we found the young German
who had cast his critical eye upon Steavens at dinner.
He introduced himself as Herr Scharlach, and in order to make matters clear, he drew from his pocket a
printed list of the passengers, which had been distrib-
uted just before we sailed, on which he put a cross against
each of our names and his own, as he had already done
with several others in the catalogue.   He was a young
man somewhere in the thirties, with a clear blue eye

that gleamed like a sword, a high forehead, and a soft complexion deepened by tropical sunburn. He could have been identified as a German anywhere, from the air he had of holding a balance of power in all earthly affairs ; and when he checked off our names, I couldn't help thinking that he was collecting data for use in some future military ·campaign, or else for a biographical dictionary of the whole human race.

"Ain't from Philadelphia, are you ?" queried Steavens, in a friendly tone, implying that the other probably *was* from that city, " We have a good many Germans there."

" No," said Scharlach, " Brazil." After which he lit a cigarette he had been rolling in his thin fingers, and puffed smoke from his nostrils in such a way as to suggest that any aperture for confidential conversation was permanently closed.

"Now here," said our confiding acquaintance, after we had pledged one another in several mild beverages suited to a first day out on the briny deep—"here's a list of places my friend made out that I want to kind of take in on my way to the springs and back." And he produced from his pocketbook a narrow crumpled white paper, on which were pencilled the weighty names of Paris, Rome, Madrid, Vienna, St. Petersburg, Dresden, Antwerp, Heidelberg, and Munich. I give them in the order in which they occurred. "I suppose that's all right, ain't it ?" he concluded, glancing at each of us in turn, as if the success of his tour depended on our good opinion.

" Why, yes," said Fearloe, " the places are all right, but you'll have to travel a good deal to include them all. I don't see how you're to get at them on the way to the baths."

"Oh, of course I shall have to branch off a little; but then the distances over there don't compare with ours," returned Mr. Steavens, hopefully.

"I'm not so sure of that," rejoined my friend, with a malicious air of there being some slight room for doubt. "Your first jaunt, from Paris to Rome, will be five hundred miles—five times as far as from Philadelphia to New York. After that you must count at least a thousand to Madrid, a thousand more from there to Vienna, and then twelve hundred, or over, to St. Petersburg." Steavens almost turned pale. He hastily set down the glass which he was carrying to his lips. "Besides," continued Fearloe, "you can't go to Rome at all before winter."

"Hold on!" cried the other, looking as if the sense of solid reality were slipping away from him. "Has anybody got a map here? Let's settle one thing at a time. You know what I want to do first is to strike down to Bad Peppers. I'd like to settle just how that stands."

Scharlach immediately went to his state-room, and returned promptly with a large and perfect map of the Continent, showing all the railroads and post-roads. Seeing this, I was tempted to make some sarcastic remark about his thorough German equipment; but I remembered Sedan, and shuddered. He was soon busily engaged in tracing out certain lines of travel with his long pink finger, the nail of which was whitish, and edged with black—according strangely with the Prussian national colors. I thought Scharlach took a peculiar interest in Pfeiffers, and seemed oddly familiar with it. He furnished our fellow-passenger with full details about the place; how it was situated on the Tamina River—which Steavens, with a friendly reminiscence of New York politics, instantly transformed into "Tammany"

River ; how the mountains were piled around its wild gorge seven or eight thousand feet high ; how the healing waters flow only in summer, and are brought to the hotel by an aqueduct ; and so on. All this seemed to reassure the rheumatic grocer very much ; and having got " Peppers " definitely fixed in his mind again, and becoming familiar with the map, he once more grew self-confident about his list of cities, and nothing could avail to dissuade him from adhering to the exact order in which his unknown adviser had jotted them down. So, for the time, we abandoned the attempt.

There is hardly a circle more merciless in its criticisms than a body of first-cabin passengers on one of the European steamers ; and Steavens soon became an object of amusement to most of us. His simplicity, openness, and perfectly good-humored, almost joyous, ignorance, made him an easy prey. But he proved to be a " good sailor," and was very gallant toward the ladies. The strangest part of it was that they rather liked him, and took his side against our covert ridicule. I suppose I must admit that this, instead of altering our opinions concerning him, only added a slight bitterness to a spirit of fun which would otherwise have been quite innocent ; and we got into a way of looking at him with sarcastic hostility. When I say " we " I refer more particularly to Fearloe, the German, Scharlach, and myself, who, having been thrown with him more than the others on the first day of the voyage, regarded him as a sort of comic exhibition under our special supervision.

This rather absurd bond of union between us led to some degree of intimacy with Scharlach, who disclosed —greatly to the enhancement of our interest in Steavens's journey—that he, likewise, was going to Pfeiffers. His errand, moreover, was a romantic one. Five years

before he had fallen in love with the orphaned niece of
a rich merchant in Berlin ; but feeling his cause to be
hopeless, at least as regarded the girl's uncle, so long as
he had nothing but his personal appearance and a very
elaborate education to support his suit, Scharlach had
preferred to retain the hold of friendship while starting
out to better his condition ; and accordingly he had
never made a positive declaration of his passion, but had
gone to Brazil, where he succeeded in gaining a moderately handsome fortune.   His friends had kept him informed of Fräulein Raslaff's movements.   As yet she
had not married, from which he augured hopefully for
his future ; but her uncle had become an invalid, and
they were now about resorting to Pfeiffers for his health,
whither Scharlach, of course, purposed following them,
in order to learn his fate.

He requested us urgently to say nothing about this to
any of our fellow-voyagers, and we even kept the secret
of his destination from Steavens.   But that could not
prevent Fearloe and myself from privately talking over
Scharlach's prospects a little.   My own opinion was that
such cool self-possession as his course showed might not
impress a woman so favorably as it did us, and I said I
was by no means sure that Scharlach would win, after all.
Fearloe did not agree with me here, and stroked his
beard with an air of restrained certainty as he replied :
" I see, Middleby, you fancy that women want something more startlingly romantic than that.   But they are
very practical, too ; and I think you'll find Miss Raslaff
will appreciate such sensible devotion as this of our Bra-
zilian emigrant."   As I have said, Fearloe knew the
effect he could produce on women, and was proud of it ;
and when he uttered this remark it was plain that he
thought he had settled the question.

II.

As I left the steamer at Southampton, and went up to London for a few days, I parted with Steavens before the voyage was completed. It was nearly a week later that I met Fearloe again, in Paris. We went together to dine at a neat little two-franc place in the Rue St. Honoré, which we had formerly haunted, and during dinner he suddenly asked, with a roguish look, " Who do you think I saw yesterday ?—Steavens !" And Fearloe here bent his head, bathing his beard in laughter. " Do you know, he has been in Paris three days and hasn't gone near the Exposition ?"

— " Well, that shows a healthy independence," said I. " Is he studying the Louvre ?"

" No," was the answer ; " he has discovered something far more important than the Louvre or the Exposition—something which seems to reward him for the whole trip."

" What can that be ?" I queried, rather blankly.

" He has discovered," said Fearloe, " that *Paris is the place to buy shirts in !*"

This, it appeared, was the topic which had engrossed Steavens's mind when Fearloe met him. The erratic man, after reaching Bremen, had abruptly decided to come over to the French capital, which he might have done much more easily and cheaply from Southampton ; and the result of this expensive détour had been a kind of shirt-intoxication. " You've no idea," added Fearloe, " how neatly he has gotten himself up. He really is making progress. And the magnificence of the fellow ! Why, he says he shall merely take a single run through the Exposition, and leave all the rest of Paris till after he has been to Pfeiffers."

"Fearloe," I said, with a measure of solemnity, "don't scoff at a man like that. I never before have met an American with quite so much originality in his treatment of Europe. He must be a genius."

Nevertheless, we continued to laugh at him, with that superiority of being less naïf and independent than he which so oddly seems to us a desirable thing nowadays. And if any one at that time had hinted that Steven Steavens, with his want of reserve and complete indifference to what is known as culture, possessed qualities of character more to be admired than our own, we should not have taken the trouble even to smile at the critic.

I did not happen to meet Steavens while in Paris; but in August I finally acted on Fearloe's chance hint aboard ship, and went to Pfeiffers myself, where I found not only our enthusiast in shirts, but also Scharlach and Miss Raslaff, together with that young lady's uncle, a shrivelled little old man, who had the air of being put away to keep in his thick white hair and whiskers, like a dried beetle in cotton-wool. To the rest of us, indeed, the old gentleman was of no more account than a beetle, and appeared to have as little influence on the lives around him as an insect might. But, as a matter of fact, though he was so nearly dead, and scarcely stirred a limb, he clutched three lives in his faded fingers, and held them fast there—his niece's life, Scharlach's life, and Steavens's life. For I was not long in discovering that my rheumatic pilgrim had fallen in love with Fräulein Raslaff almost at first sight. He himself took good care that I should not remain blind to the fact. He drew me aside, and poured his tale into my ear, though with somewhat more reserve than he had shown on the steamer in discussing his plans of travel.

"How long has this been going on ?" I inquired, as we walked together up and down the hotel terrace overlooking the wild and picturesque valley.

"Three weeks and a half," he answered. "It's a short time, and it *seems* like a short time. I've read in the story papers that when a man's in love, a few days seem to him like years, and so forth. But I don't believe it. I know exactly how long I've been here, and yet there's no doubt about it, I'm in love with that young lady, and am going to make her my wife if I can. The story papers are wrong, and I'm right."

I couldn't help reflecting that this was the same independence I had praised to Fearloe. "The man has the faculty of knowing exactly what he's about," thought I, "and that goes a good way toward securing success." Yet it seemed preposterous that he should have the least chance with a woman so far removed from him by tastes and traditions as Fräulein Raslaff. I said to him merely, "Have you spoken to her ?"

"I've tried to feel my way," was his reply. "But that uncle of hers—he's an old potato-bug, sir. He's *worse* than a potato-bug. I don't know what to call him. He won't let any one come near her, and yet he don't seem to take any pleasure in her himself. He looks just about dead, but I tell you it's only shamming ; the minute another man talks to Miss Raslaff, he wakes up ; it puts life into him, and he flies around sharp. This is a good country to operate in, though ; he can't take the walks we do with parties sometimes—up to Solitude, and the Belvedere, and around. I'd just like to see him in the gorge once ; *that* would finish him."

The gorge was a very peculiar and rather perilous cavern, higher up in the valley through which the Tamina runs.

"Then it's only the uncle that troubles you?" I queried. "You don't feel afraid of Scharlach?"

Steavens paused, looking anxious for an instant. Then the child-like expression which I had marked on my first glimpse of him came out strongly again. "Do you think he'd be mean enough to stand in my way?" he asked.

"But suppose you are standing in his?" I returned.

Steavens apparently considered this an unnatural view to take. "Scharlach can get along by himself all right," he asserted. "He might be disappointed, and it wouldn't ruin him. But me—why, take me, and what am I without *her?*" I must admit that this humbleness touched me with its pathos, and I began to range myself on Steavens's side. Then he concluded, without any pathos at all, "Well, I've got as good a right to try as he has, any way, and I'm bound to win in the end."

At length, wishing to soften a possible disappoinment, I thought I ought to tell him how long Scharlach had been hoping to gain Miss Raslaff's heart. The information startled him considerably; but after a few moments' silence he struck me on the shoulder, and exclaimed, "Well, here we are! He's rich and I'm rich; let her choose between us for something else. If he hadn't made any money out there, I'd say to him, 'Here, my man, I've got the best of you, so I'll stand by, and you can just walk in and try your chances first.' But seeing we're neck and neck on that, I don't know that there's anything to do but go ahead."

And go ahead he assuredly did from that hour. He astounded the old uncle by remonstrating with him directly against his supervision of Miss Raslaff. "It ain't fair," he said. "You don't know how to manage things in this country. I don't say a woman ought to vote ; but anyway she ought to have a right to listen to a man when he wants to tell her what he thinks of her. Do you suppose I could tell *you ?*" (With a glance by no means politic in its contempt at the desiccated little figure before him.) "And how am I to talk to her about it when you are around ?"

The result of this attack, which he made in my presence, was a violent outbreak from the old man ; and the next day Steavens was asked to meet Miss Raslaff and her uncle in their *salon*, to receive from the young woman herself a confirmation of her uncle's objection to receiving any attentions from him. The girl was pale, but composed and very beautiful. I could not make out whether or not she had taken any fancy to my brusque compatriot, but she acted her part firmly. When at last she said, in pure English, "My uncle is right ; you must not seek my acquaintance any more—more ardently ; let us be quite as we were before," I declare so sweet a suspicion of a blush came over her cheeks, and her voice died away so delicately, like a soft echo heard among the very hills around us, that I almost fell in love with her myself. A great change instantly came over Steavens. All his jauntiness, his unreserve, his child-like confidence, were extinguished at a blow. After a moment he collected his voice, and said, with great gentleness, "Miss Raslaff, I will never do anything you ask me not to, so far as speaking is concerned ; but that won't prevent my thinking about you just as much as ever, and I shall keep just as near the place where you stay as I can."

This was the end of the interview, and I thought my countryman had the best of it. He was very melancholy, though, while I remained at the baths ; and the

savage beauty of the place—the rough stream roaring out
of the cavern against whose walls of black calcareous
rock, glittering here and there with feldspar, the faint
Alpine rose bloomed pensively, the shaggy heights above
the hotel, and the glimpses of snowy peaks in the distance—was not suited to restore his cheer.   One day we
went into the gorge, with its rocky walls rising two or
three hundred feet, and gradually closing together above,
where a bridge of planks cornered into the solid stone
runs for a distance of six thousand paces to the springs,
slippery all the way from the flying river-foam.   It was
gloomy and depressing as a scene from the *Inferno*, and
bad for a rheumatic patient, as I reminded Steavens ;
but he shook his head mournfully, and said he didn't
care.   What was worse was the danger of missing a
foothold on the wet and mossy planks, and so being
precipitated into the wild stream beneath ; and I
breathed more easily when we came out safely again.
But it struck me that this would be a fearful place for
two angry rivals, such as Steavens and Scharlach now
were, to meet in.

It so happened that Scharlach that very day came to
me with *his* tale of despair.   Thinking the field was his
own, after Steavens's discomfiture, he had formally proposed for Miss Raslaff's hand, and had been rejected.
He could not understand it.   He had addressed the
young lady with her uncle's permission, and she had refused him.   I gathered from what he said that he had
pressed his claim as a matter of right, that he considered
himself to have bought her love by long patience and
the accumulation of a competence, and had put forward
this theory with undue bluntness ; for he confessed that
she had dismissed him with a cold anger and disdain that
left no hope.   We were sitting on the great stone steps

hewn in the height above the hotel as he told me this. "No," he cried, springing to his feet, at the end, in a sort of fury. "If she had shown heat of temper, I might have kept up hope. But she petrified me with her contempt. I am no better than these rocks." He ground his teeth as he spoke, looking down at the hostelry, sunk at a fearful depth below us. Then he seized a heavy stone from the earth, and flung it down the steep, madly crying, "Yes, I am stone now, and there goes my heart rolling down to crush you!" It stopped before it had gone far; but the frenzied action was enough to show that the man had lost his balance. The pent-up force of years, so well controlled till now, had broken forth at a bound, and was carrying him away. "And it was that fool from America, that friend of yours," he added, fiercely, turning upon me all at once, as if I were an enemy—"it was he that did this. It is because he is a novelty, and because her uncle opposes it, that she has taken a fancy to him, and thrown aside the man who was a slave to her for eight years. That's it, I am sure. Take him away! Take your American away!"

I need not say that I did not obey this command; but I did take myself away. The truth is, the situation was getting altogether too serious for my liking. Yet, after I had gone, I felt an incessant curiosity to know how the affair had resulted. I heard nothing more for some time, until I came across an acquaintance during the winter, who had met Steavens in Paris again. This gentleman was telling me how Steavens had been to Rome early in the winter, and now went about complaining that it was a very dirty, one-horse town, which couldn't compare with Philadelphia. He also reported Steavens as gaining some notoriety for his romantic attachment to a young German lady, whom I had no difficulty in recognizing as Fräulein Raslaff. It appeared, therefore, that he had as yet made no headway ; but I indulged in a sense of approval when I learned that he was studying hard, to enlarge his education and his knowledge of European things. Still, my acquaintance described him as a man who could never become anything but an American. He had taken the baths under the necessity of improving his health ; he was trying to take European manners, in the same way, for the sake of improving his chances with Fräulein Raslaff. Yet he remained immutably hostile to everything foreign, and to prolong his stay abroad was, therefore, the strongest sort of devotion he could have shown.

III.

FEARLOE knew nothing of these events, having gone to Egypt for the winter. But more than a year afterward, when I had been at home for some time, I was one day telling a lady at a dinner party something about Steavens's eccentricities and absurdities, when she exclaimed : " Oh, I have heard of that man before ! Your friend Mr. Fearloe was telling me about him."

I was decidedly annoyed by this, because I had frequently made an anecdote of Steavens with great effect, and now here was Fearloe spoiling my fun by telling it in advance. . Of course I had confined myself to narrating the rheumatic pilgrim's strange plan of travel, his excitement about Parisian shirts, and his unique view of Rome—things which invariably proved highly amusing

—and said nothing of his romance. I now questioned my companion at dinner, to see if I could learn anything more about that part of his history, but I could get no information on that subject. My irritation continued all the evening, for it is no slight matter when a man who painfully hoards materials for small conversation, and uses them frequently, finds an insidious friend depriving him of them. But I had an ample revenge upon Fearloe afterward, as you shall see. When I next saw him, which was some months later, he had an experience to recount which certainly put him at my mercy. I will tell it in his own words.

" I was staying at North Conway for a few days, late in July, and there was a most beautiful woman there. I hardly know whether to call her girl or woman, Middleby, there was such an immortal freshness about her face and figure, combined with a reflective sadness that showed she had had more than a girl's experiences. She dressed in black ; it was a cool thin black, that looked— perhaps on account of the calm, sweet face above it— more airy and summer-like than the most studied of the country costumes worn by other ladies at the hotel ; and she wore bracelets and a pin of Irish bog-stone set in ebony, that harmonized deliciously with her personality. You know how that sort of stone sparkles, like a clouded diamond. Well, there was something about its dim, shrouded flash that was just like the mystery in her pale face with its surroundings of black. It struck into me very deep, and excited a desire to pierce the mystery, to find out what her face meant, and what was at her heart —and perhaps to place myself in the heart, too. I'll own it frankly. You know I'm not susceptible, though I've generally made my way pretty well with the ladies." (Here a flash of Fearloe's old self-complacence

on this point came to light, but quickly died out again.)
"I have always cared more for foreign women, though,
than for our own; and this girl or woman was a German, so I was doubly taken with her. Her name was
set down on the register as— Well, I won't tell you
what the name was, just at present, but it was registered
in such a way that I couldn't tell whether she was maid,
wife, or widow. I fixed on the last, in my own mind,
from her wearing black. There was no one with her;
none of the people in the hotel, with whom I talked,
knew anything about her. There could be no question
that she was rich; but that was all I could find out concerning her.

"It was a delicate business, as you can imagine, to
make her acquaintance in the face of such a state of
things; but I managed it, fortunately, through doing
her a little service on the 'piazza,' and from that I went
on to press my society upon her cautiously. In a few
days we were on very good terms, and took a few of the
customary walks and drives in the neighborhood, with
other persons at first, and then alone. I was puzzled to
find her so easy as to this, being a foreigner; but I believe I convinced her of my trustworthiness, and she
must have found out easily, from my acquaintances in
the place, just who I was. Then she seemed to have
outgrown foreign prejudices in some way; and I confess, besides, that I accounted for it at the time by fancying that I had begun to make some impression upon her.

"I determined there shouldn't be any doubt about it.
Yes, it was a serious matter, Middleby; I had come to a
point when I meant to offer myself to her the very next
day. I got her consent to go to Artists' Falls, where I
meant to lay my passion before her. Hideous name, by
the way—Artists' Falls!" broke off Fearloe, testily.

"No affair could have prospered in a spot with such a shoppy name."

He relapsed into gloomy reflections, from which I roused him, insisting that the story should be finished.

"It was the evening before our intended excursion," he then went on. "She and I were sitting on a retired part of the piazza, just about sunset. Everything about us was rarely beautiful; the flush of the evening just dying away from old Rattlesnake, and the line of the great peaks at the distant head of the valley, with Washington's dome in the midst, looking, to the fancy—as you have probably seen them—like giant ghosts of the great men they commemorate. Then, across the intervale, with its hundreds of little brooks and its soft elms, we looked at White-horse Cliff, and that waterfall that seems to flutter from the distant hill-side like a white banner. You remember? A single star was poised above it. I shall never forget that scene. It came upon me with a kind of surprise, after all, that we could have anything so lovely here, and I began contrasting it with Europe. I wanted to hint something about going back there, you know—lead up in a sort of way to my intended declaration in the morning. So it was natural that, in talking of the other side, and the voyage, and all that, I should begin to tell her about that odd fellow on the *Weser* when we went over, you know—Steavens."

"Miserable man!" I exclaimed, at this point, remembering my discomfiture at that dinner. "You told her, and then you found she was some one I had already met and told before?"

Fearloe glared at me in amazement, then slowly smiled in a melancholy manner, and shook his head. "Don't be childish, Middleby," said he; "and please don't interrupt me. I fancy I know something more

about Steavens than *you*'ve ever told. This particular
time I'm describing to you I was surprised to find that
my listener didn't seem to enter into the fun of the
thing. I didn't mention his name, yet I almost suspected she knew something about the man. But as she
didn't relish the absurd side of him, I thought I'd give
her a proper dose of the serious. I went on to impart
what I had learned about a desperate love affair of his at
Bad Pfeiffers ; and this, by the by, is news to you, Middleby."

"Not quite," I said, with a vain smile. (It must be
kept in mind that Fearloe and I had claimed a joint
ownership in Steavens as a comic spectacle, and I was
jealous of any other kind of property in him as a sentimental one.)

"No ?" rejoined Fearloe, rather surprised, but cool.
"Well, then, you can judge how flat I felt on finding
that the beginning of his romantic episode didn't seem to
strike her much more than the rest I had said about him.

"'You seem rather to despise your compatriot,' she
said, when I had got as far as telling her what I had
heard about his rivalry with Scharlach for the favor of a
young lady whom they met at the baths. 'But why
shouldn't he feel the same love and devotion that another
might, even if he were not the most accomplished of his
nation ?'

"I answered, 'Ah, that is like you, to defend a man
for holding a generous sentiment. It is to be hoped you
would be equally kind in judging a less out-and-out
American who dared to love one of your race.' (I imagined she blushed just there.) 'But if you had seen this
man Steavens, you would understand just how I look at
him. You don't know much yet about such raw specimens of my kind.'

"The fact is, Middleby, I put something of a sneer into my words. I was angry at her liking the man even in fancy. However, I finished my story.

"'He certainly was very devoted;' I admitted that. 'He was quite as brave as the other man.'"

"'No braver, you think?' asked she, quietly, with a tone I did not comprehend.

"'You shall decide,' said I. 'The sequel was this: My German gentleman, Scharlach, got perfectly raving mad, I'm told. He looked upon the lady as his absolute right, and couldn't be quieted; while Steavens behaved so calmly that he began to get on terms with the lady and her uncle again, even after his rebuff. If you have ever been at Pfeiffers,' I said to her, 'you know the gorge of the Tamina; but you can't guess what's coming. It happened, one day, that Steavens went in there, when Scharlach had already gone to the spring, and was coming back along the foot-bridge.' I can tell you, Middleby, she looked interested when I came to this— just as you do now. She was startled, too. 'Now, by the strangest coincidence, the obdurate uncle and his niece also went down there shortly afterward, not knowing that either of the rivals was in the cave. They had gone some little way along the dangerous path, when they heard a terrible shout, like the cry of a wild man. They tried to make haste forward to see what it meant, after the first moment of terror, and came in sight of the two men just in time. Scharlach was making a rush upon Steavens, who stood perfectly still, with a pale face, but resolute and terribly stern.

"'He braced himself as well as he could. The shock came. There was a stout, short struggle, and suddenly Scharlach went over, plunging toward the rough torrent full of rocks, and was lost.'

" Then, Middleby, you should have seen that woman's
eyes as she sat there in the twilight.   How they flashed,
as she rose in her chair !   Yet there was an intense pain
in her expression.   'This is too terrible,' she·said.
'But no ; I must speak now.   Mr. Fearloe, did the
person who told you this story also tell you how, when
Scharlach fell, Steven tried to hold him—tried to save
the man who had just been seeking his life ?   Ah, there
his true and great nobility were seen ! '

" ' Good heavens, madam,' cried I, ' who are you ?
You saw them ?   Then you must be—'

" Just then, Middleby, the coach from the station had
come up, and the passengers were getting out.   Madame
was exclaiming, without heed to my questions, ' Oh, I
cannot bear this !   That scene all comes back to me.
Steven ! Steven ! why are you not here ? '   And, as if
in answer to her words, the man came up behind her
with his travelling-bag in his hand.   I felt as if lightning had struck me !   But to *her*, calmness returned in
an instant.   She rose, and with her arm in his she said,
coldly, ' Steven, do you remember Mr. Fearloe ? '   He
recalled me at once, and started to take my hand.   But
she checked him, and said to him, while looking at me
like ice, ' Ah, it's a pity you remember him, for you
must learn now to forget him ! '   And with that she
wheeled away, carrying him with her."

" It was Miss Raslaff," I cried.   " And how did it
happen you didn't know her ?"

" I had forgotten the name.   Ah, my boy, I have
been fearfully punished.   I had a conceited contempt
for that man, and see how it has been visited on me."

" Then she has married him ?"

" By this time, yes.   She clung to her savage old
uncle till he died, then came over to marry Steavens,

though by condition of the will she must forfeit all her uncle's money in doing so."

"Fearloe," I remarked, after a pause, "I think we will neither of us relate our funny encounter with Stea-vens any more. What did we, with all our fancied supremacy, gain by going to Europe, compared with this man? After all, it was a real inspiration of his to 'strike right down to Bad Peppers'!"

THREE BRIDGES.

I.

THE IMPORTANCE OF A HAT.

WITHIN a distance of about ten miles Shagford River makes three long curves, each of which is crossed by a bridge.

The first is for the railroad. The second, thrown across at a point where the ground is lower, carries a country road from bank to bank. Still further down is the third, which is of stone, and forms a paved street connecting the two parts of the factory town of Shagford.

On the afternoon of a superb summer day a fast train from the north-west swept around the curve leading to the bridge-head, and emerged upon the open iron-work structure which bore the double track above the water. The fireman was shovelling coal, and the engineer had just withdrawn his hand from a cord which blew the whistle when he caught sight of a man, in a round Bombay hat, half way across and walking in the same direction the train was taking. Again he pulled the string, sending out four hoarse notes : "Lo-ook oout, a-head!" But the man did not step aside, as would have been expected, on to the line of plank provided for foot passengers between the tracks. The engineer turned on the air-brake and shouted ; but there was a strong breeze blowing against him ; and at best a voice could hardly rouse a traveller deaf to the steam notes.   The last chance of escape appeared to have passed when the stranger, moved by an instinct of danger, though hearing nothing, turned his head.

For the space of a second he confronted the swift, trembling glitter of steel and brass and the pallid face of the engineer at the cab-window.   A look of unutterable horror convulsed his own features, and he sprang wildly into the air.   Falling again, without being hit by the engine, he went tumbling down through an interstice of the iron beams into the muddy water below.   The train was soon stopped and reversed.   Slowly the wheels revolved backward—with a solemn, funereal movement, as if conscious of the inanimate body that might soon bo added to their freight.

But to the amazement of every one on board, staring frightened into the river, the hurt man was seen to be already struggling out of the current, and clambering— wet, hatless, with dripping hair—up the steep bank they had just left.   On reaching the top he began to walk aimlessly away from the train, as if nothing had happened, but presently sat down on the ground looking weak and bewildered.

" Well, if he ain't the coolest hand !" exclaimed the brakeman.   " Must be a new sort of water-rat."   This same brakeman, however, was prompt to go with the conductor to the aid of the stranger.   They found him conscious, but stupefied, and so helped him into the train, which then continued on its way, bearing him off to Shagford.

" Where are you bound ?" asked the conductor.

The man, who was of middle age, with a sun-browned face and close iron-gray whiskers along the upper jaws, felt for his hat and, not finding it, looked uneasy. "There must be no delay," he said, half to himself. "I'll tell you in a moment," he added.

But he sat for some time without speaking; and it was evident that the shock of his terrible fall had worked confusion in his brain. Even on reaching Shagford he was unable to collect himself. But they persuaded him to consult the nearest physician, whom he sought under care of the young brakeman. This resulted in his being taken temporarily to the hospital, for, though seemingly without physical injury, he had suffered so peculiar a mental effect that rest and proper care were thought advisable.

Shortly after the occurrence of this singular accident a vehicle crossed the turnpike bridge, of which mention has been made. The vehicle was a buggy, occupied by a single figure—that of a man say about thirty-eight, clothed in a close-fitting suit of mixed brown. He was of prosperous but not portly aspect, and what was most noticeable in him was that his eyes scanned the river in a sudden, peculiar way. One might have said that, emerging from the softly massed trees upon the bank, he had an uneasy sense of being exposed to unexpected observation on the open stretch of the bridge. But perhaps the more likely explanation would be that he was an inquiring, energetic person, who habitually looked everywhere. Habit or chance, whichever it might be, his alert vision was not exercised in vain that day. He saw on the river, floating toward his point of vantage, an upturned hat. Now, this hat was the identical one which had quitted the head of the unlucky man at the railroad bridge; for, being made of cork, it was perfectly adapted to navigation.

"That's what comes of sharp eyes," said the driver

of the buggy aloud, much as though he were stating a moral maxim which it did him good to hear. "Who knows but this may turn out important? If anybody's been drowned, or—" The alternative was lost in a clucking sound with which he accompanied the urging of his horse ; for he had formed a plan.

The bridge was low ; the hat was drifting toward one of the numerous rows of spiles, hence he believed he could fish it up with his long-handled whip. Dismounting, and watching his opportunity, he succeeded after a few moment's novel angling in bringing up, by a noose made of the lash-end, his piece of flotsam.

As I have said, this man wore a comfortable mien ; his face was smooth, rosy, firm and beardless, and though the structure of his lips was rather hard and determined, the corners of the lips indicated constant readiness for a smile which, however, never culminated when he was alone. Still, at this moment, a beam of satisfaction rested on his features. The recovery of the hat presented itself to him in the light of a virtuous action. Looking into it he saw the owner's name written on the leather band : "Simeon Piper." As this conveyed no impression, he turned his attention to a small folded paper stuffed inside of the band and making a slight bulge in it. On examining what was inscribed upon the sheet, his countenance changed ; the beaming look vanished, and his eyebrows, always describing an acute angle to the temples, grew sharper than ever. It was a movement analogous to that of an animal drawing back its lips before biting, or darting a fang out. His expression, in fact, had become wolfish.

What did it mean? Merely that the name he had seen this time was his own. "Martin E. Hounshell," he read, in a half voice, finding it for an instant even

stranger than the strange name he had encountered just
before.   But he had seen other things on the page with
his name ; things which he would not articulate even
here ; certain names and dates for which he deemed
silence the fittest atmosphere.

Hounshell's next act was to toss the hat back into the
river, and he was about to tear up the paper scrap and
send it after the hat, when he changed his mind.   He
put the memorandum into an inside pocket and buttoned
up his coat, tapped the surface of the coat snugly, then
got into his buggy and drove on—thoughtful and puzzled, but with equanimity returning and ready to spring
his patent smile in a moment, should he meet an acquaintance.

Nevertheless, what had just happened was startling.
If the paper which now lay over his heart had possessed
the power of receiving a photograph from his brain he
could not have been more astonished.   The invisible had
become visible ; what had lain concealed for years in his
own mind now confronted him from without.   And who
was Simeon Piper—a total stranger—in whose hat so
mysterious a revelation had taken place ?   Hounshell's
horse dragged that question along unconsciously to the
end of the bridge, where, for the moment, it disappears
from our pen unanswered.

The small waves flashed lightly around the spiles ; a
breeze rustled in the woods, perhaps looking for something it had lost there and never could find again.   The
two bridges were deserted ; all was silent, dreamy.
Then from the unseen bridge lower down a shrill clamor
arose to break the serenity of the evening ; a chorused
shriek of twenty unearthly voices blended together.
Unexpected and wild, loudly startling it was, so that
there seemed something uncanny about it.   One might

have thought it the cry of monsters discovering human prey, or a mob of witches revelling in some crime that had been found out there. But as a matter of fact no one indulged in either of these impossible fancies. Everybody knew that the uproar came from the mills of Shagford, blowing the hour of release from work.

———

II.

FATHER, DAUGHTER, AND—WHO ELSE?

AT this signal the operatives streamed forth like school-children; and from Hounshell's flannel-mill in particular came one elderly man, who threw himself with all the energy of a boy into a row-boat that lay at the waterside, and began oaring his way lustily up-stream. He had not gone far before he turned the bow into a secluded bay where water-lilies grew thickly. Here, paddling about and causing the boat to lurch violently as he stooped over the side, he pulled a few of the flowers. He looked tired and hard-worked; there was something indescribably pathetic in his making so much effort after the day's labor. But he did not seem to see this; and so, after getting a bunch of lilies, he continued up the river with a business-like stroke that implied some past familiarity with life on the water. The end of the course was soon reached; he moored the boat close to a little cottage that stood apart from the houses of the other working-people, and wore a peculiarly well-cared-for aspect.

On one side of the path was a tomato-patch ; on the other a minute flower-garden ; a grape-vine laid its flat leaves by one of the windows, and everything about the place was neat, cosey, sheltered.   As the weaver came up toward it, however, he saw that there were two persons in the room behind the vine, instead of only one, as he had expected.   He paused, looking in, and saw that it was Hounshell with his daughter.   The mill-owner at that moment took her hand in a somewhat fervent way, addressing her eagerly, and led her toward the window. Instantly the girl withdrew her hand and came running out.

" Oh, father, dear, how lovely !   Did you bring them for me ?"

" Who else d'you s'pose, Addie ?   I'm not courting any one."

He looked at her quizzically as she received the lilies, his weather-worn face glowing mildly at the same time, with pride in her beauty and delight at having pleased her.

" That's mean of you, father," she said, half offended, yet smiling as she inhaled the delicate, sweet-almond scent of the blossoms.

" What ?   Not to be courting ?" he asked, putting his arm fondly around her.   " I can do better than that, lass, by coming home.   Four bells have struck ; time for a kiss, you know."   Whereupon she put her lips to his faded, fatherly cheek.

Addie was certainly beautiful in her way, and Scofield thought there was no way to compare with it.   She was tall, fresh, dark-eyed ; her complexion was rich with the soft, clear brown which our American sun so deftly diffuses over a healthy face that ripens in its warmth ; and she always looked as cool, as sparkling and lithe as if she had just stepped from a bath in the river. You felt that, were you to place your hand on her shoulder, she would resist springily, like a young bough in the woods.

"And you can do a good deal better than I can; that's certain," said Hounshell to Scofield, breaking in. He had come to the threshold and witnessed this little passage.

"You ought not to talk about it before me, anyway," declared Addie, whose code of propriety never allowed ceremony to stand in the way of truthfulness. And, having administered this rebuke, she blushed as if it were she who had offended modesty.

"Oh, well, don't take on about it!" said the mill-owner, apologetically. "I don't know how to talk when I get down here. Different up to the mill; ain't it, Scofield?" Here he winked at the father with humorous comradeship. Then, turning again to Addie: "All is, I want you to be my wife, and you know it, and so does the old man. So where's the harm, talking about? Lord! there ain't nothing high daddy about me. I worked my way up, and I like working-people; so, 'stid of going round among the high daddies, I come to you and say I want to marry you. I've seen you grow into a woman, just like"—the speaker, embarrassed, gazed helplessly round the garden for a comparison, and proceeded:—"Like one of those tomaytoes there, when it comes to fruit. And I know all about you."

"I don't believe I'm like a tomayto one bit," said Addie, with conviction. The next moment, allowing herself a saucy smile: "And I don't know all about you, you see. So there!"

Her mature admirer did not resent this, but stood really abashed and disconcerted. "What am I to do,

Scofield?" he asked, stepping out on to the walk. "You see how it goes."

Addie seized the moment for escaping into the house, while her father, regarding his employer meditatively, replied : " Take soundings, and then try again. That's all I can say."

" I don't know," observed Hounshell, shaking his head. He tried to bring his regulation smile into play, but the springs would not work. He was really attached to the girl ; and there was a painful longing in his mind, besides another motive, of which he could not speak. He was unnerved.

Presently they went into the house. " Won't you stay to supper ?" suggested Scofield.

" No, thank'ee. I'm going. Addie !"

" Yes, sir." She looked at him from her cool, liquid eyes as steadily and with as much unconsciousnes in her clear-lined face as if she had never heard him speak of marriage.

" I've a word to say, if you'll come ont to the gate."

" All right." Addie put the cups on the table for her father and herself, and then followed Hounshell, who bade the weaver good-night.

" I want you to treat me differently," said the miller, when they were alone. " This is a very serious matter, and there's more in it than you think. You ought to consider your father."

The girl's eyes flashed. " You don't mean," she began, " that you—"

" No, I don't mean any harm to him, of course. Take me or leave me, he'll be all right. But if you take me, my father-in-law don't remain in the weaving-room, by a long shot. I'll make him my partner instid."

Addie appeared to weigh this.

"Well, that's right," she said.   "He ought to be."
Hesitatingly, she went on : "I know it's generous of
you, but—but—"

"There's another reason, too," the suitor hastened to
explain.   "I can't tell you now, but I might afterward.
It's very serious.   Oh, I can't stand it, if you don't consent !" he almost groaned.

She was startled by his strenuous manner.

"What reason can it be ?" she asked, quivering a
little.

"It's been on my heart so long," Hounshell said,
pressing both hands on his chest.   "It's there now," he
continued, sinking his voice.   At the precise instant of
speaking his fingers felt beneath the coat that fateful fold
of paper which the river had brought him, and both
arms fell as if he had been struck.

"Good God !" he exclaimed, staring at her.

It seemed to him that she, too, must have felt the paper
and its tell-tale words.

"What have I been saying ?" he asked, in a bewildered tone.

The change in him within a few moments had been
extraordinary, and Addie experienced a shock.   Any
one who had seen the wolfish glare of his eyes on the
bridge would have been surprised at the human emotion
he now betrayed.

"You frighten me," said the girl, shrinking ; but
she was conscious of feeling more pity than fright.

"Don't be frightened," urged Hounshell, trying to
speak gently ; but his voice broke.   It sounded abject
rather than soothing.   "I s'pose I'm making mistakes
again.   You can't understand me.   Only this—think of
this : I shall never get over it if you don't have me.

You may do me a great wrong by turning me off. Can't you consider about this a little more?"

"I—I will try to consider, Mr. Hounshell," faltered Addie.

"Then I'll go; I'll bid you good-night," he said, regaining some of his customary stiffness.

"Good-night," she returned.

He got into the waiting buggy; there was a grinding of wheels, a puff of whitish dust from them, and then the dusk obliterated him, much to her relief. She went back into the house slightly paler than when she had left it.

"Father," she declared, "I never can marry that man."

"What! Hounshell?"

"Yes. There's something strange about him—and wrong."

"Careful! He's been our best friend, lass; there can't be anything wrong."

"All the same, I shall not marry him."

The old man was hurt.

"Have you thought over all?" he asked. "You wouldn't be the only gainer."

He glanced down at his arm, which still bore marks of sailor's tattooing, and at his hard hands all day in service at the loom; and then he sighed, as if despairing of rest.

"I know, dear father," said his daughter. "Mr. Hounshell would be very generous to you, so I wish I could do it. But oh, I can't, I can't!"

She put one hand on his arm and looked piteously into his face.

"I see how it is," said Scofield. "You have fixed your fancy on Jonah."

Addie softly moved away. All her color had returned, but she said nothing. They had barely seated themselves at the table when a knock was heard.

"Come in!" cried Addie, and on the entrance of the new-comer, "Oh—Jonah!"

"Did you think it was—well, never mind who."

Jonah, in whose spruce attire, as he now presented himself, it was not easy to recognize the brakeman of the afternoon train, made this enigmatical remark rather uneasily, and subsided into regretful silence.

"Sit down, Jonah, and have some supper," said old Scofield, with a slight lingering gruffness.

The young man, however, accepted without compunction; and in a twinkling Addie had spirited on to the table an extra cup, plate, knife and fork, which were suspiciously ready to her hand.

"We had a queer thing happen on the train this afternoon," said Jonah, as the hot tea roused him into talkativeness again. And he proceeded to relate the occurrence with which our narrative of these events began. "Man's name is Piper," he continued—"Simeon Piper. No one knows anything about him, and he can't tell why he was there or where he was going. The shock put a screw loose in his brain somewhere, the doctor says. May get over it, and may not. But they won't keep him at the hospital long, because there's nothing the matter with him much, except that."

"Poor fellow!" Addie murmured. "What will he do when they send him away, if he doesn't know where he wants to go?"

"Can't make it out," was Jonah's answer. "Some one ought to take hold and help him till he gets well."

Addie made a prompt resolution.

"We'll take hold ; won't we, father ? Couldn't you bring him out here, Jonah ?"

The brakeman reflected a moment. Piper was not young ; so there was no objection on that score.

"Yes," he said, "I'll bring him out when I get back from my run to-morrow. They say he seems pretty well-to-do, too. He'll pay board."

"Never mind if he does," said Miss Scofield, artlessly. "We can be kind to him just the same."

It was settled accordingly.

After supper the two men went out into the garden. They had a serious subject to talk over, and Jonah began it by saying :

"The men are pretty near all agreed, Mr. Scofield, and we've got to do something soon. How is it in your mill ?"

"Hounshell's, you mean," corrected the ex-sailor and weaver, cutting a piece of tobacco. "Well, I suppose a good many of our hands will go with you, if it comes to a strike. But I can control a number, I guess ; and I'm bound to tell you that we shall stick to work and stand out ag'in you."

"That's bad—bad," mumbled the young railroader, with a troubled air. He plucked a spear of tall grass and began biting it. "I can't see, Scofield," he burst out (dropping the "Mr." this time), "why you stick to that man against all your own interests and the interests of your fellow-workmen. What's Hounshell compared with them ?"

"He's my friend and benefactor ; that's all. Didn't he take care o' my poor wife the day she died ? And when I come back from sea, after a long cruise and a shipwreck, and my wife was dead, didn't I find that he had taken my little girl in tow, and was eddicating her ?

Look here," Scofield pushed up the sleeve of his coat and shirt and displayed the dim blue anchor on his forearm ; " as long as that stays there I'm going to be true to the man as was true to me," he said.

"I know all that," said Jonah.   " He's done a lot. The others are a little jealous of you, sometimes ; and that's one reason I want you to be with us.   If you ain't, they'll say : ' Oh, yes, it's very fine for Scofield to stay out ! The boss helped him to a nice cottage, and give his daughter a pianna.   But the rest of us have got to look out for ourselves.' That's what they'll say.   And as for me, I say it's barter and trade ; that's what ! Hounshell give Addie an education and a pianna, and now he wants her to give herself in exchange."

" That ain't the way to look at it," retorted Scofield. " It ain't fair.   And if you mean to insult my daughter by your talk about barter and trade, why, you'd better—"

" You're the first to say ' insult,' " Jonah answered, in an angry, constrained tone.   " I love Addie ; and I don't believe she'd marry in any such way.   And what's more, I—I kind of hope she'll marry me.   There again, there's another reason why I wanted you to be on our side—now that we've got everything together, and the railroad hands and mill hands are ready to move at the same time.   But I see it's no use ; I've done my best."

" No ; it's no use," assented the weaver.   " I'm doing my best, too."

Thus it happened that the young man took his departure in some heat ; but it was of her own accord that Addie followed this lover to the gate ; and she did not let him go without a few sweet words to comfort him.

III.

LISTENING.

MARTIN HOUNSHELL had three good causes for wishing to marry Addie Scofield. First, so far as in him lay, he loved her. Secondly, knowing that opposition was afoot among the men, he feared the influence that Jonah Brown might obtain over Scofield, should he succeed in his courtship of the daughter; for he relied much on the sailor-weaver's loyalty to fight off the trouble. Thirdly, he had some time since been guilty of a secret misdeed, which he hoped to repair by bestowing further benefits on the Scofields.

This evening, after going from the cottage and leaving his horse at home, he went down to the deserted mill, entered the office, locked himself in, and then spread out on his desk the discovered memorandum. The words with which it began were these : "Martin E. Hounshell. Property delivered, April 13th, 1877. Adelaide Scofield died same day. Husband returned—."

The date here was omitted. Below followed the names of certain persons in California, and two or three other brief notes.

To the mill-owner, sitting there in the dim candle-light, with a hand pressed nervously over his lips, this told the whole story. To any one it would at least suggest suspicion. Should he destroy the paper? He held it up toward the candle; then hesitated. It might be desirable first to find out who had written it, and to do this he would keep it as evidence. No place so unapproachable by others as his own pocket; so he put it away again.

The injury he had done to the unsuspecting Scofield had been crowned with success to himself, but it had tormented him, too. In spite of having given the man employment and having assisted the daughter, he could not escape his remorse. But when he should have wedded Addie, and lifted the weaver into a subordinate partnership, he felt sure that his mind would be at rest. " As it is," he muttered, " I have done more than most would have done, to make amends. I can't give up all— the whole thing. It ain't reasonable. And if I get to be his son-in-law, why, we're all together, and that squares it."

But who and where was this other man, this unknown Piper, who carried dangerous information which might at any moment, if disclosed, give a sudden check to the comforting plan thus formed ? That must be learned without delay.

It was not until the next afternoon that, looking over the Shagford *Minute-Hand* more carefully than he had had time to do in the morning, he saw an account of the accident at the railroad bridge, which accounted for the floating hat. Simeon Piper, then, was in the very town, at the hospital—perhaps at this instant telling some one the tale which had come to his knowledge ! Preposterous unkindness of fate, to deal such a blow at this late day ! Hounshell only half believed it could be dealt him ; yet when he rose from his chair he felt very weak, and the solid walls of the mill as he passed outside seemed decidedly rickety. He very nearly expected them to fall over upon him. As directly as he could he made his way to the hospital, and by the time he reached it was aware that his interest in the stranger might appear somewhat singular. To prevent this he began carelessly, to the attendant :

"Queer sort of case, that one you had yesterday from the railroad."

"Yes, a very narrow escape."

"I read about it in the *Minute-Hand*. How's he getting along?"

"Very well indeed. He's left us."

"Left a'ready!" Hounshell wondered if his face looked as white as it felt. "There's no chance, then—"

"No chance to see him now," said the attendant, far from suspecting the anxiety under that word "chance," as used by Hounshell.

"He's lucky to get off so soon," remarked the latter, a cold perspiration on his back. "Gone from town, I s'pose."

"I believe so."

Hounshell was afraid to ask anything more. He covered his retreat by discussing his ostensible errand, which was to make arrangements for possibly sending to the hospital the invalid wife of one of his men. He had no intention of actually sending her, but he went away leaving an impression of his remarkable kindness.

How dear to him was all this false reputation, which cost so little except in secret mental twinges! He doubted whether a respectability honestly worked for would have yielded him nearly so keen an enjoyment; and he was determined to hold on to that which he had gained. Where to look for Piper, and just how to dispose of him, was the problem now before him. But he began to feel easier, and his thoughts returned to the impending labor revolt.

It was desirable to see Scofield in private, and with this end in view he drove out to the cottage again at evening.

On entering the little sitting-room he was annoyed to

find a stranger there comfortably adjusted in a rocking-chair.

"I didn't know you had company here," he observed frigidly, eying Scofield.

"Oh, that won't interfere!" said Scofield. "It's only Mr. Piper; the man that—"

"Piper!" ejaculated Hounshell, in a voice harsh with horror.

The stranger looked up at him astonished.

"Yes," said the weaver. "Mr. Piper, this is our boss, Mr. Hounshell."

It was all over—so the miller thought. He stood staring, waiting for Simeon Piper to spring up with deadly denunciation on his lips. But that individual merely bowed and inspected his *vis-à-vis* with a good-natured air. The only thing worthy of remark about him was that there was a sort of pained blankness in his face; and as he met Hounshell's fixed gaze he lifted one hand and pressed his forehead vaguely for an instant. The other man was quick to take the respite offered.

"I'm glad to see you looking so well, Mr. Piper," he said, exhibiting his smile with great success. "I've heard about your escape."

Then he looked at Scofield imperiously, and they went out together.

"What is that man there for?" he demanded, taking the weaver's arm sharply.

"Why, he's come out to board; that's all. Do you know him? You seemed a good deal shaken up."

"No; I don't know him. I s'pose this labor combination is making me nervous. I kind of suspect people."

"Pshaw! This man's an outsider; comes from California. He was a rancheero, or something, out there,

I believe. I can tell you how we happen to have him here." And the explanation was given. "He's dropped the bottom out of his memory, like, and wants to wait till he can fit a new one to it."

"Oh, that's it!" exclaimed Hounshell, once more secure. He saw that his name had not been recognized by his enemy; and perhaps the memorandum in his pocket was the only connecting link that would ever lead to such a recognition. "Still," he said, "I don't like Jonah's bringing him here. It won't hurt if you let him go his way this side of next week."

They then proceeded to a discussion of the state of things in the mill; and Hounshell went home without attempting an interview with Addie. But first, after driving a little way, he stopped, went back on foot, and stealthily looked through the vine-hung window. Addie was reading something to the robust-looking invalid, who still sat in the rocking-chair, his face as blank as ever. Her father occupied himself with carving a small piece of wood, twisting his lips in sympathy with the knife. Everything was placidly reassuring.

Hounshell wondered at the thinness of the partition that stood between him and ruin; but he did not care if it was only an egg-shell, so long as it did not break.

But while he was still gazing through the pane, the sound of a distant train on the railroad came through the night. The watcher was scarcely aware of it until he saw Piper start up in his chair, listening, with a roused, intent expression. The girl ceased from her reading; Scofield stopped his work and looked at their guest. No one spoke in the little room. The noise of the train grew louder; now it became a rumbling hum or a rattle —busy, swift, determined in character. It was as if a gigantic shuttle were being driven through the woof of the darkness, to carry one more strand into that great web of civilization, woven day and night continually. But there was something mysterious and warning in the sound besides. Under the general subdued roar could be heard the sharp click of the wheels from rail to rail, in definite pulsations; the sound thus grew so precise one might have suspected that it would break into speech. Had it not some message to deliver of which this was the vague prelude?

That at least was what Piper seemed to hope as he rose excited, finally gaining his feet, with a quicker intelligence in his face than had been there before. As if it would be possible to catch the message more distinctly should he look out, he turned his eyes toward the window. Hounshell barely missed betraying himself there, but slid away into the dark swiftly.

"Was that a face?" Simeon Piper demanded. "No; I see it must have been an illusion," he added, despondently, once more putting his hand to his head.

The father and daughter exchanged looks of pity.

By this time the cars had got farther off and were less audible. Piper's agitation died away proportionately, and he sank back into his seat.

But the same sort of thing happened on the following day when he heard the distant movement of a train.

"Listen!" he cried to Addie, who was with him. "Don't you hear? It's going to say something. I shall get hold of the idea and find out what is the matter. Listen! listen!"

Then, as before, the hollow rumble diminished, gradually softened to a stir no louder than a sigh, and finally was quite lost. Only the baffled breeze continued its hopeless search among the leafy boughs by the river.

" What is it you think you might hear ?'' asked Addie, gently.

The strong man looked at her with tears in his eyes.

" A secret, young lady ; a secret ! I knew it, and now it is gone. It's strange that cars should excite me this way, but something has hurt my brain. You are very kind ; and if you go on being so perhaps my mind will get right again.''

A week passed. Piper listened each day to the passing trains ; sometimes at night too, when he lay alone, and it seemed still more likely that through its relation with this sound the lost clew might disclose itself. But all in vain ; he was unable to recover what had escaped him.

During these days Hounshell did not come out to the cottage, but the labor movement culminated, and all the railroad and mill employés demanded an advance of wages.

IV.

THE THIRD BRIDGE.

THE employers met in conference, and agreed not to yield—so the strike began. Scofield, however, and a small group with him, stoutly refused to join the movement ; and some work was still done at Hounshell's. This encouraged the other mill-owners and directors, and exasperated the men in revolt. At first everything was quiet and orderly ; but as the success of the laborers grew more doubtful to them, anger and excitement gained sway.

"I feel almost afraid for father," said Addie to Simeon Piper, on the fourth day of the strike. For, in fact, there were now serious threats of riot.

"I don't believe they would do him any harm," said the Californian, easily. "The most they'll do will be to make him stop working, and then he'll have a holiday."

"But he won't stop," the girl affirmed, excitedly. "I know father better than you."

"Well, then," suggested Piper, still seeking an easy way out, "persuade your friend Brown—my friend, too —to come over to father's side."

Piper, with a Western taste for convenience and cordiality, had adopted this mode of referring to Scofield.

"But I—I don't want to," faltered Addie, with a soft blush.

"Hoity-toity!" cried Simeon. "What does that mean?"

"I want him—the strikers, that is—to win."

"Against father?" Piper raised his good-humored eyebrows.

"Oh dear, I wish they were on the same side! I only know I'm fearful. They'll hurt him; I know they will."

"Oh, look here," said Piper, "that's all foolishness! But I'll tell you what: we'll walk down to town and see how things are going."

"Shall we? Oh, how nice you are, Mr. Piper! Come on, then."

And they started.

A great many men were standing about the streets, looking ominous of ill; but as yet no disturbance was made. The mill stood at one end of the street-bridge; and as Piper and Addie came up to it they heard the noise of a crowd approaching around one corner of it. A moment after they had gained the entrance, this crowd, which numbered some twenty-five men, armed with thick sticks and some heavy stones, arrayed itself face to face with them.

"Where do you lot on going?" asked Piper, in a leisurely manner.

"In here," said some of the group, "to stop them working."

"I guess not," observed the Californian. His tone was even genial.

"We'll see," retorted a leader, moving forward.

The mill-door was fast, but at this moment the bolts were loosed, and Scofield made his appearance.

"Addie," he commanded, sternly, "come in, and out of the muss! and you, too, Piper."

"You can send daughter in," answered Piper, indicating Addie, who—far from quailing—looked as serene and fresh as ever. "But I'm going to stand in front of this door. Now," he continued, with determination, fronting the rioters, "you leave the old man and his girl alone. If you don't you've got to fight me. One of your locomotives run me off the bridge t'other day and didn't kill me; and I guess you can't, either. I promise to corral the whole herd, if you try to come in here."

Some of the men showed defiance, but those nearest were in no hurry to attack. It had suddenly become apparent to them that their antagonist's shoulders were particularly square and rugged. Scofield wondered whether his champion knew what he was about; the Piper certainly seemed to be in possession of all his faculties.

The leaders began to confer.

As luck would have it, the owner of the mill, who had been absent, and was not aware of the immediate danger, just then came up. He had not seen the crowd until within a few yards. At once a threatening cry arose :

" Hounshell !"

A strange sensation came over Piper ; a loud, tumultuous noise following the word, filled his ears. Was it the rush of the river, or the thunder of a railroad train ? He could not tell ; but he shouted suddenly with fierce exultation :

" Hounshell — that's the name ! Hounshell's the man !"

His memory had come back to him.

The strikers, diverted by this new object, turned as if to assault the " boss ;" but Piper was before them. He had darted forward and toward Hounshell, who, blanched with fear, and thinking Piper in league with the men, took flight, making for the bridge ; the Californian after him. The little mob, itself bewildered, followed ; but Piper had already clutched the fugitive when it caught up with them.

" I've got him," he cried. " This man's a fraud. Do you want to know why ? He took the money left to the other man —Scofield—hurrah ! that's the other name. He stole the money, I tell you, and bought that mill, and it don't belong to him. The mill is Scofield's ; d'you hear ?"

" Let go," gurgled Hounshell, trying to wrench himself free. But his captor shook him once, and he was quiet.

The workmen crowded up to get a clearer understanding of this extraordinary statement ; and as it broke fully upon them, " Throw him over the bridge," became their watchword. But by this time several other persons had advanced over the street bridge, among whom were Jonah and Scofield.

"No violence, boys," said Jonah, lifting his voice, which had authority. "You're disgracing the cause."

The men became silent, but Scofield was indignant with his ally of a moment before.

"What are you doing to the boss?" he demanded, hotly. "You must be crazy."

"Yes; he's crazy," said Hounshell, trying to assume the air of a composed and meritorious person placed at a disadvantage.

"You must have been yourself," the Californian vehemently declared, "when you took that legacy to pay to Mrs. Scofield, and then stole it because she died and no one knew about it. The mill belongs to Scofield, I say, and I can prove it in a little time."

"You've got no evidence," asserted Hounshell, very pale and a trifle wolfish.

"Evidence! I've got you, and you're chock full of it. I believe I could shake it right out of you if I tried."

Piper glared at him, and then, without releasing his hold, made a dive with one hand at his captive's breast.

"It's gone," said Hounshell, huskily. "I've burned it."

"Burned what?"

"The paper," Hounshell muttered; "your memo—"

"Oh, you had it, then! You've convicted yourself by that, my fine scamp."

"I give up," said the wretched criminal. "Let's go. Take me away—the mill! Bring Scofield. I give up."

Seeing that this was best, Simeon acceded.

" Come along, Scofield," he said.

Jonah pressed up to Scofield and congratulated him as they went, but the older man scarcely responded. When they were again at the mill one striker renewed the idea of coercing the workers. But Jonah imposed his veto.

" Not now," he said.

And Scofield added :

" Boys, if the mill belongs to me it's settled beforehand. You get your advance."

This sent them off with a cheer and the prophecy that the rest of the bosses would have to follow suit.

The four men, left alone, entered the office.

" Is it true ?" asked Scofield.

Hounshell winced, but replied steadily :

" It's all true."

The weaver went to the window and put his head on his arm. It was he, the innocent man, who was overwhelmed by the disgrace of the one who had wronged him.

" But how did you find it out ?" Jonah asked of Piper.

" Roundabout," was the answer. " First off, from a man I was hiring on my ranche. He came from here and spoke about Scofield ; said he was a weaver. I'd heard something about that rich brother in 'Frisco that hadn't seen the rest of the Scofields for years, and left 'em his money ; so I saw there might be something wrong. I looked it up, and came on here."

Jonah took his hand.

" But you must have known the Scofields, or had some interest in them," he said, after a moment.

Simeon Piper looked down ; then he looked away ; finally he twirled his thumbs.

" I could afford the time," he said. " Got money

enough. Well, yes, I suppose you might call it interest.
Fact is, I knew Scofield's wife's sister when she was
young. I—didn't marry her. But, then, I never married any one, you see."

And with this he faced his questioner, turning upon
him a pair of eyes that beamed as if he had just set forth
a remarkably cheerful circumstance.

On further inquiry it was understood how Piper had
taken the wrong train for Shagford, and, finding that it
branched off, had started foolishly to walk along the
track when overtaken on the bridge. He was now convinced that a hat was not a good place in which to deposit important documents.

Finding that evidence for his conviction could soon be
obtained, in addition to his confession, Hounshell executed a deed of the mill to Scofield.

"And what do you propose to do with me?" he
asked. "Are you going to get me locked up?"

The others held a conference, before answering.
Scofield was in favor of letting the malefactor go, but
the decision was at last given to Piper, who said :

"I'm sorry for you, Hounshell. It would have been
better for you if you had emigrated some time ago. But
as it is, I guess the law'll have to decide where you're to
locate."

And, subsequently, it did so.

"Well," said the deposed malefactor, when sentence
had been passed, "I'm almost glad of it."

A soft summer rain was falling as they led him out of
court to go to prison ; and, strangely enough, he had not
felt so happy for years. Once more he was open to the
charm of the pattering drops, the sweetness of refreshed
flowers, the cool air, as he had been in boyhood.

"It's only fair to you," Scofield remarked, forgivingly, "to say that you showed conscience."

"Yes—if I'd only followed it," Hounshell answered. "A man ought to trust his conscience instead of letting it trust him. I tell 'ee it's an awful sharp creditor when the time does come to pay up."

IN EACH OTHER'S SHOES.

I.

JOHN CROMBIE had taken a room at the new apartment building, The Lorne ; having advanced so far in his experience of New York as to be aware that if he could once establish himself in a house associated by name with foreign places and titles his chance of securing " position" would be greatly increased. He did not, however, take his meals in the expensive café of that establishment, finding it more economical to go to an outlandish little French restaurant, some distance away, which had been nicknamed among those of his acquaintance who resorted to it, " The Fried Cat." This designation, based on a supposed resemblance to the name of the proprietor, Fricat, was also believed to have value as a sarcasm.

It was with no pleasant sensations, therefore, that Crombie, waking on a gray and drizzling morning of November, remembered that he must hie him to the " Fried Cat" for an early breakfast. He was in a hurry that day ; he had a great deal to do. His room was very small and dark ; he bounced up and dressed himself, in an obscure sort of way, surreptitiously opening the door and reaching vaguely for his shoes, which stood just outside, ready blacked. Nor did it add to his comfort to know that the shoes were very defective as to their soles, and would admit the water freely from the accumulated puddles of the sidewalks. In fact, he had been ashamed to expose their bad condition to the porter when he put them out every night, as he was forced to do, since they were his only pair. Drawing them on hastily, in order to conceal his mortification from even his own mind, he sallied forth ; and though at the moment of putting them on a dim sense of something unfamiliar crossed his mind, it was not until he reached " The Fried Cat" that he became fully aware that he had carried off some one else's shoes. He turned up the soles, privately, underneath the low-hanging table-cloth, and by a brief examination convinced himself that the gaiters did not belong to him. The test was simple : his feet were unaccountably dry, and there were none of those breaks in the lower surface of their leather covering which he had so often been obliged to contemplate.

He saw at once that the porter of The Lorne had made a mistake, and must have deposited at another apartment his own very insufficient foot-gear ; but there was no chance now to remedy the confusion. Crombie had barely time to reach the office where he was employed.

On an ordinary occasion he would perhaps have gone back to The Lorne and effected an honorable exchange. This particular day, however, was by no means an ordinary occasion. Crombie had made up his mind to take a momentous step ; and it was therefore essential that he should appear at his desk exactly on time.

He was a clerk in an important engraving company. For several years he had occupied that post, without any opportunity having presented itself for a promotion. At the best, even should he rise, what could he expect ?

To be cashier, perhaps, or possibly, under exceptional circumstances, a confidential private secretary. This prospect did not satisfy him ; he was determined to strike for something higher.

It will naturally be inferred that he was ambitious. I am not in a position to deny this ; but all I can be certain of is, that he was in love—which is often about the same thing.

Several times at The Lorne he had met in the hallways or in the elevator a young lady, who was in no small degree beautiful, and charmed him still more by her general presence, which conveyed the idea of a harmonious and lovely character. She had light hair and blue eyes, but these outward attributes were joined with a serenity and poise of manner that indicated greater stability than is attributed, as a rule, to individuals of her type.

Once he happened to arrive at the main entrance just as this vision of beauty emerged to take her place in a coupé which was waiting by the curbstone. She dropped her card-case upon the sidewalk, and Crombie's heart throbbed with delight as he picked it up, gave it to her, and received her smiling thanks for his little service. Another time, as he was descending in the elevator, a door opposite the shaft, on the second floor, stood open, and he caught a glimpse of the apartment to which it gave access. The room was finished in soft tints, and was full of upholstery and hangings that lent it a dim golden atmosphere. In the middle of it stood the young girl, clad in the palest blue, above which her hair shone like a golden cloud on some dim evening sky.

Slight occurrences of this sort had affected him. He learned that she was the daughter of Littimer, the rich, widowed banker : her name was Blanche.

II.

In these new, stout shoes that did not belong to him Crombie trod with a buoyancy and assurance strongly in contrast with the limp and half-hearted pace to which his old, shabby gaiters had formerly inclined him. He rattled down the stairs of the elevated station with an alacrity almost bumptious ; and the sharp, confident step that announced his entrance into the company's office made the other clerks quite ashamed of their own want of spirit.

He worked at his desk until noon ; but when the bells of Trinity rang twelve in solemn music over the busy streets, he dropped his pen, walked with a decisive air the length of the room, and, opening a door at the other end, presented himself before Mr. Blatchford, the treasurer, who was also an influential director.

"Crombie, eh ? Well, what is it ?"

"I want to speak with you a moment, sir."

"Anything important ? I'm busy."

"Yes, sir ; quite important—to me. Possibly it may be to you."

"Fire away, then ; but cut it short." Mr. Blatchford's dense, well-combed gray side-whiskers were directed toward the young man in an aggressive way, as if they had been some sort of weapon.

Crombie nonchalantly settled himself in a chair, at ease.

"I am tired of being a clerk," he said. "I'm going to be a director in this company."

"I guess you're going to be an inmate of a lunatic asylum," Mr. Blatchford remarked, with astonished cheerfulness.

"That seems as unlikely to me as the other thing does to you," said Crombie.

Hereupon Mr. Blatchford became sarcastically deferential. "And just about when do you propose to become a director?" he asked.

"In the course of a month. The election, I believe, takes place in December."

"Quite right," said his senior, whose urbanity was meant to be crushing. "Meanwhile, you will need leisure to attend to this little matter. Suppose I oblige you by saying that the company has no further need of your services?"

"Suppose you do. What then?"

Mr. Blatchford gave way to his anger. "What then? Why, then you would have to go; that's all. You would be thrown out of employment. You would have to live on your principal, as long as there was any; and afterward you would be obliged to find some other work, or beg, or borrow, or—"

"That's enough," said Crombie, rising with dignity.

"No, it isn't," the treasurer declared, "for you don't seem to understand even now. I discharge you, Mr. Crombie, on the company's behalf, and you may leave this office at once."

Crombie bowed and went out. "I'm going to be a director, all the same," he told Mr. Blatchford before he closed the door. Then he collected the few articles that belonged to him from his desk, and departed, a free man. He had his future to himself; or else he had no future worth speaking of; he wasn't sure which. Nevertheless, he felt quite happy. Such a result as this had seemed to him, in the prospect, hardly possible; but now that it had arrived he was not discomfited. Unbounded courage seemed to rise from the stout soles of the alien boots, percolating through his whole system. He was surprised at himself. He had intended to use more diplomacy with Mr. Blatchford, and it was no joke to him to lose his place. But instead of feeling despondent, or going at once in search of new employment, he cheerfully went about making calls on several gentlemen who, he thought, might be induced to aid in his ambitious project. His manner was that of a person sure of his powers and enjoying a well-earned leisure. It had its effect. Two or three stockholders of the company joined in agreeing with him that improved methods could be introduced into its management, and that it would be a good thing to have in the board, say, two young, fresh, active men—of whom Crombie, by reason of his experience and training, should be one.

"I own a little stock," said the deposed clerk, who had taken the precaution to obtain a couple of shares by great effort in saving. "Besides, not having any other engrossing interests at present, I could give my whole attention to the company's affairs."

"Quite so," said the merchant whom he was addressing, comfortably. "We must see if we can get together a majority; no time to be lost, you know."

"No, sir. I shall go right to work; and perhaps you will speak to some of your friends, and give me some names."

"Certainly. Come in again pretty soon; will you?"

Crombie saw that he had a good foundation to build upon already. Blatchford was not popular, even among the other directors; and sundry stockholders, as well as people having business with the company, had conceived a strong dislike of him on account of his overbearing manners. Therefore it would not be hard to enlist sympathy for a movement obnoxious to him. But it was imperative that the self-nominated candidate should acquire more of the stock ; and to do this capital must be had. Crombie did not see quite how it was to be got ; he had no sufficient influence with the bankers.

The afternoon was nearly spent, and he trudged uptown, thinking of the ways and means. But though the problem was far from solved, he still continued in a state of extraordinary buoyancy. Those shoes, those shoes ! He was so much impressed by their comfort and the service they had done him in making a good appearance that he resolved to get a new pair of his own. He stopped and bought them ; then kept on toward The Lorne, carrying his purchase under his arm without embarrassment. The cold drizzle had ceased, and the sunset came out clear and golden, dipping its bright darts into the shallow pools of wet on the pavement, and somehow mingling with his financial dreams a dream of that fair hair that gave a glory to Miss Blanche's face.

On regaining his modest apartment he sent for the boot-boy, and inquired the whereabouts of his missing shoes.

"Couldn't tell you, sir," said the servant. "Pretty near all the men's boots in the house has gone out, you see, and they'll only be coming back just about now. I'll look out for 'em, sir, and nab 'em as soon as they show up."

"All right. Whose are these that I've been wearing ?"

The boy took them, turned them over, and examined them with the eye of a connoisseur in every part. "Them ? I should say, sir, them was Mr. Littimer's."

Crombie blushed with mortification. Of all the dwellers in The Lorne, this was the very one with whom it

was the most embarrassing to have such a complication
occur ; and yet, strange inconsistency ! he had been
longing for any accident, no matter how absurd or fantastic, that could bring him some chance of an acquaintance with Blanche.

"Take these boots, dry them right away, and give
'em a shine. Then carry them up to Mr. Littimer's
rooms." He gave the boy a quarter : he was becoming
reckless.

Now that he had embarked upon a new career, he
perceived the impropriety of a future director in the
Engraving Company going to dine at the "Fried Cat,"
and so resolved to take his dinner in the gorgeous café of
The Lorne. While he was waiting for the proper moment to descend thither, he could not get the shoe question out of his mind. Surely, the boot-boy could not
have been so idiotic as to have left that ancient, broken-
down pair at Littimer's threshold ! And yet it was possible. Crombie felt another flush of humility upon his
cheeks. Then he wandered off into revery upon the
multifarious errands of all the pairs of boots and shoes
that had gone forth from the great apartment-house that
day. Patter, patter, patter ! tramp, tramp !—he imagined he heard them all walking, stamping, shuffling
along toward different parts of the city, with many
different objects, and sending back significant echoes.
Whither had his own ruinous Congress gaiters gone ?—
to what destination which they would never have reached
had he been in them ? Had they carried their tempo-
rary possessor into any such worriment and trouble as he
himself had often travelled through on their worn but
faithful soles ?

Breaking off from these idle fancies at length, he went
down to the café ; and there he had the pleasure of din-

ing at a table not far from Blanche Littimer. But, to his surprise, she was alone. Her father did not appear during the meal.

III.

THE fact was that the awful possibility, mere conjecture of which had frightened Crombie, had occurred. Littimer had received the young man's shoes in place of his own.

They happened to fit him moderately well ; so that he, likewise, did not notice the exchange until he had started for his office. He believed in walking the entire distance, no matter what the weather ; and to this practice he made rare exceptions. But he had not progressed very far before he became annoyed by an unaccustomed intrusion of dampness that threatened him with a cold. He looked down, carefully surveyed the artificial casing of his extremities, and decided to hail the first unoccupied coupé he should meet. It was some time before he found one ; and when finally he took his seat in the luxurious little bank parlor at Broad Street, his feet were quite wet.

His surprise at this occurrence was doubled when, on taking off the shoes and scrutinizing them more closely, he ascertained that they were the work of his usual maker. What had happened to him ? Was he dreaming ? It seemed to him that he had gone back many years ; that he was a poor young man again, entering upon his first struggle for a foothold in the crowded, selfish, unhomelike metropolis. He remembered the day when *he* had worn shoes like these.

He sent out for an assortment of new ones, from which, with unnecessary lavishness, he chose and kept three or four pairs. All the rest of the day, nevertheless, those sorry Congress boots of Crombie's, which he had directed his office-boy to place beside the soft-coal fire, for drying, faced him with a sort of haunting look. However much he might be occupied with weightier matters, he could not keep his eyes from straying in that direction ; and whenever they rested on that battered " right" and that way-worn " left," turned up in that mute, appealing repose and uselessness at the fender, his thoughts recurred to his early years of trial and poverty. Ah ! how greatly he had changed since then ! On some accounts he could almost wish that he were poor again. But when he remembered Blanche, he was glad, for her sake, that he was rich.

But if for her sake, why not for others ? Perhaps he had been rather selfish, not only about Blanche, but toward her. His conscience began to reproach him. Had he made for her a large life ? Since her mother's premature death, had he instilled into her sympathies, tastes, companionships that would make her existence the richer ? Had he not kept her too much to himself ? On the other hand, he had gratified all her material wants ; she could wear what she pleased, she could go where she chose, she had acquaintances of a sort becoming to the daughter of a wealthy man. Yet there was something lacking. What did she know about old, used-up boots and all that pertains to them ? What did she know about indigence, real privation, and brave endurance, such as a hundred thousand fellow-creatures all around her were undergoing ?

Somehow it dawned upon the old banker that if she knew about all these things and had some share in them, albeit only through sympathy and helping, she might be happier, more truly a woman, than she was now.

As he sat alone, in revery, he actually heaved a deep sigh. A sigh is often as happy a deliverance as a laugh, in this world of sorrows. It was the first that had escaped Littimer in years. Let us say that it was a breathing space, which gave him time for reflection ; it marked the turning of a leaf ; it was the beginning of a new chapter in his life.

Before he left the bank he locked the door of the private parlor, and was alone for two or three minutes. The office boy was greatly puzzled the next morning, when he found all the new pairs of shoes ranged intact in the adjoining cupboard. The old ones were missing.

Littimer had gone away in them, furtively. He was ashamed of his own impulse.

This time he resolutely remained afoot instead of hiring a carriage. He despatched a messenger to Blanche, saying that sudden business would prevent his returning to dinner, and continued indefinitely on his way— whither ? As to that he was by no means certain ; he knew only that he must get out of the beaten track, out of the ruts. For an hour or two he must cease to be Littimer, the prosperous moneyed man, and must tread once more the obscure paths through which he had made his way to fortune. He could hardly have explained the prompting which he obeyed. Could it have had anything to do with the treacherous holes in the bottoms of those old shoes ?

As it chanced, he passed by the " Fried Cat ;" and, dingy though the place was, he felt an irresistible desire to enter it. Seating himself, he ordered the regular dinner of the day. The light was dim ; the tablecloth was dirty ; the attendance was irregular and distracted. Lit-

timer took one sip of the sour wine—which had a flavor
resembling vinegar and carmine ink in equal parts—and
left the further contents of his bottle untasted. The
soup, the stew, and the faded roast that were set before
him, he could scarcely swallow ; but a small cup of coffee
at the end of the well-nigh Barmecide repast came in
very palatably.

In default of prandial attractions, Littimer tried to occupy himself by looking at the people around him. The
omnifarious assembly included pale, prim-whiskered
young clerks ; shabby, lonely, sallow young women,
whose sallowness and shabbiness stamped them with the
mark of integrity ; other females whose specious splen-
dor was not nearly so reassuring ; old men, broken-down
men, middle-aged men of every description, except the
well-to-do.

"Some of them," Littimer reflected, "are no worse
than I am. But are any of them really any better ?"

He could not convince himself that they were ; yet his
sympathies, somehow, went out toward this motley
crowd. It appeared to him very foolish that he should
sympathize, but he could not help it. "And, after all,"
was the next thought that came to him, "are we to give
pity to people, or withhold it, simply because they are
better or worse than ourselves ? No ; there is something
more in it than that."

Leaving the "Fried Cat" abruptly, he betook himself to an acquaintance who, he knew, was very active in
charities—a man who worked practically, and gave time
to the work.

"Do you visit any of your distress cases to-night ?"
he asked.

"Yes, I shall make a few calls," answered the man
of charity. "Would you like to go along ?"

"Very much."

So the two started out together. The places they
went to were of various kinds, and revealed a considerable diversity of misfortune. Sometimes they entered
tenement-houses of the most wretched character ; but in
other instances they went to small and cheap but decent
lodgings over the shops on West Side avenues, or even
penetrated into boarding-houses of such good appearance that the banker was surprised to find his friend's
mission carrying him thither. All the cases, however,
had been studied, and were vouched for ; and several
were those of young men and women having employment, but temporarily disabled, and without friends who
could help them.

"You do well to help these beginners, at critical
times," said the banker, with satisfaction. "I take a
special interest in them."

It was almost the same as if he were receiving relief
himself. Who knows? Perhaps he was ; but to the
outward eye it appeared merely that, with his friend's
sanction, he was dispensing money and offers of good
will to the needy. What a strange freak it was, though,
in Littimer ! He kept on with the work until quite late
in the evening, regardless of the risk he ran by continu-
ing out-of-doors when so ill shod.

I think he had some idea in his mind that he was per-
forming an act of penance.

IV.

Having waited a reasonable length of time after dinner, Crombie again left his room, resolved to make a call upon Mr. Littimer, on the plea of apologizing for having marched away with his shoes.

He would not run the risk, by sending his card, of being denied as a stranger; so, notwithstanding much hesitation and tremor, he approached the door which he had once seen standing open, and knocked. A voice which he now heard for the second time in his life, but which was so sweet and crept so naturally into the centre of his heart that the thought of it seemed always to have been there, answered: "Come in." And he did come in.

"Is Mr. Lit—is your father at home?" It seemed to bring him a little nearer to her to say "your father."

Blanche had risen from the chair where she was reading, and looked very much surprised. "Oh," she exclaimed, with girlish simplicity, "I thought it was the waiter! N–no; he hasn't come home yet."

"I beg pardon. Then perhaps I'd better call later." Crombie made a feeble movement toward withdrawal.

"Did you want to see him on business? Who shall I tell him?"

"Mr. Crombie, please. It's nothing very important."

"Oh," said Blanche, with a little blush at her own deception, "haven't I seen you in the house before? Are you staying here?"

She remembered distinctly the incident of the card-case, and how very nice she had thought him, both on that occasion and every time she had seen him. But as for him, his heart sank at the vague impersonality with which she seemed to regard him.

"Yes, I'm here, and can easily come in again."

"I expect my father almost any moment," she said. "Would you like to wait?"

What an absurd question, to one in his frame of mind! "Well, really, it is such a very small matter," he began, examining his hat attentively. Then he glanced up at her again, and smiled: "I only wanted to —to make an apology."

"An apology!" echoed Blanche, becoming rather more distant. "Oh, dear! I'm very sorry, I'm sure. I didn't know there'd been any trouble." She began to look anxious, and turned her eyes upon the smouldering fire in the grate. So this was to be the end of her pleasant, cheerful reveries about this nice young man. And the reveries had been more frequent than she had been aware of until now.

"There has been no trouble," he assured her, eagerly. "Just a little mistake that occurred; and, in fact, I was hardly responsible for it."

Blanche's eyes began to twinkle with a new and amusing interpretation. "Ah!" she cried, "are you the gentleman who—" Then she stopped short.

Crombie was placed in an unexpected embarrassment. How could he possibly drag into his conversation with this lovely young creature so commonplace and vulgar a subject as shoe-leather! Ignoring her unfinished question, he asked: "Do you know, Miss Littimer, whether the—a—one of the servants here has brought up anything for your father—that is, a parcel, a—"

"A pair of shoes?" Blanche broke in, her eyes dancing, while her lips parted in a smile.

"Yes, yes; that's what I meant."

" They came up just after dinner," Blanche returned. " Then you *are* the gentleman."

" I'm afraid I am," Crombie owned, and they both laughed.

Blanche quietly, and with no apparent intention, resumed her chair ; and this time Crombie took a seat without waiting to be invited again. Thus they fell to talking in the friendliest way.

" I can't imagine what has become of papa," said Blanche. " He sent word, in the most mysterious manner, that he had an engagement ; and it is so unusual ! Perhaps it's something about the new house he's building—up-town, you know. Dear me ! it does make so much trouble, and I don't believe I shall like it half as well as these little, cosey rooms."

The little, cosey rooms were as the abode of giants compared with Crombie's contracted quarters ; but he drew comfort from what she said, thinking how such sentiments might make it possible to win even so unattainable an heiress into some modest home of his own.

" You don't know till you try it," he replied. " Just think of having a place all to yourself, belonging to you."

Blanche lifted her eyebrows, and a little sigh escaped her. She was reflecting, perhaps, that a place all to herself would be rather lonely.

" You have never met my father ?" she asked.

" No. I have seen him."

" Well, I think you will like him when you know him."

" I don't doubt it !" Crombie exclaimed with fervor, worshipping the very furniture that surrounded Blanche. " I hope we may become better acquainted."

" Only I think, Mr. Crombie, he will owe *you* an apology now."

" Why ?"

" For keeping your shoes out so late."

"*My* shoes !" said the young man, in vehement surprise.

" Why, yes. Didn't you know they came to him ? The porter said so."

Crombie grew red with the sense of his disgrace in having his poverty-stricken boots come to the knowledge of the banker. Really, his mortification was so great that the accident seemed to him to put an end to all his hopes of further relations with Blanche and her father.

" Oh, I assure you," he said, rising, " that makes no difference at all ! I'm sorry I mentioned the matter. Pray tell Mr. Littimer not to think of it. I —I believe I'd better go now, Miss Littimer."

Blanche rose too, and Crombie was on the point of bowing a good-night, when the door opened, and a weary figure presented itself on the threshold ; the figure of a short man with a spare face, and whiskers in which gray mingled with the sandy tint. He had a pinched, half-growling expression, was draped in a light, draggled overcoat, and carried an umbrella, the ribs of which hung loose around the stick.

" There's papa this moment !" cried Blanche.

Crombie perceived that escape was impossible, and, in a few words, the reason of his presence there was made known to the old gentleman.

Littimer examined the visitor swiftly, from head to foot—especially the foot. He advanced to the fire, toasted first one and then the other of the damp gaiters he had on, and at length broke out, in a tone bordering on reproach : " So you are the owner, are you ? Then my sympathy has all been wasted ! Why, I supposed, from the condition of these machines that I've been lugging around with me half the day, that you must be in the greatest distress. And, lo and behold ! I find you a young fellow in prime health, spruce and trim, doing well, I should say, and perfectly happy."

"I can't help that, sir," retorted Crombie, nettled, but speaking with respect. "I confess I was very happy until a moment or two ago."

"What do you mean by that ?" the other demanded, with half-yielding pugnacity. "Till I came in—is that the idea ?"

"Oh, papa !" said Blanche, softly.

"Well, honey-bee, what's the matter ?" her father asked, trying to be gruff. "Can't I say what I like, here ?" But he surrendered at once by adding : "You may be sure I don't want to offend any one. Sit down, Mr. Crombie, and wait just a few moments while I go into the other room and rejuvenate my hoofs, so to speak—for I fear I've made a donkey of myself."

He disappeared into an adjoining room with Blanche, who there informed him artlessly of Crombie's consideration and attentiveness in restoring the errant shoes. When they came back Littimer insisted upon having the young man remain a little longer and drink a glass of port with him. Before taking his departure, however, Crombie, who felt free to speak since Blanche had retired, made a brief statement in satisfaction of conscience.

"You hinted," he said, "that you judged me to be doing well. I don't want to leave you with a false impression. The truth is, I am not doing well. I have no money to speak of, and to-day I lost the position on which I depended."

"You don't tell me !" Littimer's newly roused charitable impulses came to the fore. "Why, now you
begin to be really interesting, Mr. Crombie."

"Thanks," said Crombie; "I'm not ambitious to
interest people in that way. I told you only because I
thought it fair."

"Don't be touchy, my dear sir," answered the
banker. "I meant what I said. Come, let's see what
can be done. Have you any scheme in view ?"

"Yes, I have," said Crombie, with decision.

Littimer gave a grunt. He was afraid of people with
schemes, and was disappointed with the young man's
want of helplessness. Dependence would have been an
easier thing to deal with.

"Well," said he, "we must talk it over. Come
and see me at the bank to-morrow. You know the ad-
dress ?"

V.

THE next day Crombie called at the bank; but Littimer was not there. He was not very well, it was said;
had not come down-town. Crombie did what he could
toward organizing his fight for a directorship, and then
returned to The Lorne, where he punctually inquired
after Mr. Littimer's health, and learned that the banker's
ardor in making the rounds among distressed people the
night before had been followed by reaction into a bad
cold, with some threat of pneumonia. Blanche was
plainly anxious. The attack lasted three or four days,
and Crombie, though the affair of the directorship was

pressing for attention, could not forbear to remain as near as possible to Blanche, offering every aid within his power, so far as he might without overstepping the lines of his very recent acquaintance. But the Littimers did not, according to his observation, number any very intimate companions in their circle, or at least had not many friends who would be assiduous in such an emergency. Perhaps their friends were too busy with social engagements. Consequently, he saw a good deal of Blanche, and became to her an object of reliance.

Well, it was simply one of those things that happen only in fairy-tales or in romances—or in real life. Littimer recovered without any serious illness, and, after a brief conference with Crombie, entered heartily into the young man's campaign. Crombie showed him just what combinations could be formed, how success could be achieved, and what lucrative results might be made to ensue. He conquered by figures and by lucid common-sense. Littimer agreed to buy a number of shares in the Engraving Company, which he happened to know could be purchased, and to advance Crombie a good sum with which to procure a portion of the same lot. But before this agreement could be consummated, Crombie, with his usual frankness, said to the banker :

"I will conceal nothing from you, Mr. Littimer. I fell in love with Blanche before I knew her, and if this venture of mine succeeds, I shall ask her to become my wife."

"Let us attend to business," said Littimer, severely. "Sentiment can take care of itself."

Their manœuvre went on so vigorously that Blatchford became alarmed, and sent an ambassador to arrange a compromise ; but by this time Crombie had determined to oust Blatchford himself and elect an entirely new set of men, to compose more than half the Board, and so control everything.

He succeeded.

But Littimer did not forget the charitable enthusiasm which had been awakened by a circumstance on the surface so trivial as the mistake of a boot-boy. He did not desist from his interest in aiding disabled or unfortunate people who could really be aided. Some time after Crombie had achieved his triumph in the Engraving Company, and had repaid Littimer's loan, he was admitted to a share in the banking business; and eventually the head of the house was able to give a great deal of attention to perfecting his benevolent plans.

When the details of their wedding were under discussion, Crombie said to Blanche : "Oughtn't we to have an old shoe thrown after the carriage as we drive away ?"

She smiled; looked him full in the eyes with a peculiar tenderness in which there was a bright, delicious sparkle of humor. "No; old shoes are much too useful to be wasted that way."

Somehow she had possessed herself of that particular, providential pair; and, though I don't want anybody to laugh at my two friends, I must risk saying that I suspect Mrs. Crombie of preserving it somewhere, to this day, in the big new house up-town.

THE END.

www.ingramcontent.com/pod-product-compliance
Lightning Source LLC
Chambersburg PA
CBHW020347030726
47496CB00007B/2042